Anonymous

Acts of the Legislature of the State of Michigan

SALZWASSER
VERLAG

Anonymous

Acts of the Legislature of the State of Michigan

Reprint of the original, first published in 1858.

1st Edition 2023 | ISBN: 978-3-37513-863-9

Verlag (Publisher): Salzwasser Verlag GmbH, Zeilweg 44, 60439 Frankfurt, Deutschland
Vertretungsberechtigt (Authorized to represent): E. Roepke, Zeilweg 44, 60439 Frankfurt, Deutschland
Druck (Print): Books on Demand GmbH, In de Tarpen 42, 22848 Norderstedt, Deutschland

ACTS

OF

THE LEGISLATURE

OF THE

STATE OF MICHIGAN,

PASSED

AT THE EXTRA SESSION OF 1858,

WITH AN APPENDIX,

Containing Certified Statements of Boards of Supervisors relative to the Erection of New Townships; also, State Treasurer's Annual Report for the year 1857.

By Authority.

LANSING:

Hosmer & Kerr, Printers to the State.

1858.

LIST OF ACTS

PASSED BY THE LEGISLATURE OF 1858.

JOINT RESOLUTIONS.

LAWS OF MICHIGAN.

[No. 1.]

AN ACT to provide rooms for holding the sessions of of the Supreme Court, and the collection and preservation of the records of the Supreme Court of the Territory of Michigan.

SECTION 1. *The People of the State of Michigan enact,* That the Attorney General be and he is hereby author-ized to procure apartments in the city of Detroit, in which to hold the sessions of the supreme court, and to provide the necessary furniture for fitting up the same; and also proper desks, cases, tables and other furniture for the safe keeping and preservation of the records, books and papers of the court, to be kept and preserved in such apartments; and in the name of the people of the State, to sign and execute any lease of such apartments upon such terms as he shall see fit: *Provided,* Such lease shall not be for a longer term than five years, and shall be de-terminable whenever any three of the judges of the court shall give, or cause to be given, three months notice to that effect to the lessor, his heirs, executors or assigns, or the person or persons claiming under him or them: *And provided further,* That the State shall not be responsible for any damage to such apartments by fire, which lease, or a duplicate thereof, shall be deposited with the Auditor General.

Sec. 2. The Auditor General is required to draw his warrant on the State Treasury for the amount of rent from time to time falling due on such lease; and also for

1

such necessary furniture, upon the certificate of one of the justices of the court that the same has been duly delivered, and upon the presentation and allowance of the same, as in other cases provided, by the Board of State Auditors.

Duties of clerk of Supreme Court of Wayne county.

Sec. 3. It shall be the duty of the clerk of the supreme court in Wayne county, to collect and obtain possession of all the books of record, files and papers of the supreme court of the Territory of Michigan, belonging to said court in the county of Wayne or elsewhere, and to deposit them in such apartments, in proper order, to be there kept and preserved until removed to some other place by order of the supreme court.

Rooms at the capitol to be fitted up.

Sec. 4. Three apartments in the capitol, at Lansing, are assigned for the use of the supreme court, to be fitted up under the direction of the Auditor General, at the expense

Duties of St. Librarian.

of the State, which expenses are to be credited [audited] and allowed by the said Board of Auditors; and the State Librarian is hereby directed to allow such portion of the law books belonging to the state library as the justices shall select, to be removed from the room in which they now are, and placed in one of such apartments for the use of the justices, there to remain during the session of said court.

Sec. 5. This act is ordered to take immediate effect.

Approved January 29, 1858.

[No. 2.]

AN ACT to authorize the Supervisor of the township of Macomb, in the county of Macomb, to make a new assessment of the real and personal property of said township, and to extend the time for the collection of taxes in said township.

Supervisor to make new assessment.

SECTION 1. *The People of the State of Michigan enact,* That the supervisor of the township of Macomb, in the county of Macomb, shall have authority to make a new assessment of the real and personal property of said town--

ship for the year one thousand eight hundred and fifty- Tax roll to seven, and that he shall make a new tax roll therefrom in accordance with existing laws, and shall deliver the same, with the proper warrant affixed thereto, to the treasurer of said township, on or before the second Monday in February, one thousand eight hundred and fifty-eight.

Sec. 2. The treasurer of said township shall, within five, Duty of township days after the receipt of said tax roll and warrant, pay treasurer. over to the county treasurer of his county all moneys collected by him upon a former tax roll, and execute a bond according to law to the said treasurer.

Sec. 3. The township treasurer, when he shall have Time extended for col-complied with the provisions of section two of this act, lection of taxes. shall proceed to collect the unpaid taxes levied in said roll, and the time for the collection and return of said taxes be extended to the last Monday of March, 1858, and the county treasurer of the county of Macomb shall make return, as in other cases, within fifty days from the time of the return made by the township treasurer.

This act shall take effect immediately.

Approved January 29, 1858.

[No. 3.]

AN ACT to amend section sixty-two of chapter seventeen of the Compiled Laws of eighteen hundred and fifty-seven, entitled "Of the assessment and collection of taxes."

SECTION 1. *The People of the State of Michigan enact,* Section amended. That section sixty-two of chapter seventeen of the compiled laws of eighteen hundred and fifty-seven, entitled "Of the assessment and collection of taxes," be, and the same is hereby amended, so that the same shall read as follows:

Sec. 62. If any township treasurer, ward collector, or Penalty. other collecting officer in the city shall neglect or refuse to pay to the county treasurer the sums required by his warrant, or to account for the same as unpaid, as required by law, the county treasurer shall, within ten days after the time when such payment ought to have been made, issue a warrant under his hand, directed to the sheriff of the county, commanding him to levy such sum as shall remain unpaid and unaccounted for, together with his fees for collecting the same, of the goods and chattels, lands and tenements of such township treasurer, ward collector or other collecting officer, and their sureties, and to pay the said sums to such county treasurer and return such warrant, within forty days from the date thereof.

Duty of Co. treasurer.

Sec. 2. This act is ordered to take immediate effect.

Approved January 29, 1858.

[No. 4.]

AN ACT to amend the Revised Statutes of 1846, and other statutes, so as to adapt them to the organization of the present Supreme Court, and to define more accurately the duties of Judges of the Circuit Courts and of Circuit Court Commissioners.

SECTION 1. *The People of the State of Michigan enact,* That the following alterations and amendments be and the same are hereby made in the statutes of this State, that is to say : the following sections of the revised statutes of 1846 shall be altered and amended as follows :

CHAPTER 90.

Condition of Injunction.

Section nineteen of chapter ninety shall read thus:

If an application for an order that an injunction or a writ *ne exeat* issue be made to the circuit judge or any person authorized to grant the same, and such order be refused, in whole or in part, or be granted conditionally or on terms, no subsequent application for the same purpose and in relation to the same matter shall be made to any other circuit judge or any other person authorized to grant the same.

Sec. 2. Section one hundred and nine of said chapter is hereby repealed, and the following enacted in its stead:

The circuit judges, and each injuction master within the circuit for which he may be appointed, shall severally have power to grant injunctions to stay proceedings at law. *Power to grant injunctions, to whom vested.*

Sec. 3. Section one hundred and forty-four of said chapter shall read as follows:

Such appeal shall be claimed and entered [returned] within forty days from the time of the making of such decree or final order; and the appellant shall, within said forty days, file with the register or clerk who entered such decree or order a bond to the appellee with sufficient sureties, to be approved by a judge of the circuit court or a circuit court commissioner, and in such sum as such judge or commissioner shall direct, conditioned to pay, satisfy or perform the decree or final order of the supreme court, and to pay all costs, in case the decree or order of the circuit court in chancery shall be affirmed. *Limit of appeal.* *Bond to be filed and approved.*

Sec. 4. Section one hundred and forty-six of said chapter shall be so amended as to read as follows:

When such appeal shall be perfected it shall be the duty of the clerk or register, in thirty days thereafter, to make a copy of the bill or other pleadings, papers and proceedings in the cause, and transmit the same to the clerk of the supreme court whose office shall be nearest, by the usual traveled route, to the place where such circuit court was held, unless otherwise ordered by the supreme court or one of the justices thereof. *Duty of clerk in relation to appeals.*

Sec. 5. Section one hundred and forty-nine of said chapter is hereby repealed.

Section fifty-seven of chapter ninety, and the act amendatory thereto, is hereby amended so as to read as follows:

Sec. 57. Either party to a cause in chancery may, within

Witnesses
may be ex-
amined on
claim of ei-
ther party. ten days after issue joined in said cause, apply to the circuit court or to the circuit judge at chambers for an order for the examination of witnesses in open court, and upon good cause shown, the court or judge may, by an order under his hand, direct the examination of witnesses in open court, and a certified copy of such order shall be served upon the

Order to be
served with-
in five days. solicitor of the opposite party within five days thereafter; in which case no commission shall be issued, nor examination of witnesses had before a circuit court commissioner, but the cause shall be heard in its course on the calendar by examination of witnesses in open court, unless the court, on legal cause shown, shall otherwise direct as in a

Proviso. suit at law: *Provided,* That if an application shall not be made to the court or judge within ten days after the joining of issue as aforesaid, and a certified copy of said order served upon the solicitor of the opposite party within five days after the date of said order as aforesaid, a commission may be issued and the testimony of the witnesses in said cause taken before a circuit court commissioner, as provided by the rules and practice of said court: *And*

Proviso. *provided further,* That in case any cause in chancery shall be so tried in open court, either party shall be entitled to make and settle a case, setting forth the evidence at large before the judge who tried the same, at such time and in such manner as said judge shall direct, or as shall be prescribed by the rules of said court. And upon the making and filing of such case within three months after such trial, the same shall be taken and deemed to be the evidence in said cause, to the same extent and with like effect as if the said testimony had been taken before a circuit court commissioner and certified by him.

Section eighty of said chapter is hereby amended so as to read as follows :

Sec. 80. After the filing of a bill, the circuit judge or circuit court commissioner shall make an order for the appearance of a defendant, at a future day therein to be specified, as hereinafter directed in the following cases: '

When the defendant resides out of this State, upon proof by affidavit of that fact;

Provision for ordering the appearance of a defendant in certain cases.

When the defendant is a resident of this State, upon proof by affidavit that the process for his appearance has been duly issued, and that the same could not be served by reason of his absence from, or concealment within this State, or by reason of his continued absence from his place of residence.

CHAPTER 95.

Sec. 6. Section four of chapter ninety-five shall be so altered and amended as to read as follows:

Circuit court commissioners, qualified according to law, shall severally be authorized and required to perform all the duties and to execute every act, power and trust which a judge of the circuit court may perform and execute out of court, according to the rules and practice of such court, and pursuant to the provisions of any statute, in all civil cases, except as herein otherwise provided.

Circuit co'rt commiss'n'r authorized to perform the duties of circuit judge.

Sec. 7. Section five of said chapter shall be so altered and amended as to read as follows:

But when any power is given in express terms, by any statute, to a circuit judge or to circuit judges, without naming circuit court commissioners in such statute, such commissioners shall not be authorized to exercise any such powers.

When not allowed to perform such duties.

Sec. 8. Section twelve of said chapter is so altered and amended as to read as follows:

If an application for any order be made to any justice of the supreme court, judge of a circuit court, or circuit court commissioner, and such order be refused, in whole or in part, or granted conditionally or on terms, no subsequent application in reference to the same matter and in the same stage of the proceedings, shall be made to any other circuit

Order issued on second application shall be revoked.

court commissioner; and if, upon a subsequent application, any order be made by a circuit judge or circuit court commissioner, it shall be revoked by such judge or commissioner, or by any justice of the supreme court, upon due proof of the facts.

CHAPTER 98.

Sec. 9. Section one of chapter ninety-eight is altered and amended so as to read as follows:

Recognizance, before whom taken.   In all cases where special bail shall be required to be put in, a recognizance thereof may be taken before any justice of the supreme court, any circuit judge, circuit court commissioner, clerk of any court of record, and shall be filed in the office of the clerk of the court in which the action is pending.

Sec. 10. Section twenty of said chapter is altered and amended so as to read as follows:

Special bail, surrender made, before whom.   The special bail of any defendant may surrender him, or such defendant may surrender himself in exoneration of his bail, before any judge of a circuit court, or a circuit court commissioner.

CHAPTER 102.

Sec. 11. Section sixty-four, of chapter one hundred and two, is altered and amended so as to read as follows:

Power to discharge witnesses.   Every justice of the supreme court, circuit judge and circuit court commissioner, shall have the like authority to discharge any witness arrested contrary to the foregoing provisions.

CHAPTER 110.

Sec. 12. Section seven, of chapter one hundred and ten, is altered and amended so as to read as follows:

Suit for the recovery of land.   After the commencement of any action on the case for waste, or of any action for the recovery of land, or of the possession of land, the defendant shall not make any waste of the land in demand, or premises in question, during the pendency of the suit; and if such defendant shall commit any waste thereon, or shall threaten to make preparations to commit waste thereon, the court in which such suit is pending, or any circuit judge, or circuit court commissioner, Defendant either in term or vacation, shall have power, on the appli- may be restrained cation of the plaintiff, to make an order restraining the from the commission defendant from the commission of any waste, or further of waste. waste thereon.

Sec. 13. Section eight of said chapter shall be so altered and amended as to read as follows:

If any person shall commit, or threaten, or make prepa- Ib. rations to commit any waste on any real estate which shall be attached or levied upon by execution in any civil action, the court from which such execution or attachment shall have issued, any circuit judge or circuit court commissioner, may, on the application of the plaintiff, either in term or vacation, make an order restraining such person from committing any waste or further waste thereon.

CHAPTER 115.

Sec. 14. Section three of chapter one hundred and fifteen is altered and amended so as to read as follows:

Such appointment shall be made as follows:

If the suit be intended to be brought in the circuit Appointment court, by any judge thereof, or circuit court commissioner.

Sec. 15. Section nine of said chapter one hundred and fifteen, is altered and amended so as to read as follows:

Such appointment shall be made upon the request of How made. such defendant, and upon the written consent of any competent person proposed as guardian, by the court, or any circuit judge, or any circuit court commissioner for the county.

CHAPTER 122.

Sec. 16. Section two, of chapter one hundred and twenty two, is altered and amended so as to read as follows:

2

Warrant to enforce claim.

Any person having any such claim or demand as is specified in the preceding section, may make application to any officer authorized to perform the duties of a circuit judge at chambers, or to any judge of any court of record in the county within which such ship, boat or vessel shall then be, for a warrant to enforce the lien of such claim or demand, and to collect the amount thereof.

CHAPTER 123.

Sec. 17. Section three, of chapter one hundred and twenty-three, is altered and amended so as to read as follows:

Suit for the recovery of lands.

The person entitled to the possession of the premises, his agent or attorney, may make complaint in writing and on oath, and deliver the same to a circuit court commissioner, or a judge of the circuit court for the county, setting forth that the person complained of is in possession of the lands and tenements in question, describing them, and that he entered into the same with force, or that he unlawfully holds the same by force, as the case may be.

Sec. 18. Section thirteen of said chapter is altered and amended so as to read as follows:

Ib.

In the cases specified in the preceding section, the person entitled to the possession of the premises, his agent or attorney, may make complaint in writing and on oath, and deliver the same to a circuit court commissioner, or judge of the circuit court for the county, setting forth that the person complained of is in possession of the lands or tenements in question, describing them, and that such person holds the same unlawfully and against the right of the complainant.

CHAPTER 134.

Sec. 19. Section three of chapter one hundred and thirty-four, is altered and amended so as to read as follows:

Such writs may also be issued by any justice of the supreme court, judges of a circuit court, or any officer authorized to perform the duties of such circuit judge, upon the like application of a party to any suit or proceeding pending in a court of record, or pending before any officer or body who may be authorized to examine witnesses in any suit or proceeding. Writs, when and by whom issued.

Sec. 20. Section nine of said chapter is altered and amended so as to read as follows:

Application for such writ shall be made by petition, signed either by the party for whose relief it is intended, or by some person in his behalf, as follows: Application for writs.

To the supreme court during its sitting;

The supreme court or to any of the circuit judges or any officer who may be authorized to perform the duties of a circuit judge at chambers, or to a circuit court commissioner, being or residing within the county where the prisoner is detained; or, if there be no such officer within such county, or if he be absent, or for any cause be incapable of acting, or having refused to grant such writ, then to some officer having such authority, residing or being in any other county. To whom made.

Sec. 21. Section forty-three of said chapter is altered and amended so as to read as follows, to wit:

Upon the production of such order to any circuit court commissioner of any county in which such prisoner may be, or to any judge of a court of record, he shall be authorized to take the recognizance of the person so detained, and of two sufficient sureties, in the sum so directed, with a condition for the appearance of such person at the court designated in such order; but previous to taking such recognizance, such officer shall be satisfied by the oath of persons offering themselves as sureties, that they are householders of the county, and are severally Recognizance. Sureties.

worth double the sum in which they shall be required to
be bound, over and above all demand against them.

CHAPTER 138.

Sec. 22. Section seven of chapter one hundred and
thirty-eight is altered and amended so as to read as follows :

Writs of error. Writs of error upon judgments in all other criminal
cases shall issue of course, but they shall not stay or delay
the execution of the judgment or sentence, unless they
shall be allowed by one of the justices of the supreme
court, or a circuit judge, with an express order thereon
for a stay of proceedings on the judgment or sentence.

Sec. 23. Section fifteen of said chapter is altered and
amended so as to read as follows :

Writs of certiorari. Writs of certiorari may be allowed by any justice of the
supreme court, or judge of the circuit court, or circuit court
commissioner.

CHAPTER 141.

Sec. 24. Section three of chapter one hundred and forty-
one is altered and amended so as to read as follows :

Power of plaintiff to arrest defendant. In all cases whereby the preceding provisions of this
chapter, a defendant cannot be arrested or imprisoned, it
shall be lawful for the plaintiff who shall have commenced
a suit against such defendant, or shall have obtained a
judgment or decree against him, in any court of record, or
justice's court, to any judge of the court in which such suit
is brought, or to any circuit judge or circuit court commissioner, or to any justice of the peace before whom such
suit is pending or judgment obtained, or before whom such
proceedings shall have been transferred, for a warrant to
arrest the defendant in such suit.

CHAPTER 142.

Sec. 25. Section three of chapter one hundred and forty-
two is altered and amended so as to read as follows :

Executors and administrators may become petitioning Petitioning creditors. creditors for the discharge of an insolvent, under the order of the judge of probate, to whom they may be liable to account, or of a judge of the circuit court; and shall be chargeable only for such sum as they shall actually receive on the dividend of the insolvent estate.

Sec. 26. Section six of said chapter is altered and amended so as to read as follows:

Every such petition may be presented to a judge of the Petition. circuit court, or a circuit court commissioner.

CHAPTER 162.

Sec. 27. Section one of chapter one hundred and sixty-two, is altered and amended so as to read as follows:

The justices of the supreme court, the several circuit Security may be required for the preservation of peace. judges, circuit court commissioners, all mayors and recorders of cities, and all justices of the peace, shall have power to cause all the laws made for the preservation of the public peace, to be kept, and in the execution of this power, may require persons to give security to keep the peace in the manner provided in this chapter.

CHAPTER 163.

Sec. 28. Section one of chapter one hundred and sixty-three is altered and amended so as to read as follows:

For the apprehension of persons charged with offences, Power to issue process, in whom vested. excepting such offences as are cognizable by justices of the peace, the justices of the supreme court, the several circuit judges and circuit court commissioners, mayors and recorders of cities, and all justices of the peace, shall have power to issue processes to carry into effect the provisions of this chapter.

Sec. 29. Section twenty-six of said chapter is altered and amended so as to read as follows:

Officers before whom persons charged with crime shall Power to mit to bail be brought, shall have power to let them to bail, as follows:

In whom vested. Any justice of the supreme court, judge of a circuit court, circuit court commissioners, in all cases, except for capital offences, or for murder in the first degree, where the proof is evident or the presumption great;

Bail. Any justice of the peace, or mayor or recorder of a city, in all cases where the punishment for the offence charged shall be less than imprisonment for life in the State prison.

Sec. 30. The second section of the act entitled "an act to provide for the transfer of causes from one circuit court to another, in certain cases," approved February twelfth, one thousand eight hundred and fifty-five, is altered and amended so as to read as follows :

Transfer of suit. Any party desiring to transfer any such suit or proceeding as is hereinbefore mentioned, may apply to a circuit court commissioner of the county where said suit is pending, or to the judge of any adjoining circuit, who is not within the disqualifications mentioned in the first section of this act, for an order to transfer such suit; such application shall be in writing and shall set forth the grounds specifically for such transfer. The parties to any such suit may, by stipulation in writing, consent to the tranfer of such suit or proceeding without any application to the judge or commissioner; in which case the stipulation shall have the same effect as an order duly made for such transfer under the provisions of this act.

Approved January 29, 1858.

[No. 5.]

AN ACT to amend an act entitled "an act to define the limits, jurisdiction and powers of Circuit Courts," approved April 8, 1851.

SECTION 1. *The People of the State of Michigan enact,* That section one, of an act entitled "an act to define the limits, jurisdiction and powers of Circuit Courts," approved April 8, 1851, be amended so that said section shall read as follows:

SECTION 1. *The People of the State of Michigan enact,* Limits of circuits. That the State shall be composed of ten judicial circuits, to be denominated the first, second, third, fourth, fifth, sixth, seventh, eighth, ninth and tenth circuits, respectively, and to be composed as follows:

The first circuit shall be composed of the counties of Monroe, Lenawee and Hillsdale.

The second circuit shall be composed of the counties of Branch, St. Joseph, Cass and Berrien.

The third circuit shall be composed of the counties of Wayne and Cheboygan.

The fourth circuit shall be composed of the counties of Washtenaw, Jackson and Ingham.

The fifth circuit shall be composed of the counties of Eaton, Calhoun, Kalamazoo and Van Buren.

The sixth circuit shall be composed of the counties of St. Clair, Macomb, Oakland and Sanilac.

The seventh circuit shall be composed of the counties of Livingston, Shiawassee, Genesee, Lapeer, Tuscola and Saginaw.

The eighth circuit shall be composed of the counties of Ionia, Clinton, Kent, Montcalm and Barry.

The ninth circuit shall be composed of the counties Counties attached for certain purposes. of Allegan, Ottawa, Newaygo, Oceana, Mason, Manistee, Manitou, Grand Traverse, and the following unorganized counties shall also form a part of said circuit, and be attached to the following organized counties for judicial and municipal purposes—to the county of Grand Traverse there shall be attached for the purposes aforesaid, the counties of Emmet, Charlevoix, Antrim and Kalcaska—to to the county of Manistee there shall be attached for the purposes aforesaid, the counties of Wexford and Missaukee—to the county of Mason, shall be attached for the purposes aforesaid, the county of Lake—to the county of Newaygo there shall be attached for the purposes aforesaid, the counties of Mecosta and Osceola.

The tenth circuit shall be composed of the counties of Gratiot, Isabella, Midland, Iosco and Alpena, and the following unorganized counties shall also form a part of said circuit, and be attached to the following organized counties for judicial and municipal purposes—to the county of Midland, there shall be attached for the purposes aforesaid, the counties of Arenac, Gladwin, Clare and Roscommon— to the county of Iosco, there shall be attached for the purposes aforesaid, the counties of Ogemaw, Oscoda, Alcona and Crawford—to the county of Alpena, there shall be attached for the purposes aforesaid, the counties of Otsego, Montmorency and Presque Isle.

Sec. 2. There shall be elected on the first Monday of April, in the year one thousand eight hundred and fifty-eight, one circuit judge and one regent of the University in each of the ninth and tenth judicial circuits, as organized by the provisions of this act, in the manner provided for the election of judges and regents of the University in the several circuits of the State, according to the provisions of an act entitled "an act to provide for the election of circuit judges and regents of the University," approved March 10, 1851, and the subsequent elections for such officers, and the termination of their respective terms, shall be at the times required by the constitution for judges and regents in other circuits, and each of the judges for said circuits respectively, shall, on or before the first day of June, A. D. 1858, and every two years thereafter, fix and appoint the time of holding the several terms within his circuit for the period of two years, which appointment when so made, shall remain unalterable for two years thereafter, and he shall immediately transmit to the

county clerk of each county within his circuit, a notice of
the appointment of terms so made by him, and it shall be
the duty of said clerk to preserve and file such notice, and
said county clerk shall cause a copy of such notice to be Duty of Co.
posted in some conspicuous place in his office, at least six clerk.
successive weeks before the holding of any term in pursuance thereof.

Sec. 3. All acts and parts of acts contravening the provisions of this act, are hereby repealed.

This act shall take effect immediately.

Approved January 29, 1858.

[No. 6.]

AN ACT authorizing a loan to pay those parts of the
State indebtedness falling due before and on the first
day of January, A. D., (1859,) eighteen hundred and fifty-
nine, and providing for a temporary loan, if necessary.

Section 1. *The People of the State of Michigan enact*, Governor &
That the Governor and State Treasurer are hereby au- State Treas-
thorized and directed in the name and behalf of the loans.
people of this State, to negotiate and contract for a loan
or loans not exceeding in all two hundred and sixteen
thousand dollars, redeemable at the pleasure of the State,
at any time after the expiration of twenty years from and When to be
after the first day of July, in the year one thousand eight redeemable.
hundred and fifty-eight, on the best and most favorable
terms and conditions, that in their judgment can be obtained, at an interest not exceeding six (6) per centum per Rate of in-
annum, payable half yearly, to be expended and applied terest.
solely in taking up and canceling outstanding bonds issued Funds, how
pursuant to the provisions of an act entitled "an act to pro- ed.
vide for the relief of the Detroit and Pontiac railroad
company," approved on the fifth day of March, in the year
A. D. (1838) eighteen hundred and thirty-eight; outstanding bonds issued pursuant to the provisions of an act enti-

3

tled "an act authorizing the building of the State penitentiary," approved on the twenty-second day of March, in the year A. D. 1838, and outstanding bonds issued pursuant to the provisions of an act "entitled an act to authorize a loan of a certain sum of money to the University of Michigan," approved on the sixth day of April in the year A. D. (1838) eighteen hundred and thirty-eight.

Certificates of stocks or bond.. Sec. 2. For the purpose of affecting the loan or loans aforesaid, the Governor and State Treasurer are hereby empowered and directed, after having first advertised for such loan in one of the daily papers in each of the cities of Detroit, Boston and New York, for at least thirty days prior to negotiating said loan, to cause to be made and **Amount of each.** issued certificates of stock or bonds, in sums of not less than one thousand dollars each, to be signed by the Governor and countersigned by the Secretary of State and State Treasurer, with the great seal of the State affixed thereto, which said certificates of stock or bonds shall be **Are to be transfera-ble.** drawn in favor of the Auditor General, and being endorsed by him, shall become transferable and be delivered to the Governor and State Treasurer, and be transferable by them in such form as they shall decide, to be redeemable as **Interest, when and where paya-ble.** aforesaid, and to bear interest as aforesaid, payable on the first days of July and January in each year, in the city of New York, or elsewhere in the United States, should the Governor and State Treasurer find it convenient and advantageous so to contract; and it is hereby further declared· that it shall be deemed a sufficient execution of said power to borrow, that the Governor and State Treasurer have caused the said certificates of stock or bonds to **Proviso. Bonds, how sold** be executed and sold : *Provided*, That said certificates of stock or bonds shall not be sold for less than their par **Money, how to be appli-ed.** value, and the money obtained from said loan or loans shall be paid over to the State Treasurer, to be applied for the purposes directed in this act.

Sec. 8. The faith of the State is hereby pledged for the payment of any loan or loans that shall be made pursuant to the provisions of this act. Faith of the State pledged.

Sec. 4. All necessary contingent expenses incurred by the Governor and State Treasurer in carrying out the provisions of this act, shall be audited by the Board of State Auditors and paid out of any moneys in the treasury not otherwise appropriated: *Provided*, That the State Treasurer shall not sit as a member of said Board, nor have a vote in auditing any claim or claims under this section. Expenses. Proviso.

Sec. 5. The certificates of stock or bonds, the issue of which is authorized by this act, shall be numbered and registered in a proper book to be prepared and kept for that purpose by the Auditor General in his office; which register shall contain the number, amount and when each certificate of stock or bond becomes due, the rate of interest, and when and where the interest is payable. And the Auditor General shall keep full minutes of the certificates of stock and bonds taken up and paid under the provisions of this act, in a book to be provided and kept by him in his office for that purpose, and immediately after said minutes shall have been taken as aforesaid, the same certificates and bond shall be canceled in writing across the face of each, which cancelments shall be signed by the Secretary of State and State Treasurer, and said certificates and bonds, thus canceled, shall be filed in the office of the Secretary of State. Duties of Aud. Gen'l. Canc'lment, by whom signed.

Sec. 6. The Governor and State Treasurer are hereby authorized and directed, in the name of the people of the State of Michigan, to negotiate and contract for a temporary loan or loans, not exceeding in all fifty thousand dollars (should it become necessary to do so, to meet deficiencies in the revenue) upon the same terms and conditions as the loan or loans hereinbefore are authorized, redeemable at the pleasure of the State at any Temporary loan. When to be redeemable.

time after the expiration of two years from and after the first day of July next, at an interest not exceeding seven per centum per annum, to meet deficiencies in the ordinary revenues of the State, should any exist—and all the provisions of the preceding sections of this act shall govern and control the proceedings under this section, so far as they are applicable and not inconsistent herewith : *Provided*, That the Governor and State Treasurer shall not be compelled to advertise for the loans authorized under this section.

This act is ordered take immediate effect.

Approved January 30, 1858.

Marginal notes: Rate of interest. Proviso.

['No. 7.]

AN ACT to authorize the Township of Holland, and other Townships, in the Counties of Ottawa and Allegan to make loans and levy taxes for the improvement of the harbor at the mouth of North Black River, in Ottawa County.

SECTION 1. *The People of the State of Michigan enact,* That the township of Holland, in the county of Ottawa, is hereby authorized and empowered to borrow money on the faith and credit of said township, and issue its bonds therefor, or levy taxes to an amount not exceeding one per centum upon its taxable property, in any one year, which money shall be expended in improving the entrance from Lake Michigan to Black Lake harbor, in said township.

Sec. 2. Said township bonds may be issued for sums not less than ($100 00) one hundred dollars each, and for a time payable not less than (5) five years, and at a rate of interest not exceeding (7) seven per centum, payable by coupons, annually, which bonds shall be signed by the supervisor and countersigned by the clerk of said township: *Provided*, That a majority of all the taxable inhabitants of said township, voting at any annual or special meeting

Marginal notes: Loan or tax authorized. How the money is to be expended. Amount of bonds, when payable. Rate of interest. Proviso.

thereof, shall vote by ballot for such loans, and not other- ^{Taxable inhabitant to vote on the question.} wise; *And provided also*, That said bonds shall in no case be sold for less than their par value.

Sec. 3. If said loans are authorized by a majority of the ^{Powers of township board.} electors, the township board may order the issue of said bonds from time to time, and may appoint one or more agents to negotiate the same, requiring such bonds for the faithful performance of their duty, as to such board may seem proper, and the moneys so obtained shall be paid over to the treasurer of the township, to be known as the "Black ^{Duties of township treasurer.} Lake Harbor Fund," who shall give such bonds for the faithful performance of his duty in this behalf, as the township board may require.

Sec. 4. Said township board shall appoint (7) seven free- ^{Persons appointed to improve the harbor.} holders of the township, to hold their office for such length of time as said board shall determine, and to appoint their successors, and fill all vacancies as necessities may require, ^{Their powers and duties.} whose duty it shall be to build, widen, excavate, improve and keep in repair the harbor at the mouth of North Black River aforesaid, in such manner as they shall deem best, and to such end shall use and disburse all moneys raised ^{Condition of the drawing and disbursement of the fund.} for such purpose, and the same shall be drawn out of the fund aforesaid, only upon the order of the supervisor, signed by himself and countersigned by the clerk thereof: *Provided*, That the letting of the work of improvement ^{Proviso} herein contemplated, shall first be advertised for (4) four successive weeks in a newspaper published in the city of Detroit, and in the village of Holland at least (6) six weeks ^{Contracts given to the lowest bidder.} before the letting of said work; and said letting shall be given to the lowest bidder therefor, who shall give suffi- ^{Security required,} cient security for the faithful performance of said work.

Sec. 5. The supervisor of said township, shall, from time ^{Duties of supervisor in relation to a tax.} to time, as shall be necessary, levy and assess a tax upon the taxable property of said township, sufficient to meet the bonds issued by the township as aforesaid, and interest thereon, as they shall from time to time become due, and

all necessary expenses and said tax shall be assessed and collected in the same manner as other taxes are by provisions of law assessed and collected, and the tax thus collected shall be exclusively applied and appropriated to the payment of the loans, bonds, expenses and interests aforesaid.

Sec. 6. For the purposes herein provided for, it shall be lawful for said township to take, receive and hold such voluntary grant, or donation of land or other property, as shall be made in aid of said improvement, and to purchase, take and hold such real estate or other property, as may be necessary for such purpose, and for the acquiring of such title, said township board shall proceed in all respects as near as may be applicable, in accordance with the provisions of an act entitled "an act to provide for the incorporation of railroad companies, approved February 12th, twelfth, (1855,) eighteen hundred and fifty-five, and all other acts amendatory thereto.

Sec. 7. The provisions of this act shall apply to any other township in the counties of Ottawa and Allegan, for the object aforesaid, and said townships shall, in the same manner act jointly with the township of Holland in prosecuting the said improvement of Black Lake harbor, each township thereupon, having a voice in the prosecution of said work, and all matters connected therewith, relatively, according to and in proportion to the amount of moneys raised by each of said townships.

This act is ordered to take immediate effect.

Approved February 2, 1858.

[No. 8.]

AN ACT to enlarge the boundaries of the Township of
Teal Lake, in Marquette county.

SECTION 1. *The People of the State of Michigan enact,* Boundaries defined.
That so much of the county and township of Marquette,
as is designated in the United States survey as township
forty-seven north, of range twenty-six west, be included
in the township of Teal Lake, and subject to the provisions of the act providing for the organization of the same,
approved February 10, 1857.

This act is ordered to take immediate effect.

Approved February 3, 1858.

[No. 9.]

AN ACT extending the powers of the Board of Control,
having in charge the grants of lands made to the State
of Michigan for Railroad purposes, approved February
(14) fourteenth, (1857) eighteen hundred fifty-seven.

SECTION 1. *The People of the State of Michigan enact,* Board of control may allow the flat bar iron rail to be used on rail roads in the Upper Peninsula.
That the board of control named in the act aforesaid, be
and they are hereby authorized and empowered to allow
the substitution of a flat bar iron rail, instead of the T or
continuous rail, in the construction of the several railroads
in the Upper Peninsula of this State, if in their opinion
the same shall be most advantageous for the interests of
the State, and of the several companies constructing the
same.

This act is ordered to take immediate effect.

Approved February 3, 1858.

[No. 10.]

AN ACT to amend an act entitled an act to re-organize the county of Emmet, approved February thirteenth, one thousand eight hundred and fifty-five.

Sections amended. SECTION 1. *The People of the State of Michigan enact,* That sections two and nine of an act entitled an act to re-organize the county of Emmet, approved February thirteenth, one thousand eight hundred and fifty-five, be and the same is hereby amended so as to read as follows:

Election, when held. Sec. 2 There shall be elected on the third day of August next, all the several county officers to which by law the county is entitled, and the said election and the canvass *How to be conducted.* shall in all respects be conducted in the manner prescribed by law for holding elections and canvasses for *Where held.* county and State officers; and the canvass shall be held at Mackinac City, in said county, on the Tuesday next suc- *Officers, when to be qualified.* ceeding said election, and the said county officers shall immediately be qualified and enter upon their respective *When their terms of office shall expire.* offices, and their respective offices shall expire at the same time they would have expired had they been elected at the last general election.

County seat. Sec. 9. The county seat of said county of Emmet shall be and hereby is established at Mackinac City, being on part of sections twelve and thirteen in town thirty-nine north of range four west.

Sec. 4. This act shall take immediate effect.

Approved February 3, 1858.

[No. 11.]

AN ACT to authorize the District Judge of the Upper Peninsula to convey lands held in trust in the town site of the village of Ontonagon, in the county of Ontonagon.

Preamble. *Whereas,* The Congress of the United States, by an act approved May twenty-third, one thousand eight hundred and forty-four, provided as follows: "That whenever any portion of the surveyed public lands has been or shall be settled and occupied four years as the site of a town, and therefore not subject to entry under the existing pre-emption laws, it shall be lawful for the corporate authorities thereof, and if not incorporated, for the judge of the county court for the county in which such town may be situated, to enter at the proper land office, and at the minimum price, the land so settled and occupied, in trust for the several use and benefit of the occupants thereof, according to their respective interests; the execution of which trust, as to the disposal of the lots in such town, and the proceeds of the sale thereof, to be conducted under such rules and regulations as may be prescribed by the legislative authority of the State or Territory in which the same is situated: *Provided*, That the entry of the lands intended by this act shall be made prior to the commencement of the public sale of the body of land in which it is included, and that the entry shall include only such land as is actually occupied by the town, and be made in conformity to the legal sub-divisions of the public lands authorized by act of the twenty-fourth of April, one thousand eight hundred and twenty, and shall not in the whole exceed three hundred and twenty acres: *And provided also*, That any act of said trustees not made in conformity to the rules and regulations herein alluded to, shall be void and of no effect. *And whereas*, Allen Gardiner, John Greenfield and others settled upon and occupied certain lands, as a town site, known as "Gardiner's addition" to the town of Ontonagon, in the county of Ontonagon, in the State of Michigan, the same being subject to entry as in said act provided; *And whereas*, The county courts are abolished, and the jurisdiction heretofore possessed by them is vested in the district court, the judge of which is sole judge of the Upper Peninsula, of the courts held in said county of Ontonagon, and the only per-

4

són now authorised to make such entry and hold such lands in trust, said town being unincorporated: *And whereas*, The United States have, agreeable to the act aforesaid, heretofore conveyed to Daniel Goodwin, judge of the district court of the Upper Peninsula, and of the courts of the county of Ontonagon, certain lands in trust for a town site known as "Gardiner's addition" to the town of Ontonagon, being lot number one of section number thirty-six, in township number fifty-two north, of range forty west; *therefore*,

'Powers of district judge.

SECTION 1. *The People of the State of Michigan enact*, That the Hon. Daniel Goodwin, district judge of the Upper Peninsula, and judge of the courts held in and for the county of Ontonagon, in the State of Michigan, be, and he and his successors in office are hereby authorised and empowered to dispose of the following lands now held by him, in trust, for the benefit of the occupants thereof, to wit:

Lands to be sold.

lot number one of section number thirty-six, in township number fifty-two north, of range forty west, in said county of Ontonagon, it being known as "Gardiner's addition" to to the town of Ontonagon, in pursuance to the act mentioned in the foregoing preamble, and in conformity thereto, and under the rules and regulations hereinafter contained.

Deeds to be given to occupants.

Sec. 2. Said judge shall, as trustee of the occupants of that part of the town site of Ontonagon, in the county of Ontonagon, described as lot number one, of section number thirty-six, in township number fifty-two north, of range number forty west, deed and convey unto the occupants severally of the lots, or tracts of land held by them by virtue of contracts made with Allen Gardiner and John Greenfield, aforesaid. Such deeds, so to be made and delivered

Conditions of the delivery of deed.

on the compliance of the person claiming, with the conditions and terms of the contract under which he, she or they so claimed, whether such contract be written or verbal; and all such deeds to be delivered only after such compliance and on the payment by or for the person to whom any such lot is to be conveyed, of his, or her or their pro-rata amount of such sum as may be sufficient to defray all necessary expenses. The amount to be determined by such judge, thereon.

Sec. 3. Said judge shall, after conveying to each and every person having a legal claim to any part or parcel of said lot of land, ·by virtue of any contract made by said Allen Gardiner and John Greenfield, convey the remainder thereof to the said Allen Gardiner and John Greenfield, their heirs, executors or representatives, according to their respective interests in said land. *Balance of land to be conveyed to Gardner & Greenfield.*

Sec. 4. Should any controversy or matter of difference arise between the respective parties claiming any of the lots aforesaid, such judge shall proceed summarily to determine the same upon such testimony, such notice to the parties interested, and at such times as he may prescribe and direct; and his decision thereon shall be conclusive and final, subject only to review, reversal, modification or affirmance by the supreme court, in such manner as said supreme court may determine, on application duly made for that purpose, within six months after such decision of the judge thereon. *Matters of difference, how determined.*

Sec. 5. The supreme court are hereby authorized on application made as aforesaid, to review and decide upon such decision of such judge, and may direct a re-hearing of such controversy in such manner as the circumstances of the case may seem to require. *Duties of Supreme Court.*

Sec. 6. This act shall take immediate effect.

Approved February 3, 1858.

[No. 12.]

AN ACT for the Relief of the Genesee and Oakland Railroad Company.

Time extended. SECTION 1. *The People of the State of Michigan enact,* That the time for complying with the terms of the act incorporating the Genesee and Oakland railroad company, is hereby extended to said company for three years from and after the first day of December next.

Sec. 2. This act is ordered to take effect in thirty days after its approval.

Approved February 3, 1858.

[No. 13.]

AN ACT to amend an act entitled "an act to repeal chapter (25) twenty-five of the Revised Statutes of (1846) eighteen hundred and forty-six; also, act (88) eighty-eight, entitled "an act to amend chapter (25) twenty-five of the Revised Statutes of (1846) eighteen hundred and forty-six, relative to laying out, altering, and discontinuing highways," approved March (18) eighteenth, (1848) eighteen hundred and forty-eight; also, act No. (72) seventy-two, entitled "an act to amend chapter (25) twenty-five of the Revised Statutes of (1846) eighteen hundred and forty-six, approved March (15) fifteenth, (1848) eighteen hundred and forty-eight, and to provide for altering, laying out and discontinuing highways," approved February (17) seventeenth, (1857) eighteen hundred and fifty-seven.

SECTION 1. *The People of the State of Michigan enact,* That an act entitled an act to repeal chapter (25) twenty-five of the revised statutes of (1846) eighteen hundred and forty-six; also, act (88) eighty-eight, entitled an act to amend chapter (25) twenty-five of the revised statutes of (1846) eighteen hundred and forty-six, relative to laying out, altering and discontinuing highways, approved March (18) eighteenth, (1848) eighteen hundred and forty-eight; also, act No. (72) seventy-two, entitled an act to amend

chapter (25) twenty-five of the revised statutes of (1846)
eighteen hundred and forty-six, approved March (15) fifteenth, (1848) eighteen hundred and forty-eight, and to
provide for altering, laying out and discontinuing highways, approved February (17) seventeenth, (1857) eighteen
hundred and fifty-seven, be so amended as to read as follows:

"That whenever any (10) ten or more freeholders of any *No. of freeholders ne-*
township shall wish to have a highway in any part of such *cessary to
make appli-*
township, not included within the corporate limits of any *cation.*
city or village, altered, laid out or discontinued, they may,
by writing under their hands, make application to the commissioners of highways of the township for that purpose,
who shall proceed to alter, lay out, or may discontinue such
highway, as hereinafter directed: *Provided*, That no sec- *Application,
to whom
made.*
ond application shall be made within twelve (12) months
for the same purpose: *Provided*, That whenever the person or persons through whose land the proposed highway
is to be altered or laid out, shall give his, her or their consent, in writing, according to the provisions of section (17)
seventeen of this act, and release any claim for damages,
the commissioners of highways shall have power to alter *Powers of
commission-*
or lay out the proposed highway, without the intervention *ers.*
of a jury or commissioners appointed by a court of record,
as hereinafter provided, and shall certify their action to
the township clerk.

Sec. 2. Whenever the commissioners of highways shall *Provision for
a jury.*
be applied to as mentioned in the preceding section, to
alter or lay out any highway, they, or one of them, shall,
within five (5) days thereafter, make application to a justice of the peace of the same or adjoining township, for
the appointment of a jury of twelve (12) freeholders of
the county, to ascertain the necessity of taking the property described in such application, and to appraise the
damage thereon, which application shall be in writing, and

describe the premises through which it is proposed to alter or lay out such highway.

Duty of justice.

Sec. 3. Upon the receipt of such application, the justice shall appoint a time and place for that purpose, and shall issue a citation or notice stating the object, time and place of such meeting, which shall be served by the highway commissioners on the owner or occupants of lands through which it is proposed to alter or lay out such road, at least (10) ten days before such time; and in case any such land is unoccupied, the notice may be served by posting up the same in three public places in the township, (10) ten days before the time of meeting.

Sec. 4. If the commissioners, or any one of them, and the owners or occupants of such lands, or such as may be present, cannot agree upon any other mode of appointing such jurors, they shall be appointed in the following manner:

Mode of appointing jurors.

The justice may make a list of twenty-four disinterested freeholders residing in the county, and each party may object to six on the list, and if either party fail to appear, or refuse to act, the justice and the other party, or the justice alone, may strike out the names of twelve, and the remaining twelve (12) shall be the jurors selected, and the justice may continue the hearing of the application for not less than six, nor more than (12) twelve days.

Sec. 5. The justice shall then annex to the application a warrant under his hand, returnable on said adjourned day, and issue the same, directed to any constable of the county, commanding him to summon the said jurors to be and appear at the place appointed on the said adjourned day, to serve as jurors, to ascertain the necessity of taking certain property for highway purposes, and to appraise the damages thereon; and if all the jurors shall not appear, the justice shall cause a sufficient number of talismen to be summoned to make a full jury. And if said jury shall fail to agree and return a verdict to the parties (justice) within the time provided by this act, they shall be, by such justice, discharged, and a new jury empannelled within (12) twelve days, upon the same application and in the same manner and form as herein provided for empanneling a jury.

Sec. 6. The jurors shall be sworn by such justice, to ascertain the necessity of taking the property described in the application, and justly and impartially to appraise the damage thereon, if any is claimed. They shall then proceed to view the premises described, and shall, within (5) five days thereafter, make return to the said justice in writing, to be signed by them of their doings, which shall state, if such road be altered or laid out, the necessity of taking the property described in such application, the amount of damages appraised, if any, to whom payable if known, and a statement of the time spent by them for that purpose, which return shall be certified by such justice, and filed in the office of the township clerk.

Sec. 7. Such jurors shall be entitled to receive ($1) one dollar per day, and fifty (50) cents for each half day, and the justice and constable each ($1) one dollar for their fees; and the damages which shall be assessed as hereinbefore provided, upon altering or laying out any highway, and all the lawful charges against the township for services, fees and expenses consequent upon altering or laying out such highway, shall be levied and collected in the township within which such highway is situated, and shall be paid upon the order of the township board as other township charges, except as hereinafter provided.

Sec. 8. Whenever the commissioners of highways of one township shall disagree with the commissioners of an adjoining township, whether in the same or another county, in any matter relating to a highway on the line between the two townships, the commissioners of both townships, or a majority of them shall meet at the request of the commissioners of either township, and make their determination upon such subject of disagreement.

Proceedings as to roads between two townships. Sec. 9. Whenever it shall become necessary to have a highway altered or laid out upon the line between two townships, application for that purpose may be made to the commissioners of either township, who shall proceed to lay out or alter such road in the manner provided by this act; but they shall cause the survey, or a copy thereof certified by them, to be filed in the office of the township clerk of each township. Upon proceeding to alter or lay out such road, application may be made to a justice of the peace of either township for the appointment of jurors who may be drawn equally from the townships on the line between which said road runs. The said jurors shall appraise the amount of damage to be paid by each township, and the return of their doings shall be certified by the justice and filed in the office of the township clerk of each township.

Duties of commissioners. Sec. 10. The commissioners of highways of such adjoining townships, upon altering or laying out a highway upon the line thereof, shall determine what part of such highway shall be made and repaired by each township, and each township shall have all the rights and be subject to all the liabilities in relation to the part of such highways to be made and repaired by such township as if the same was located wholly in such township.

Width of road. Sec. 11. Public roads to be laid out according to the provisions of this act, shall not be less than (4) four rods wide, except in cities or villages, where the commissioners or other proper authorities may otherwise determine.

Length of notice. Sec. 12. Whenever commissioners of highways are applied to, as provided in section (1) one of this act, to discontinue a road, they shall give at least (10) ten days notice, in writing, to the owners or occupants of lands through

which said road runs, of the time when and place where
they will meet for that purpose; and in case such land or
any part is unoccupied, such notice may be given by posting up the same in (3) three public places in the township.
In case the commissioners shall deem it advisable to dis- Order filed
with town-
continue such road, they shall make and sign an order to ship clerk.
that effect, and cause the same to be filed in the office of
the township clerk, from and after the time of filing which,
such road shall cease to be a public highway, unless an
appeal shall be taken from the determination of said commissioners, as hereinafter provided.

Sec. 13. The commissioners of highways, or (1) one of Appointm't
of commis-
them, may, instead of making application for the appoint- sioners.
ment as (of) jurors, as provided in section (2) two, of this
act, make application to any court of record, for the appointment of (3) three commissioners, whose duty it shall
be to ascertain the necessity of taking the property described in such application, and to appraise the damage
thereon, if any is claimed. The application shall be in Notice given
to owners.
writing, and describe the premises proposed to be taken
for such highway purposes, and notice thereof shall be
given, at least (5) five days previous to making such application, to the owners or occupants of lands described in
the application, and such notice may be served by the
highway commissioners, in the same manner as provided
in section three (3) of this act, and such court shall be en- Compensation of the
titled to receive for his services on each application for the court.
appointment of commissioners, as provided in this act, the
sum of ($1) one dollar.

Sec. 14. The commissioners so appointed, shall be sworn Commissioners, their
by one of the commissioners of highways, to ascertain the duties and
compensa-
necessity of taking the property described in the applica- tion.
tion, and justly and impartially to appraise the damage
thereon, if any is claimed. They shall then proceed to
view the premises, and shall, within (5) five days thereaf-

5

tar, make return of their doings in writing, signed by them, to the township clerk, which return shall state if such road is altered or laid out, the necessity of taking the property described in such application, the amount of damage appraised thereon, to whom payable, if known, and shall be filed in the office of the township clerk. The said commissioners shall be entitled to the same compensation as jurors are, under the provisions of this act. The damages appraised by said commissioners, together with all the costs of the proceeding, shall be levied, collected and paid in the manner prescribed in this act.

Damages, &c. Sec. 15. If any discontinued highway shall be attached to a tract of land through which a new highway shall be laid out, the same may be taken into consideration, in estimating the damages sustained by the owners, and in estimating the damages which may be sustained by any person owning or interested in said lands, by reason of laying out or altering any highway, the benefit which such persons shall receive thereby, shall be taken into consideration.

Existing highways legalized. Sec. 16. All highways heretofore regularly laid out and established in pursuance of existing laws, or statutes heretofore passed by the Legislature and approved by the Governor, are hereby declared to be legal highways, and it shall be the duty of the township clerk to record, in a book to be kept by him for that purpose, all papers filed in his office, relating to the laying out, altering or discontinuing of roads, as provided in this act.

Lands given for highway purposes. Sec. 17. Whenever the owner or owners of lands shall give the same or any part thereof, to the township for highway purposes, such owner or owners shall make a statement in writing, signed by him or them, to that effect, and cause the same to be filed in the office of the township clerk, of the township in which such lands are situated, and if a road shall be opened and worked thereon within the time limited by the (25) twenty-fifth section of this act, for opening and working highways, the person or persons signing such statement, or any one claiming under him or them, shall be precluded from having any action to recover possession of such land, or any compensation therefor, so long as the same shall be used for such highway purposes.

Sec. 18. Any person who shall conceive himself aggrieved by any determination of the commissioners of highways of any township, in discontinuing or refusing to discontinue any road, may, within (10) ten days after such determination, appeal to the township board of such township, but an appeal by one person shall not conclude nor affect the rights of any other person, who shall appeal within the time limited; and the said township board shall suspend all proceedings upon appeals received by them, from any such determination, until the time limited for such appeals shall have expired, to the end that their decision, when made, may embrace the whole subject.

Sec. 19. In case of an appeal from a determination of the commissioners of highways of adjoining townships in the same county, or in different counties, relating to a road upon the line of such township, such appeal may be made to the township boards of the said adjoining townships, who shall act jointly in deciding upon the determinations of the said commissioners: *Provided*, That any commissioner who may be a member of the township board shall not act on such appeal.

Sec. 20. Every appeal from a determination of commissioners of highways shall be in writing, addressed to the township board or boards, as the case may be, and signed by the party appealing, and shall briefly state the grounds upon which it is made, and whether it is brought to reverse entirely the determination of the commissioners, or only to reverse a part thereof, and in the latter case it shall specify what part.

Duty of
township
boards.

Sec. 21. It shall be the duty of the township boards, to whom the appeal is made, as soon as may be after the time limited for taking such appeals shall have expired, to give notice to the appellant, and to one or more of the commissioners from whose determination such appeal was taken, of the time when they will proceed to view the premises and hear the appeal.

Sec. 22. Every such notice shall be in writing and served at least (4) four days before the time mentioned therein, by delivering a copy of the same to the appellant and to one of such commissioners, or by leaving a copy thereof at the dwelling house of such appellant and commissioner.

Sec. 23. The said township board or boards shall proceed at the time specified in the notice, to view the premises and to hear the proofs and allegations of the parties, and may adjourn from time to time as may be necessary, and their decision shall be conclusive in the premises, and every such decision shall be reduced to writing, be signed by the township board or boards making the same, and filed by them in the office of the clerk of the proper township, who shall file the same, and give notice thereof to the commissioner of highways, but nothing herein contained shall be construed to prevent a new application under the provisions of this act.

Survey may
be made.

Sec. 24. Whenever a highway shall be altered or laid out and the same does not run upon a section line, the commissioners of highways shall, if they shall deem the same necessary, cause an accurate survey to be made of the line of said road, and shall file the minutes of such survey in the office of the township clerk of the township in which such road is situated : *Provided*, That in all cases where the premises taken for a highway are required to be set out or described, the said premises or the said highway shall be construed to be the parcel of land not less

Line of survey, how
construed.

than (2) two rods wide on each side of the line of survey, and shall be sufficiently set forth and described for all the purposes of this act by setting forth the line of survey.

Sec. 25. Whenever a public highway shall have been laid out and established, or altered through any enclosed or improved land, and the ascertained damages for such highway shall have been paid or tendered to the owner or occupant, or an order on the treasurer of the proper town-ship for the amount of such damages, shall have been exe-cuted and delivered, or tendered to such owner or occu-pant by said commissioners, said commissioners of high-ways shall then give the owner or occupant of the land through which said road shall have been laid out or altered, notice thereof, and require him to remove his fence or fences, within such time as they shall deem reasonable, not less than (60) sixty days after giving such notice, and in case such owner or occupant shall neglect or refuse to remove his fence or fences, within the time specified in such notice, the said commissioners shall have full power and authority, and it shall be their duty to enter with such aid and assistance as shall be necessary upon the premises and remove such fence or fences, and open such highway without delay, after the time specified in such notice shall have expired: *Provided*, No person shall be required to remove his fence or fences between the (1st) first day of April and the (1st) first day of November.

Sec. 26. Every public highway already laid out, no part of which shall have been opened and worked within (4) four years from the time of the time of its being so laid out, and every such highway hereafter to be laid out, no part of which shall be opened and worked within the like period, shall cease to be a road for any purpose whatever.

Sec. 27. All public highways now in use, heretofore laid out and allowed by any law of this State, or of the late Territory of Michigan, of which a record shall have been made in the office of the clerk of the county or township, and all roads not recorded, which have been used (10) ten years or more, and all roads which shall be hereafter laid out and not recorded, and which shall be used (10) years or [more, shall be deemed public highways, but may be altered or discontinued according to the provisions of this act.

Powers of corporations in relation to highways

Sec. 28. In cities and villages, application may be made by (10) ten freeholders, as provided in section (1) one of this act, to the corporate authorities of such city or village, as (and) the corporate authorities of such city or village shall have power, upon such application, to lay out and establish, open, alter or discontinue such streets, commons, lanes, alleys, sidewalks, highways, water-courses and bridges, as may be necessary for the public convenience.

Sec. 29. In case the corporate authorities of any city or village, should require the lands of any person for such purposes, such corporate authorities may cause notice to be given to the owner or party interested, his, her, or their agent or attorney, either by personal service, or by written or printed notice, posted up in at least (3) three public places in said city or village, (3) three weeks next preceding the meeting of the corporate authorities for the purpose aforesaid, and the said corporate authorities of such city or village, are hereby authorized to contract for and purchase such lands for the purposes aforesaid.

Provision for calling a jury.

Sec. 30. In case the owner or owners of such lands, shall refuse to sell the same for the purpose aforesaid, or if the parties fail to agree, it shall and may be lawful for the corporate authorities of such city or village, to cause the clerk or recorder of the same, to issue a *venire facias*, directed to the marshal or other proper officer of such city or village, directing him to summon and return a jury of (12) twelve freeholders to appear before such clerk or recorder, at a time to be therein stated, to inquire into the necessity of taking said lands or premises, and the just compensation therefor to the owners of, or to those interested in said lands and premises, which jury shall be duly sworn by such clerk or recorder, faithfully and impartially to inquire into the necessity of taking such lands or premises, and the just compensation to be made therefor.

Sec. 31. The said jury shall then proceed to view the lands and premises proposed to be taken for such public use, and if they shall deem it necessary for such city or village to take such lands or premises for the public use, shall inquire and assess such damage and recompense as they think proper to award to the owner or owners of such lands and premises, according to their respective estates and interests therein, and the said clerk or recorder shall, upon the return of such assessment or verdict, report the same to the corporate authorities of such city or village, at their next meeting, and the said corporate authorities may thereupon enter an order confirming the same, or may refuse to confirm the same, and order another jury to be summoned in the manner aforesaid; and such second jury when summoned and sworn as aforesaid, shall proceed to inquire into the necessity of taking such lands and premises for the public use, and assess such damages as aforesaid. *Duties of jury.*

Sec. 32. If one or more of such jurors shall fail to attend at the time and place mentioned in the *venire facias,* the justice, clerk or recorder before whom such jury were summoned to appear, shall order the constable, marshal or person summoning such jury, forthwith to summon a sufficient number of talismen to make up said jury. *Non attendance of jurors.*

Sec. 33. The damage or compensation so assessed by said jury, together with the costs and expenses of such proceedings, shall be assessed, levied and collected upon the property of such city or village in the same manner as other taxes or moneys are levied; such damage and recom- *Damages, &c., how paid.*

pense shall be paid or tendered to the claimant or person entitled thereto, before such street, common, lane, alley or highway shall be opened, established or altered; when the damage aforesaid shall have been paid or tendered to the person or persons entitled thereto, it shall be lawful for the corporate authorities of such city or village, to cause the said lands and premises to be used and occupied for the purposes aforesaid.

Sec. 34. The clerk or recorder aforesaid may, instead of procuring the summoning of a jury as hereinbefore provided, make an application to a court of record for the appointment of (3) three commissioners, whose duty it shall be to ascertain and determine the necessity of taking the property described in such application, and to appraise the damage thereon, if any is claimed; such application shall be in writing, and describe the premises proposed to be taken for such purpose, and notice thereof shall be given at least (5) five days previous to the time of making such application, to what court such application will be made, and the time of making the same, to the owner or occupant of the lands described in the application, his, her or their agent or attorney, and such notice may be given by the commissioner of highways, clerk or recorder, as the case may be, in the manner provided in section (4) four of this act.

Sec. 35. The commissioners so appointed, shall, before they proceed to the performance of their duties prescribed in the preceding section, be sworn to ascertain and determine the necessity for taking the property described in the application, and justly and impartially to appraise the damage thereon, if any is claimed; such commissioners shall then proceed to view the premises proposed to be taken for such public use, and shall within (5) five days thereafter, make return of their doings in writing, signed by them, to the township, city or village clerk or recorder, which return shall state if such highway, street, common, lane or alley is laid out or altered, the necessity therefor, the amount of damage appraised and to whom payable, if known, and shall be filed in the office of the township, city or village clerk or recorder. The commissioners so appointed shall be entitled to receive the same compensation as jurors are entitled to under the provisions of this act.

Sec. 36. Jurors who have been regularly summoned under the provisions of this act, who shall, without good cause shown therefor, neglect or refuse to appear and act in pursuance to said summons, shall forfeit the sum of (5) five dollars, to be recovered by action as other forfeitures to townships.

Sec. 37. The commissioners of highways of the several townships may cause a statement to be presented at the annual township meeting, of the improvements necessary to be made in the roads and bridges in such townships for the ensuing year, and an estimate of the probable expense thereof, beyond what the labor to be assessed for that year will accomplish; and such meeting may vote for the raising of a sum not exceeding ($\frac{1}{2}$) one-half of (1) one per cent. upon the agggregate valuation of the property in the the township, according to the assessment roll of the preceding year, and the sum so voted shall be levied and collected in the same manner as other township expenses.

Sec. 38. Chapter (25) twenty-five of the revised statutes of (1846,) eighteen hundred and forty-six, also act (88) eighty-eight, entitled an act to amend chapter (25) twenty-five of the revised statutes of (1846,) eighteen hundred and forty-six, relative to laying out, altering and discontinuing highways, approved March (18) eighteenth, (1848) eighteen hundred and forty-eight; also, act (72) seventy-two, entitled an act to repeal (amend) chapter (25) twenty-five of the revised statutes of (1846) eighteen hundred and forty-six, approved March (15) fifteenth, (1848) eighteen

6

hundred and forty-eight, be and the same are hereby repealed, and all acts and parts of acts inconsistent with the
provisions of this act, except acts of incorporation of cities
and villages, are hereby repealed.

This act is ordered to take immediate effect.

Approved February 3, 1858.

[No. 14.]

AN ACT to authorize Directors of the Detroit and Milwaukee Railway Company to be represented at Board of Directors by proxy.

Directors allowed to vote by proxy.

SECTION 1. *The People of the State of Michigan enact,*
That it shall be lawful for the Board of Directors of the
Detroit and Milwaukee railway company to provide by
"by laws" for allowing any directors of said company, who
may reside out of this State, to be represented and vote
at all meetings of said board of directors by proxy; such

Proxy to be in writing & filed with the secretary.

proxy to be in writing and signed by such directors, and
the same, or a true copy thereof, to be filed with the secretary of said company: *Provided,* That no proxy shall be
valid unless held by a director of said company.

This act is ordered to take immediate effect.

Approved February 3, 1858.

[No. 15.]

AN ACT to amend an act entitled "an act to provide for the construction of a State road from Saginaw City, by way of St. Louis and Ithaca in Gratiot county, (to St. Johns in Clinton county.")

Section amended.

SECTION 1. *The People of the State of Michigan enact,*
That section two of an act entitled "an act to provide for
the construction of a State road from Saginaw City, by
way of St Louis and Ithaca in Gratiot county, to St. Johns
in Clinton county," shall be amended to stand as follows:

Sec. 2. That the non-resident highway tax for three **Non-resident taxes appl'd to improvement of road.** miles on each side of the established line of said road, that shall be assessed upon the same, be and the same is hereby appropriated for the establishment and improvement of such road for the perod of three years from the first of January, eighteen hundred and fifty-seven, to be expended as hereinafter provided. Said act otherwise to be and remain in all respects as when first enacted.

Sec. 2. This act shall take immediate effect.

Approved February 3, 1858.

[No. 16.]

AN ACT granting to the River Raisin and Grand River Railroad Company the right of way over certain lands of this State.

SECTION 1. *The People of the State of Michigan enact,* **Right of way over State lands granted.** The right of way over any of the unimproved lands belonging to this State is hereby granted to the River Raisin and Grand River railroad company one hundred feet in width along the line of said road, on the line which has been heretofore surveyed, or as the same may be hereafter changed so as not materially to alter said route from the city of Jackson, Jackson county, to the township of Lansing.

Sec. 2. This act shall take immediate effect.

Approved February 3, 1858.

[No. 17.]

AN ACT to amend an act entitled "an act disposing of certain grants of land made to the State of Michigan for railroad purposes by act of Congress, approved June third, eighteen hundred and fifty-six," approved February 14, A. D. 1857.

SECTION 1. *The People of the State of Michigan enact,* **Section amended.** That section nineteen of an act entitled "an act disposing

, of certain grants of land made to the State of Michigan for railroad purposes by act of Congress, approved June third, one thousand eight hundred and fifty-six," approved February 14, A. D. 1857, be amended by striking out the word "next" where it first occurs in said section, and inserting in place thereof the words "one thousand eight hundred and fifty-eight;" also, by striking out the words "fifty-nine" in the fifteenth line of said section and insert in the place thereof the word "sixty," so that said section as amended shall read as follows:

Time extended.

Sec. 19. Each and every one of the aforesaid railroad companies shall complete and put in good running order at least twenty continuous miles of its road during each year from and after the first day December, one thousand eight hundred and fifty-eight, and shall complete the entire length of its road within seven years from the fifteenth day of November next, except the railroads in the Upper Peninsula herein named; and as to these, each and every one of them shall complete the first twenty miles of their several roads within three years from the first day of December next, and the entire lines of their several roads within the time above limited; so much of the Amboy, Lansing and Traverse Bay Railroad as shall lie between Hillsdale and Lansing, and between Lansing and the point of intersection of said road with the Detroit and Milwaukee railroad, shall be completed, fully and entirely, and put in readiness for a train of cars, on or before the first day of November, eighteen hundred and sixty, and said Amboy, Lansing and Traverse Bay railroad company shall build and finish at least twenty continuous miles of its road each year thereafter, until the whole of its line is completed ; *Provided always*, That the entire length of its road from Amboy to some point on or near Traverse Bay shall be finished by the first day of November, eighteen hundred and sixty-five ; *Provided, also*, That said Amboy,

Lansing and Traverse Bay railroad company shall locate their depot buildings at Lansing, within twenty rods of a line drawn east or west of the capitol square, situated on section sixteen in the township of Lansing. Location of depot build-ings.

Sec. 2. This act shall take immediate effect.

Approved February 3, 1858.

[No. 18.]

AN ACT to provide for the payment of the Members and Officers of the Extra Session of the Legislature, for the year eighteen hundred and fifty-eight.

SECTION 1. *The People of the State of Michigan enact,* Amount appropriated. That there be appropriated out of any money in the treasury, to the credit of the general fund, a sum not exceeding twelve thousand dollars, for the payment of the members and officers of the Legislature.

Sec. 2. The compensation of the President and members Compensation of members. of the Senate, and the Speaker and members of the House of Representatives, shall be three dollars per day for actual attendance, and when absent on account of sickness, for the first twenty days of the session, and ten cents for every mile actually traveled in going to and returning from the place of meeting of the Legislature, on the usually traveled route, and to the members of the Senate and House of Representatives from the Upper Peninsula, two dollars per day additional, for the first twenty days of the session. Each member of the Senate and House of Representatives shall also be entitled to receive five dollars Stationery. for stationery and newspapers. The compensation of the Secretary, Engrossing and Enrolling Clerk, and Sergeant-Officers of the legisla-at-Arms of the Senate, and their assistants, and of the ture. Clerk, and Engrossing and Enrolling Clerk and Sergeant-at-Arms of the House of Representatives, and their assistants, and of the Reporters of either House, shall be three

Mileage.

dollars per day for actual attendance during the session, and ten cents for every mile actually traveled in going to and returning from the place of meeting of the Legislature, on the usually traveled route. The compensation of the clerks employed, with the consent of either the Senate or the House of Representatives, by any of the standing or the special committees of either of said Houses, shall be three dollars per day for actual service during the session. The compensation to the Senate to pay their firemen, shall be three dollars per day during the session, and the compensation to the House of Representatives to pay their firemen, shall be four dollars per day during the session. The compensation of the Messengers of the Senate and of the House of Representatives shall be two dollars per day for actual attendance during the session.

Accounts, how certified.

Sec. 3. Such sums as may be due under the provisions of this act, to the Secretary of the Senate and the Clerk of the House of Representatives, shall be certified by the presiding officer of the respective Houses, and countersigned by the Auditor General; such sums as may be due to the President of the Senate, and the Speaker of the House of Representatives, shall be certified by the Secretary and Clerk of the respective Houses, and countersigned by the Auditor General; and such sums as may be due the members and officers of either House, shall be certified by the Secretary or Clerk, and countersigned by the presiding officers of the respective Houses; and the State Treasurer, upon the presentation of any such certificates, countersigned as aforesaid, shall pay the same.

This act is ordered to take immediate effect.

Approved February 3, 1858.

[No. 19.]

AN ACT to repeal act number one hundred and forty-five of the session laws of eighteen hundred and fifty-seven, being an act to provide for laying out and establishing a State road in the counties of St. Clair, Sanilac and Tuscola.

SECTION 1. *The People of the State of Michigan enact,* Act repealed. That act number one hundred and forty-five of the session laws of eighteen hundred and fifty-seven, approved February sixteenth, eighteen hundred and fifty-seven, being an act to provide for laying out and establishing a State road in the counties of St. Clair, Sanilac and Tuscola, be and the same is hereby repealed.

Sec. 2. This act is ordered to take immediate effect.

Approved February 4, 1858.

[No. 20.]

AN ACT to provide for the laying out and establishing a certain State Road in the counties of Midland, Isabella and Gratiot.

SECTION 1. *The People of the State of Michigan enact,* Section amended. That section six of the act to provide for the laying out and establishing of a certain State road in the counties of Midland, Isabella and Gratiot, be amended so that said section shall read as follows:

Sec. 6. For the purpose of improving said 'road, there Appropriation of non-resident highway taxes. shall be appropriated all such of the non-resident highway taxes of the year eighteen hundred and fifty-seven, and for three years thereafter, as may be collected for the several organized townships through which said road may pass, except the non-resident highway tax of the east half of the townships of Arcada, Newark and Fulton, in the county of Gratiot; and the highway commissioners of the several organized townships through which said road may pass, are required to expend said

Exceptions. appropriation on said road—and also one-half of the non-resident highway tax of the township of Midland, in Midland county be, and the same shall be expended by the proper authorities on that part of the said road to be established within said township.

Sec. 2. This act is ordered to take immediate effect.

Approved February 4, 1858.

[No. 21.]

AN ACT to amend act number sixty-three of the session laws of one thousand eight hundred and fifty-seven, being an act entitled "an act to lay out and establish a State road in the counties of Sanilac and Tuscola."

SECTION 1. *The People of the State of Michigan enact,* That section two of said act shall be amended so as to read as follows:

Appropriation of non-resident highway taxes.

Sec. 2. For the purpose of improving said road there shall be appropriated all such of the non-resident highway taxes for the year eighteen hundred and fifty-seven, and for three years thereafter as may be collected upon any legal subdivision of land, an equal or a greater part of which shall be within two lines running parallel with said road, one mile each way from the centre of said road; and where said road passes through the unsettled ranges of townships, to wit: ranges fourteen, thirteen and twelve, there shall be applied, on said road, all such of the non-resident highway taxes as may be collected on any of the non-resident lands in said townships.

Sec. 3. This act is ordered to take immediate effect.

Approved February 4, 1858.

[No. 22.]

AN ACT to incorporate the City of St. Clair.

SECTION 1. *The People of the State of Michigan enact,* That so much of the townships of St. Clair and China, in the county of St. Clair, as is embraced within the following boundaries, to-wit:

Commencing at the north-east corner of the south part Boundaries. of fractional section number twenty-nine, (29,) in township number five, (5,) north of range seventeen (17) east; thence west on the quarter line, across sections twenty-nine (29) and thirty, (30,) to the north-west corner of the south part of fractional section thirty, (30,) in said township and range; thence south, on the west line of said section thirty, (30,) to the north line of private claim three hundred and five, (305;) thence along the north line of said private claim, westerly, to the north-west corner thereof; thence along the west line of said private claim, southerly, to the south-west corner thereof; thence along the south line of said private claim, easterly, to the north-west corner of private claim three hundred and four, (304;) thence southerly along the west line of private claim three hundred and four, (304,) to the north-west corner of out lot number fourteen, (14;) thence east, along the north line of said out lot, to Pine River; thence southerly, along said river, up stream, to the north-west corner of out lot number seventeen, (17;) thence easterly, along the north line of out lots seventeen (17) and nineteen, (19,) to the River St. Clair; thence along said river, northerly, to the place of beginning.

Also, all that part of private claim number three hundred and six, (306,) which lies north and east of Pine River, and also the waters of Pine and St. Clair rivers, within and in front of the above limits, is hereby set off from the townships of St. Clair and China, and constituted the city of St. Clair, by which name it shall be hereafter known.

7

Body corpo-
pamte. Sec. 2. The freemen of said city, from time to time,
being inhabitants thereof, shall be and continue a body
coporate and politic, to be known and distinguished by
Title. the name and title of the mayor, recorder and aldermen of
the city of St. Clair, and shall be and are hereby made
Powers. capable of suing and being sued, pleading and being impleaded, of answering and being answered unto, and of
defending and being defended in all courts of law and
Seal. equity, and in all places whatever, and may have a common seal which they may alter and change at pleasure,
and by the same name shall be and are hereby made capa-
Real and ble of purchasing, holding, conveying and disposing of
personal es-
tate. any real and personal estate for said city.

Wards. Sec. 3. The said city shall be divided into two wards, as
follows, to wit: All that part of the city lying north of a
line commencing on the border of the river St. Clair, in
the centre of Jay street, thence west along said street to
to the east line of five acre lot number seventy-nine (79,)
thence north to the north-east corner of said five acre lot
number seventy-nine (79,) thence west along the north
line of said five acre lot numbers seventy-nine (79,) and
eighty (80,) and fifty acre lot number four (4,) to the west
line of private claim three hundred and five (305,) shall
be the first ward, and all that part of the city lying south
of said line shall be the second ward.

Govern-
ment. Sec. 4. The municipal government of the city shall
consist of a common council, composed of a mayor, recorder and four aldermen, of whom the mayor or recorder,
and three aldermen, or any four of them, shall constitute
a quorum.

Officers. Sec. 5. The following officers shall be elected from
among the electors of said city, to-wit: one mayor, one recorder, who shall be ex-officio school inspector and city
clerk, one treasurer, one marshal, who shall be ex-officio
collector of taxes, one street commissioner, two school in-

spectors, two directors of the poor, and two justices of
the peace, who shall be elected in the following manner,
to-wit: the mayor, recorder, treasurer, marshal and street
commissioner, shall be elected annually, and shall hold
their offices for one year, and until their successors shall
have been elected and qualified. There shall also be elected annually, one school inspector and one director of the
poor, for the term of two years: *Provided*, That at the Proviso.
first election there shall be elected two school inspectors
and two directors of the poor: *And provided also*, That im- Proviso.
mediately after said first election, the common council
shall meet and determine by lot which of the school inspectors and which of the directors of the poor so elected
shall serve for one year, and which for two years. There
shall also be elected once in two years, one justice of the Justices of
the peace.
peace for the term of four years: *Provided* That at the Proviso.
first election there shall be elected two justices of the
peace: *And provided also*, That immediately after the first Proviso.
election the common council shall meet and determine by
lot which of the justices of the peace so elected shall
serve for two years, and which for four years: *Provided*, Proviso.
That no justice of the peace shall be elected unless there
be a deficiency in the number of two, occasioned by the
expiration of the term of office, or otherwise, of one or
more of the justices of the peace heretofore elected in the
township of St. Clair, and who shall reside within the limits of said city at the time this act shall take effect; such
justices shall be justices of the peace of said city, and shall
hold their offices during the term for which they were
elected, unless a vacancy shall occur from some other
cause.

Sec. 6. There shall be elected at the same time, one su- Ward officers elect'd.
pervisor, one treasurer, one constable and one alderman in
and for each of said wards, the said supervisor, treasurer
and constable shall hold their offices respectively for the

term of one year and until their successors are elected and qualified, the said aldermen shall hold their offices for the term of two years, and until their successors are elected

Proviso. and qualified: *Provided*, That at the first election there shall be elected in each ward two aldermen, one for the term of one year and one for the term of two years. The

Supervisors. supervisors in and for the several wards shall represent the said wards in the board of supervisors of the county and shall be entitled to all the rights, privileges and powers, and shall be subject to all the obligations of super-

Treasurers of wards. visors of townships. The said treasurers in their respective wards, for the purpose of the collection and return of State, county, school library and school house taxes, shall be deemed township treasurers, and shall for those purposes have all the powers, and perform all the duties, and be subject to all the liabilities of township treasurers.

Treasurers' bond to the county. The treasurer of each ward shall, on or before the fifth day of November in each year, give to the county treasurer a bond in double the amount of the State and county taxes apportioned to his ward, with good and sufficient sureties, to be approved by the supervisor of his ward or the county treasurer, with like conditions as that required of township treasurers, and shall also, within the same

Treasurers' bond to the city. time, give to the city treasurer and his successors in office a bond in such sum, with such sureties as the supervisor of his ward or the city treasurer shall direct and approve, conditioned to the faithful discharge of the duties of his office, and that he will faithfully and truly account for and pay over according to law all moneys which shall come to his hands as such treasurer, and the city treasurer shall file

Vacancies in treasurer's office, how filled. the same in his office. In case the treasurer of any ward shall refuse to serve or shall die, resign, or remove from the ward before he shall have entered upon or completed the duties of his office, or shall be disabled from completing the same from any cause, the common council shall forthwith appoint a treasurer for the remainder of the year who shall give like security and be subject to like penalties and duties, and shall have the same powers and compensation as the treasurer in whose place he was appointed, and the recorder shall immediately give notice of such appointment to the county treasurer, but such appointment shall not exonerate the former treasurer or his sureties from any liabilities incurred by him.

Sec. 7. The annual elections under this act, shall be held on the first Monday in March in each year, at such places in each ward as the common council shall designate, notice of which shall be given by the recorder, at least ten days before the election, by posting the same in three public places in each ward. The supervisor and alderman of each ward shall be inspectors of such election, and they shall also be the inspectors of the State, district and county elections. The supervisor, if present, shall act as chairman of said inspectors, and the alderman shall act as clerk of said elections, and in case of the absence of one or more of such inspectors, the electors present may choose *viva voce* from their number, one or more to fill such vacancy or vacancies in said board of inspectors, and cause a return of the result of said election to be delivered to the county clerk in the same manner as is required of township clerks, and in case two or more shall receive for the same office an equal number and plurality of votes given at such election, the common council shall immediately proceed to determine by lot, between the persons so receiving the highest number of votes, which shall be elected to such office. The treasurer and marshal shall, respectively, before entering upon the discharge of their duties, give such security to the common council as said council shall direct and approve, and in case any of the officers so elected, shall neglect, for the term of ten days, to qualify as aforesaid, or to give such security, the office shall become vacant.

Vacancies in city offices, how filled.   Sec. 8. In case of a vacancy in either of the city offices, the common council may order a special election in and for the whole city, at some proper place, for the purpose of electing some person to fill such vacancy, and such election shall be conducted, and the votes canvassed by the common council of said city, or any three (3) of them. In case of a vacancy in any of the offices of the wards, the

Vacancies in ward offices, how filled.   common council may order a special election in such ward to fill such vacancy, which election shall be conducted in all respects in the same manner as annual elections for ward officers. The common council shall designate the time and

Special election to all vacancies.   place for holding such special elections, notices of which shall be posted up in three or more public places in the city or ward, as the case may be, or published in at least one newspaper published in said city, at least ten days prior to such election, which notice shall state what office or offices are to be filled, and any person so elected shall serve for the remainder of the term of such office.

Powers and duties of officers in relation to elections.   Sec. 9. The president, recorder, and trustees of the village of St. Clair, shall have all the powers and are hereby required to discharge all the duties in relation to the first election to be held under this act, that are conferred on the mayor, recorder and alderman of the city of St. Clair, any two of whom may act as inspectors of election in either of the wards at such election, and in case no two of them shall appear at the time and place appointed for such election, two of the electors present shall be chosen by the voters present to act as such inspectors.

Duties of mayor.   Sec. 10. It shall be the duty of the mayor to preside at all meetings of the common council, and in his absence the common council may appoint any one of their number to preside at such meeting. And it shall be the duty of the recorder to attend all meetings of the common council, and keep a fair and accurate record of their proceedings. Duty of recorder.

Sec. 11. The common council shall meet regularly, on the first Monday in every month, for the purpose of attending to any business that may be properly brought before them, at such places as the mayor, or in his absence, the recorder shall appoint; and the common council shall have power to impose, lay and collect such fines as they may deem proper, for the non-attendance of the officers and members thereof, at any such meeting, and also to require the attendance of any of the other officers of the city, and to impose fines for non-attendance: *Provided*, No such fine shall exceed five dollars for each offence. Meetings of common council. Fines for non-attendance. Non-attendance of officers. Proviso.

Sec. 12. The common council shall have power to organize, regulate and maintain a police of the city, and to make all such by-laws and ordinances as they may deem necessary for the promotion of the public peace, and shall have full power and authority to make all such by-laws and ordinances relative to all nuisances within the limits of said city and for the abatement of the same, and for the punishment by fine of all persons occasioning or permitting the same on his or her premises, to suppress all games of chance or hazard, and for the suppression of every species of gambling in said city, and for the suppression of disorderly and low houses, to prevent the vending, sale, or giving away of any spirituous liquors by any person or in any place within said city, to prohibit and prevent the running at large of dogs, to require them to be muzzled, and to authorize their destruction when running at large in violation of any ordinance of the common council. The common council shall have full power and authority to make all by-laws and ordinances for the suppression of riots and riotous conduct and for the dispersion of crowds in the streets, the discharge of fire-arms, fire-crackers, or making any improper noises that Powers and duties of common council. Police. Nuisance. Games and gambling. Disorderly houses. Spirituous liquors. Dogs. Riots. Fire-arms.

Vagrants, drunkards and idle persons. may tend to disturb the peace and good order of the city, for the apprehension and punishment of vagrants and drunkards and idle persons, and to make all other by-laws and ordinances as they shall deem just and proper for the safety, good order and government of said city not inconsistent with the laws and constitution of this State or of the United States.

Hay, wood, &c. Sec. 13. The common council shall also have power to make by-laws and ordinances relative to the weighing of hay, measuring of fire wood, and sale of the same, and for that purpose may appoint proper persons to measure all fire wood brought into the city for the purpose of sale in **Drays, carts and other vehicles.** the streets, or public grounds, and also relative to drays, carts and other vehicles, kept and used for the transportation of persons or property in said city, prescribe the amount of charges for services, and designate the stands for drays, carts and other vehicles, and also the stands for the sale of hay, fire wood, produce, and all other things exposed for sale in the streets, or within the limits of the **City market.** city; and also for the regulation of a city market, to pre-**Immoderate driving.** vent and punish all immoderate driving in any of the **Bathing.** streets of said city, to prohibit any public bathing within the limits of said city, to prevent the improper driving **Sidewalks.** over or upon the sidewalks, or incumbering the said sidewalks; to compel the occupants of lots to clear the sidewalks in front of and adjacent thereto, of snow, ice, dirt, mud, boxes, and every incumbrance and obstruction **Grave yards and burial of the dead.** thereon, and to regulate all grave yards and burial of the dead within or for said city; also, relative to common show-**Common Showmen.** men, the restraining of swine, horses and all other ani-**Swine, &c., prohibited fr'm run'ing at large.** mals from running at large in the streets or other public places in said city, and to regulate and establish one or **Pounds.** more pounds in said city.

Public health. Sec. 14. The common council shall have power and it shall be their duty to adopt measures for the preservation

of the public health of said city, to restrain or prohibit
the exercise of any unwholesome or dangerous avocation
within the limits of the said city, and shall be a board of
health and invested with such powers and subject to such
duties as shall be necessary to secure the inhabitants of
said city from contagious, malignant and infectious diseases,
to provide for its proper organization and for the appointment of the proper officers, and they shall have
authority to make all such by-laws and for the government of such board of health, and for the preservation of
the health of the inhabitants of said city, as shall secure
a prompt and efficient discharge of the duties imposed
upon the common council by this act; they shall also have
full power and authority to make all such by-laws and
ordinances as may be deemed by the common council expedient or necessary for the preservation of the salubrity
of the waters of Pine River and St. Clair River or other Pine River
and St.
streams within the limits of said city, relative to the open- Clair River
ing of sluices and building of wharves, relative to the
filling up all low grounds or lots covered or partially covered with water, relative to the embankment of the
margin of said rivers, within said limits, and shall also
have full power and authority to prevent and remove all Obstruct'ns
to naviga-
obstructions to the navigation of said rivers within the tion.
limits of said city and to regulate or prevent the erection
of booms, stopping of tugs, rafts of lumber or timber or
any other obstruction, and to cause said rafts of logs, timber, lumber, booms, or other obstructions in any manner
affecting the free navigation, or affecting the salubrity of
said waters, to be removed and prevented, and may cause
such rafts of logs, lumber, timber, booms, &c., to be seized
and held, to be sold or to make the owner or owners
thereof, or any person having the same in charge, person-
ally liable for any fine or penalty imposed by the ordinances or by-laws for any such obstructions or delay in

removing the same as shall be provided in such ordinances. or by-laws.

Abatement of nuisances.   Sec. 15. The common council shall have power and authority, and it is hereby made their duty to require and compel the abatement and removal of all nuisances within the limits of said city, and such regulations as shall be prescribed by ordinances, to cause all grounds therein where water shall become stagnant, to be raised, filled up or drained, and to cause all putrid substances, whether animal or vegetable, to be removed to a distance beyond the limits of said city, and when it may become necessary for the abatement of such nuisances to pull down any building or to fill up or level any ground, it shall be lawful for the common council to assess the costs or expenses of such pulling down, filling up, or leveling or removing buildings, upon the property improved, and should the owner or occupant, on reasonable notice being had, neglect or refuse to pay the full amount of said assessment, the said common council shall have full authority to sell or lease such property or premises at public auction, for the least number of years that will defray such expenses or charges, giving thirty days previous notice of the time and place of such sale or leasing, in some newspaper published in said city; and such sale shall vest a full and legal title to the purchasers for such term as the same may be sold. *Provided,* **Proviso.** That the said costs and expenses, or any part thereof, may be, at the discretion of the common council, and with the consent of the freeholders, by a two-thirds vote, in legal meeting assembled, paid or provided for by a general assessment upon the property of the whole city.

Streets.   Sec. 16. The common council shall have full power and authority to levy and collect highway taxes, and to make by-laws and ordinances relative to the time and manner of working upon the streets, lanes and alleys of said city, and also relative to the time and manner of assessing, levying and collecting all highway and sidewalk taxes.

Sec. 17. The common council shall have power and autho- Sewers and reservoirs, rity to construct sewers and reservoirs, and to provide for &c. supplying such reservoirs with water, to cause bridges to be Bridges and paving sts. built or repaired, streets to be graded, paved or planked, within the bounds of the city, whenever they shall deem the same necessary or proper; they shall also have power to cause sidewalks to be constructed or repaired, when and Side walks. where they shall deem necessary and proper, and cause the expense thereof, and of such grading, paving and planking of streets, to be assessed on lots or premises adjoining or in front of such streets or sidewalks, or by general assessment, as they may direct; to fix and establish the grades of all such streets and sidewalks, and also to establish lines upon which buildings may be erected, and beyond which such buildings shall not extend.

Sec. 18. The common council shall have authority to lay out and establish, open, make and alter such streets, lanes, and alleys, sidewalks, highways and water courses, market places, public parks and bridges within the limits of said city as they may deem necessary for the public convenience, and if in doing so they shall require for such purpose the grounds of any person, they shall give notice Proceedings when private property is to be taken. thereof to the owners or parties interested, or his or their agent or representative, by personal service, or by a notice published in some newspaper published in said city, at least three weeks previous to the meeting of the common council for the purpose aforesaid, and the said common council are hereby authorized to treat with such persons for such grounds or premises, and if for any cause a stipulation between such parties shall not be perfected, it shall be lawful for the said council to direct the recorder of said city to issue a venire facias, directed to the marshal of said city, or to any constable of said county, commanding him to summon a jury of twelve disinterested free-holders, to be taken from within the limits of said city, to appear before any justice of the peace of said city, and at any time therein to be stated, to enquire into and assess the damages in the case, which jury being duly sworn by said justice faithfully and impartially to inquire into and assess the damages in the case in question, and having viewed the premises, if necessary, shall inquire of and assess such damages as they shall judge fit to be awarded to the owner or owners, or parties interested in such grounds or premises, for their respective interests and estates therein, and the said justice shall, upon the return of such assessment or verdict, enter judgment thereon confirming the same, and such sum or sums so assessed, together with his or their costs, shall be paid or legally tendered to the claimant thereof before such street, lane, alley, sidewalk, highway, market place, public park, or bridge, shall be made, opened, established or extended; but if such jury shall find that the claimant is not entitled to any damages, then it shall be competent for such justice to render judgment against such claimant for costs, and issue execution therefor, and in either case it shall thereupon be lawful for the common council to cause the same grounds or premises to be converted to and for the purposes aforesaid: *Proviso ap-* *Provided*, That any party claiming damages may have the right to remove such proceedings, by appeal to the circuit court, for the county of St. Clair, upon giving notice of his or their intention so to do to such justice in writing within ten days after the verdict of such jury and the judgment of such justice thereon aforesaid, and upon filing of a transcript of the proceedings aforesaid in the said circuit court, the same proceedings shall be had as prescribed by law in cases of appeals: *Provided*, That if the final judgment for damages of said circuit court shall not exceed the damages assessed before said justice, the party appealing shall pay all costs occasioned by such appeal. The said common council shall have full control of all streets, lanes, alleys, bridges, sidewalks and other public grounds within the said city and the property belonging to said city, and it shall be their duty, and they are hereby empowered, to make all such by-laws and ordinances, not inconsistent with the constitution and laws of this State or the United States, as shall by them be deemed necessary and proper for the best interest of said city.

Sec. 19. The assessment in the several wards of said city shall be made at the same time, and the assessment rolls completed, and all other proceedings had thereon, in the same time and the manner as is required by law of township assessors; *Provided*, That for the purpose of assessing all property equally in the whole city, the assessors shall act jointly in assessing each ward, and shall meet at the time required by the statute, at the office of the recorder of said city, for the purpose of reviewing and completing their assessments and assessment rolls for each of their several wards, and two of said assessors shall be authorized to perform all the duties required by the whole number.

Sec. 20. When such assessment rolls shall be completed they shall be delivered to the recorder, who shall immediately proceed to make therefrom a full and complete condensed copy from such assessment rolls, for the use of the common council, which shall be deemed the city assessment roll for that year. When such copy shall be completed, and within fifteen days after receiving the same, the said recorder shall deliver said rolls to the respective supervisors of each ward, to be used for State and county purposes.

Sec. 21. The common council shall have power and authority to levy and collect a capitation or poll tax upon all male inhabitants between the ages of twenty-one and fifty years, of said city, and also taxes on all real estate and personal property within the limits of said city, by them deemed necessary to defray the expenses, and for the public improvement of said city, not to exceed one-half of one per cent. on the valuation thereof, exclusive of the expenses for the fire department, which shall not exceed one-fourth of one per cent. in addition thereto, and shall have power and authority to make and establish all necessary by-laws and ordinances for the collection of the same. And every assessment of tax lawfully imposed or laid by the said common council on any lands, tenements and hereditaments or premises whatsoever in said city, shall be and remain a lien on said lands, tenements and hereditaments, from the time of imposing such tax until paid, and the owner or occupants, or parties interested respectively in said real estate, shall be liable on demand to pay all and every such tax to be made as aforesaid. And in default of such payment, or any part thereof, or in default of the payment of the assessment upon any lot, for grading, paving or planking the streets, or the construction or repair of sidewalks adjoining such street, lot or premises, it shall be lawful for the marshal of said city to sell personal property, and for want thereof to sell real estate, rendering the overplus, if any, after deducting the charges of such sale, to such owner, occupant or lesee. *Provided,* That whenever any real estate shall be sold by said marshal, notice thereof shall be published in a newspaper published in said city, once a week for at least one month next preceding such sale, and the said marshal, or his successor in office, shall give to the purchaser or purchasers of any such lands, a certificate in writing, describing the lands purchased, and the time when the purchaser will be entitled to a deed for said land. And if the person claiming title to said land described in the said certificate, shall not, within two years thereafter, pay to the treasurer of said city, for the use of the purchaser, his heirs or assigns, the sum mentioned in such certificate, together with the interest thereon at the rate of twenty-five per cent. per annum from the date of such certificate, the said marshal, or his successor in office, shall, at the expiration of the said two years, execute to the purchaser, his heirs or assigns, a conveyance of the land so sold, which conveyance shall vest in the person or persons to whom it shall be given, an absolute estate in fee simple, subject to the claims the estate shall have thereon. And the said conveyance shall be *prima facie* evidence that such tax was lawfully enforced and imposed, and that all the proceedings thereon, including such sale, were regular, according to the provisions of this act. And every such conveyance executed by the marshal, under his hand and seal, and witnessed and acknowledged and recorded in the usual form, may be given in evidence in the same manner and with the like effect as a deed regularly executed and acknowledged by the owner, and duly recorded, may be given in evidence. And all personal estate so sold, shall be sold according and in such manner as the common council may direct.

Sec. 22. If the said common council shall deem it expedient for the purposes of said city to levy a larger tax than is allowed by section twenty-one of this act, they may, by giving ten days notice, either by publishing the same in a newspaper published in said city or posting a written notice thereof in three public places in said city, call a meeting of the inhabitants of said city, at some place therein, who may then and there vote to levy, assess and collect a further money tax upon all the real and personal property in said city, in such sum as the said meeting shall direct, and such tax shall be levied, assessed and collected in the same manner as is provided for the levying or collection of the other taxes mentioned in this act: *Provided*, That no person shall vote at such meeting who is not a freeholder in said city. The mayor of said city, and in his absence the recorder, shall preside at such meeting.

Taxes, how paid over. Sec. 23. All moneys raised to defray expenses of said city within the limits thereof shall be collected and paid over by the marshal to the treasurer of said city at such time and under such regulations as shall be provided for by the ordinances of the common council.

Tax roll. Sec. 24. It shall be the duty of the common council whenever they shall have completed their tax roll for one year, to make out a duplicate; charging each individual or premises therein an amount of tax in proportion to the amount of personal and real estate in said city, to which they shall attach a warrant, signed by the mayor or recorder, directed to the marshal of said city, commanding said marshal to collect from the several persons named in said roll the several sums mentioned in the last column of such roll opposite their respective names and to pay over the same as they shall direct in such warrant, and the said warrant shall authorize the said marshal, in case any person named in the assessment or tax roll shall neglect to pay over his tax, to levy the same by distress and sale of the goods and chattels of such person.

Powers and duties of certain officers to be prescribed by the common council Sec. 25. The common council shall have power and authority to make all by-laws and ordinances relative to the powers, duties and liabilities of the recorder, treasurer, marshal and street commissioner, and allow them respectively such compensation for their respective services as they shall deem just and reasonable; they shall also credit and allow to each assessor one dollar and fifty cents a day for the time actually spent in taking the assessment and copying rolls, and also one dollar and fifty cents per day for each inspector of elections, and no compensation shall be allowed to the mayor or aldermen for their services.

Sec. 26. The common council shall, on or before the first Monday in each year, settle and audit the accounts of the treasurer, and the accounts of all the officers and persons having claims against the city, or accounts with it, and cause all balances due to any person to be paid out of any money in the treasury not otherwise appropriated, and shall make out in detail, a statement of all receipts and expenditures, which statement shall fully specify all appropriations made by the common council, and the objects and purposes for which the same were made, and the money expended [on] such appropriation, the amount of taxes raised and the amount of contingent expenses, the amount expended on highways, streets and bridges, and all such information as shall be necessary to a full and perfect understanding of the financial concerns of the city, and shall cause the same to be published in one or more newspapers published in the city, before the next ensuing election. *Settlement with treasurer.*

Sec. 27. The common council shall have power and authority to make all by-laws and ordinances that may be necessary to secure the said city and all the inhabitants thereof, against injuries by fire; to establish and organize all such fire companies, and hose and hook and ladder companies, as shall be necessary to extinguish fires and preserve the property of the inhabitants of said city from destruction, to appoint from among the inhabitants of said city, such number of men, willing to accept, as may be deemed proper and necessary to be employed as firemen; and such fire, hose and hook and ladder company, shall have power to appoint their own officers, pass their own by-laws for their organization and government of said companies, subject to the approval of the common council, and may enforce and collect such fines for the non-attend- *Injuries by fire.* *Fire companies.* *Fines.*

9

ance or neglect of duty of any of its members, as may be established by such by-laws and regulations of every such company; and every person belonging to such company, shall obtain from the recorder of said city a certificate to that effect, which shall be evidence thereof; and the members of such company, during their continuance as such, **Exemptions of firemen.** shall be exempt from serving on juries or paying a poll tax in said city; and it shall be the duty of every such company to keep in good and perfect repair the fire engine in their charge, hose, ladders and other instruments of such company; and it shall be the duty of each fire company to assemble at least once in each month, and as often as may be directed by the chief engineer, for the purpose of working and examining the fire engine and other implements, with a view to their perfect repair; and the said firemen, so appointed, shall annually elect one of their number chief engineer, who shall have command of the whole fire department of said city; and also to elect from their number, assistant engineers, at the same time. The **Fire warden** common council shall appoint a fire warden in each ward of the city, whose powers, duties and compensation, shall be prescribed by the common council; and also to appoint **City watch.** a city watch of one or more persons, not exceeding five, if the common council shall deem it necessary for the safety of the persons and property of the said city, and to prescribe their duties and compensation when in actual service, and to remove them at pleasure.

Fire.   Sec. 28. Upon the breaking out of any fire in said city, the marshal shall repair immediately to the place of such fire and aid and assist as well in extinguishing the fire as in preventing any goods or property from being stolen or injured, and in protecting, removing and securing the same, for which purpose, and as chief of police, he may require the assistance of all bystanders, and in performance of his said duties the marshal shall in all respects be subject to the orders of the mayor or such of the aldermen as may be present.

Sec. 29. The common council shall have power to appoint an attorney for the city and one or more commissioners, and such other officers whose election is not herein specially provided for as they may deem necessary to carry into effect the powers granted by this act, and to remove the same at pleasure; they shall also have power to remove the marshal, treasurer, or street commissioner, for any violation of the ordinances of the common council, and in case of death, resignation or removal from office, or neglect to qualify, or removal from the city or from the ward for which he has been elected, of any officer of the corporation, the common council shall, as soon as may be, appoint an officer to fill such vacancy for the unexpired term of the year, and all officers so appointed shall be notified and qualified as herein directed.

Sec. 30. The marshal of said city shall, before entering upon the discharge of the duties of his office, give such security for the faithful discharge of his duties, as the common council shall direct and require. He shall be chief of the police, and it shall be his duty to serve all processes that may be lawfully [given] to him for service, to see that all by-laws and ordinances of the common council are promptly and efficiently enforced, and especially those that may be passed to carry into effect the powers of sections twelve, thirteen, fourteen and fifteen, of this act. He shall obey all the lawful orders of the mayor, and may command the aid and assistance of all constables and all persons, in the discharge of the duties imposed upon him by law. He may appoint such number of deputies as the common council shall direct and approve, who shall have the same powers and perform the same duties as the marshal, and for whose official acts he shall be in all respects responsible; and the marshal and his deputies shall have the same power to serve and execute all processes on behalf of the corporation of said city, or of the people of this State, as sheriffs or constables have by law to execute similar processes.

Sec. 31. The street commissioners, and such other officers as the common council shall direct and appoint, shall, under the direction of the common council, superintend the making, paving, planking, repairing and opening of all streets, lanes, alleys, bridges and sidewalks within the limits of their respective wards, in such manner as he or they may from time to time be directed.

Sec. 32. The common council shall have authority to make all by-laws and ordinances relative to the powers and duties and compensation of the officers of said corporation, subject to the restriction as to the compensation of officers mentioned in this act, to direct the number of, and license inn-keepers and common victualers, to provide for the collection and disposition of all fines and penalties which may be incurred under the by-laws and ordinances of said city, and to make all such other by-laws, ordinances and regulations for the purpose of carrying into effect the powers conferred by this act which they may deem necessary, to provide for the safety and good government of the city, and to preserve the health and protect the property of the inhabitants thereof, and to this end the common council may impose fines and penalties for any violation of the by-laws and ordinances which may be made by them aforesaid: *Provided*, That no by-law or ordinance shall impose a fine exceeding one hundred dollars, nor subject the offender to imprisonment in the city or county jail exceeding thirty days; also relative to the calling of meetings of electors of the city.

Sec. 33. All fines imposed by any by-laws or ordinance of the common council may be sued for in the name of the city attorney or in the name of the corporation, before

any justice of the peace for a violation of any ordinance
of the common council, it shall be the duty of the justice
forthwith to issue execution to the marshal of the city,
commanding him to collect of the goods and chattels of
the person so offending, the amount of such fine, with
interest and costs, and for the want of goods and chattels
wherewith to satisfy the same, that he take the body of
the defendant and commit him to the city or county jail,
and the marshal or sheriff shall safely keep the body of
the person so committed until discharged by due course
of law, and the defendant shall remain imprisoned until
the execution, with the fees of the sheriff or marshal,
shall be paid: *Provided*, That the common council may Proviso.
remit such fine in whole or in part, if it shall be made to
appear that the person so imprisoned is unable to pay the
same.

Sec. 34. In all suits in which the corporation of the city Competency of witnesses
of St. Clair shall be a party or shall be interested, no inhabitant of said city shall be deemed incompetent as a witness
or jurors, on account of his interest in the event of such suit
or action: *Provided*, Such interest be such only as he has Provided.
in common with the inhabitants of said city.

Sec. 35. In all trials before any justice of the peace of Jury.
any person charged with a violation of any by-law or ordinance of the common council, either party shall be entitled
to a jury of six persons, and all the proceedings for the Proceedings and trials.
summoning of such jury and in the trial of the cause shall
be in conformity, as near as may be, with the mode and
proceedings in similar cases before justices of the peace;
and in all civil cases and criminal, the right of appeal from Appeals.
the justice's court to the circuit court for the county of St.
Clair, shall be allowed, and the party appealing shall enter
into a recognizance, conditioned to prosecute the appeal in
the circuit court and abide the order of the court therein,

or such other recognizance as is or may be required by law in appeals from justice's court in similar cases.

Sec. 36. The common council of said city is hereby authorized and required to perform the same duties in and for said city, as are by law imposed upon the township boards of the several townships of this State, in reference to schools, school taxes, county and State taxes, the support of the poor, and State, district and county elections; and the supervisors, assessors, justice of the peace, recorder, school inspectors, directors of the poor, and all other officers of said city, who are required to perform the duties of township officers of this State, shall take the oath, give the bond, perform like duties, and receive the same pay, and in the same manner, and be subject to the same liabilities as is provided for the corresponding township officers, except as is otherwise provided in this act, or as may be provided by the ordinances of the common council.

Sec. 37. The president, recorder and trustees of the village of St. Clair, shall be the common council, and shall respectively discharge all the duties of mayor, recorder and alderman, and the treasurer, marshal and other officers of said village, shall be such officers of the city of St. Clair, until others are elected and qualified in their stead; and all the by-laws, ordinances and other regulations now in force, not inconsistent with this act, or the provisions of the statutes of this [State,] shall be and remain in force until altered or repealed by the common council of the city or village; and no suit, or other proceedings in which the common council or any officer of said village shall be a party, or any duties to be performed by such officer, shall be affected in any manner whatever by this act, except as herein specified, and all property belonging and all demands due to the village of St. Clair, shall be the property of the city of St. Clair, and the said city shall be liable for all legal demands against said village of St. Clair.

Sec. 38. All town officers of the township of St. Clair, residing within said city, may continue to discharge all the duties of such offices for said town, until after the first day in April next. The next township meeting for the township of St. Clair, shall be held at the town hall in the village of St. Clair. It shall be the duty of the school inspectors of the township of St. Clair, to pay over the school moneys by them received for the present year, in the same manner as if this act had not passed.

Sec. 39. The treasurers of the several wards, shall, on or before the first day of February in each year, pay the amount of moneys raised for school and library taxes, to the city treasurer, to be by him paid on the order of the school inspectors or school district officers, as the case may be, and the warrant for the collection of taxes, given to the said ward treasurers, shall command them accordingly.

Sec. 40. The city of St. Clair, for all purposes in regard to common schools, and school moneys, shall be deemed a township, and the recorder shall discharge all the duties and be subject to all the liabilities of a township clerk. The city treasurer and school inspectors shall discharge the duties of such corresponding township officers, except the collection of taxes.

Sec. 41. All acts incorporating the village of St. Clair, and all acts amendatory thereto, are hereby repealed.

Sec. 42. This act is ordered to take effect on the twentieth of February next.

Approved February 4, 1858.

[No. 28.]

AN ACT to provide for the laying out and establishing a certain State Road in the counties of Newaygo, Lake, Wexford and Grand Traverse.

Commissioners appointed. SECTION 1. *The People of the State of Michigan enact,* That William T. Howell, Samuel Rose and Daniel Weaver be and they are hereby appointed commissioners to lay out **Line of road.** and establish a State road, commencing at the south line of Newaygo county, at the north-west corner of Kent, and the north-east corner of Ottawa counties, running thence northerly to the village of Newaygo, and from thence through the townships of Fremont and Dayton, on the most practicable route to some point on Traverse Bay.

Duty of commissioners. Sec. 2. That the above named commissioners shall file so much of the survey of said record [road] in the office of the township clerk of each township through which said road shall pass, as shall be laid out in said township ; and it **Duty of township clerks.** shall be the duty of the several township clerks to record the same in their respective offices, and post such notice as shall be required by law.

Duty of commissioners of highways. Sec. 3. That it shall be the duty of the commissioners of highways in any organized township through which said road may pass, to open and work the same, in the same manner, and by virtue of the same law, as township roads are required to be opened and worked.

Damages. Sec. 4. That in all cases in which damages may be claimed, by reason of the laying out and establishing of said road, the same proceedings shall be had thereon as may be required by the laws in force at the time such claim is made, for the assessment of damages in case of roads laid out by township commissioners.

Non-resident taxes, how expended. Sec. 5. That all non-resident taxes on any lands which may be returned by the township treasurer, on each and every section, or parts of sections of land lying within two miles of said road, shall be laid out and expended in opening, bridging and repairing said road, by and under the control of commissioners of highways, in the same manner that non-resident highway moneys are appropriated by law.

Sec. 6. That the State shall not be liable for any expenses incurred or damages sustained by reason of this act, and if said road is not laid out and established within two years from the passage of this act, the provisions herein shall be void. *State not liable for expense or damage.*

Sec. 7. This act is ordered to take immediate effect.

Approved February 4, 1858.

[No. 24.]

AN ACT to amend an act entitled "an act to provide for laying out, establishing, and improving a State Road in Clinton, Gratiot, Shiawassee, Saginaw and Genesee counties," approved February seventeenth, eighteen hundred and fifty-seven.

SECTION 1. *The People of the State of Michigan enact,* That section two of said act be amended by striking out the word "seven," where it occurs in the third line of said section, so that the same shall read as follows, to-wit: *Section amended.*

Sec. 2. It shall be the duty of said commissioners, or a majority of them, on or before the first day of June, eighteen hundred and fifty-eight, to assemble, and proceed to lay out said road, and survey the same, and cause the same to be filed with the township clerk of each of the respective townships on the line thereof, so far as said road shall run through each of the respective townships; whose duty it shall be to record the same, and such record shall be prima facia evidence of the existence of said road. *Duty of commissioners. Survey of road to be filed with township clerks.*

Sec. 3. This act is ordered to take immediate effect.

Approved February 4, 1858.

' [No. 25.]

AN ACT to provide for laying out a State Road from Saginaw to Cheboygan.

Comm'ners SECTION 1. *The People of the State of Michigan enact,*
appointed.
That Daniel Carter, of Fremont; Henry Raymond, of Saginaw county; D. D. Oliver, of Devil River; A. Terry, of
Sauble River, and C. C. Whittemore, of Ottawa Bay; be,
and the same are hereby appointed commissioners to lay
Line of road. out and establish a State Road from Saginaw, in the county
of Saginaw, to Cheboygan, in the county of Cheboygan,
touching as near as may be at Ottawa Bay, Sauble River,
and Fremont, on Thunder Bay.

Commission- Sec. 2. The above name commissioners shall file so much
ers to file
surveys of the survey of the above named road, in the office of the
with county
clerks. county clerk of each county through which said road shall
pass, as shall be laid out in such county; and it shall be
Duty of Co. the duty of the several county clerks to record the same
clerks.
in their respective offices, and post such notice as may be
required by law.

Highway Sec. 3. It shall be the duty of the commissioners of
commis'ne's
to open and highways, in any organized township through which said
work road.
road shall pass, to open and work the same, in the manner
and by virtue of the same law as township roads are
opened and worked.

Compensa- Sec. 4. Said commissioners shall be entitled to receive
tion of com-
missioners. for their services while engaged in laying out and establishing said road, the sum of two dollars a day for each
and every day they are actually so engaged, to be paid
pro rata by the counties through which said road shall
pass.

State liable Sec. 5. The State shall not be liable for any expenses in-
for no ex-
pense or curred, or damages sustained, by reason of this act, and if
damage.
said road is not laid out and established within five years

from the passage of this act, then the provisions therein _{Road to be laid out within five years.} contained shall be void.

Sec. 6. This act is ordered to take immediate effect.

Approved February 4, 1858.

[No. 26.]

AN ACT to amend section six of act No. one hundred and forty-seven, of the session laws of eighteen hundred and fifty-seven.

SECTION 1. *The People of the State of Michigan enact,* That section 6 of said act shall be amended so as to read as follows:

Sec. 6. The said commissioners shall contract for the Duty of commissioners. said drainage, and the construction and completion of said canal or channel across said flats, and all works connected therewith, necessary to its usefulness and safe navigation, and of all other necessary work for the improvement of said river, at such other time as they shall think proper, not later that the first of January, eighteen hundred and Time limited. sixty, making payment for all of said work out of the sum by this act appropriated, and no payment shall be made on account of said works, or any of them, until the said drainage and the canal or channel across the said flats, and all works connected with or necessary to the usefulness thereof, are Condition of payment. completed to the satisfaction of the said commissioners, and approved by the Governor, and in accordance with the terms of the contract to be made in pursuance of this act.

Sec. 2. This act is ordered to take immediate effect.

Approved February 4, 1858.

[No. 27.]

AN ACT to aid in the Improvement of a certain State
Road.

Extension.   SECTION 1. *The People of the State of Michigan enact,*
That the provisions of act number sixty-eight of the session laws of eighteen hundred and fifty-five, approved
February tenth, eighteen hundred and fifty-five, be, and
the same are hereby extended for a period of two years
from and after the time limited in said act.

Sec. 2. This act shall take immediate effect.

Approved February 4, 1858.

[No. 28.]

AN ACT to provide for laying out and establishing a State
Road in the county of Sanilac.

Commission-
ers appoint-
ed.   SECTION 1. *The People of the State of Michigan enact,*
That Henry Wideman, Daniel Wixson and Peter W. Ash-
ley, of the county of Sanilac in the State of Michigan, be,
and they are hereby appointed commissioners to lay out
Line of road. and establish a State road, running from and commencing
at the village of Lexington, in the county of Sanilac aforesaid, thence as near as may be in a due west line from said
village, to the west line of the county of Sanilac: *Provided,* That the western terminus of the said State road shall
be within one of the townships nine, ten or eleven north,
in said county of Sanilac.

Commission-
ers to file
survey.   Sec. 2. It shall be the duty of said commissioners to
cause a description of said State road, signed by them, or
at least two of them, to be filed in the office of the township clerk of each of the respective townships through
which said road or any part thereof may pass, on or before the first day of December next; and it shall be the
Township
clerks to re-
cord survey. duty of the several township clerks to record the same in
the books of the highway commissioners of their town-

ships, and such survey, record and description of such road
when so filed and recorded, shall be conclusive evidence
of the existence of such State road; and if any township
clerk shall neglect or refuse to record the same, he shall Penalty.
be liable to indictment and punishment as for a misdemeanor, as in other cases of neglect of duty on the part of
any officer.

Sec. 3. For the purpose of improving said road, there Certain taxes appropri-
shall be and is hereby appropriated all of the non-resident ated.
highway taxes that shall be collected in the year eighteen
hundred and fifty-seven, and for three years thereafter,
upon any legal sub-division of land, an equal or the
greater part of which shall be within the two lines running
parallel with said road, one mile each way from the center
of said road, in the townships through which it may be
laid out.

Sec. 4. It shall be the duty of said commissioners to su- Duties of
commission-
perintend the expenditure of all such sums of money as ers.
shall be collected for the benefit and improvement of said
State road, and to direct and determine the manner in
which said labor shall be applied and laid out upon said
road.

Sec. 5. It shall be the duty of the said commissioners, Commissioners to exe-
before entering upon the duties of their office, to execute cute and file
bond.
and deliver each a bond to the people of the State of
Michigan, in the penal sum of one thousand dollars each,
with one sufficient surety, to be approved by the county
treasurer of Sanilac county, and filed in his office, which
bond shall be conditioned for the faithful performance of
the duties of his office, imposed upon him by this act,
and any default thereof shall render such commissioners, Penalty.
or any one of them (liable) to prosecution in the same
manner as county officers; and any moneys recovered upon
any such prosecution, shall be paid over by the proper
officers to the county treasurer of said county, to be by

him placed to the credit of the fund created by this act, for the improvement of the road herein named.

Duties of commissioners. Sec. 6. It shall be the duty of said commissioners, on or before the first day of December next, to make out a list of all non-resident lands coming under the provisions of this act, and deliver the same to the county treasurer of **Duties of Co. treasurer.** the county of Sanilac, who shall thereupon open an account with said commissioners, and credit to said commissioners all moneys that may thereafter be paid into his office as non-resident highway taxes upon any of the lands described in such list, according to the provisions of this act, and charge said commissioners with all moneys which may be drawn by their order, for the improvement of said road.

Expenses, how paid. Sec. 7. It shall be the duty of the said commissioners, or any two of them, in the payment for any labor performed, or materials furnished in the improvement of the said road, to issue their certificate to any person or persons to whom they may be indebted by virtue of their office, for work and labor done upon said road, or for materials furnished as aforesaid, and may attach to such certificate an order upon the county treasurer of said county of Sanilac for the amount thereof, payable out of the fund created by this act for the improvement of said road, who shall pay the same out of said fund, and charge the same as provided in section six of this act.

Duties of commissioners in relation to receipt and disbursem't of moneys. Sec. 8. It shall be the duty of said commissioners to render to the board of supervisors of the county of Sanilac, at their annual meeting, a true account of the receipts and disbursements of all moneys they may have received or expended under the provisions of this act, and the said board in their discretion may examine any one of such commissioners on oath, touching the correctness of such account.

Sec. 9. Any overseer of highways or any township

treasurer of any of the townships in which are situate who shall receive the whole or any part of any non-resi- *Duties of overseers of highways & township treasurers.*
any of the lands coming under the provisions of this act, who shall receive the whole or any part of any non-resi-
dent highway tax on such lands, shall immediately pay
over the same to the county treasurer of said county of
Sanilac, to be by him placed to the credit of the said commissioners, as provided for in other cases.

Sec. 10. Said commissioners may receive donations and *Donations.*
subscriptions for the benefit of said State road, and shall
cause the same to be faithfully expended and applied to
the improvement of said State road.

Sec. 11. The said commissioners shall receive as com- *Compensation.*
pensation for their services, one dollar and fifty cents per
day, while actually engaged in the performance of the duties imposed upon them by this act, which amount shall be *How paid.*
paid out of the fund created by this act, after their accounts for the same, verified by their oaths, shall have been
audited by the board of supervisors of said county of
Sanilac.

Sec. 12. The right of way for said road through any *Right of way*
lands belonging to this State is hereby granted and confirmed to the several townships in which the lands may be,
and the State shall not be liable for any expenses incurred
or damage sustained by virtue of this act.

Sec. 13. In case any vacancy shall occur in the office of *Vacancies, how filled.*
commissioner, as created by this act, upon application be-
ing made by five freeholders of said county, the county
treasurer, sheriff and prosecuting attorney of said county,
shall proceed at once to appoint a commissioner or commissioners to fill such vacancy, which appointment shall be in
writing, and signed by at least two of such officers, and
filed in the office of the county treasurer of said county,
and such appointee or appointees shall give bonds in like
manner and have the same powers as the commissioners
appointed by this act.

Commissioners for determining the necessity for taking private property.

Sec. 14. The commissioners appointed by this act may make application to the circuit court of the county of Sanilac, during any session thereof, for the appointment of the [three] commissioners by an order of such circuit court, whose duty it shall be, when private property is taken for the use of said State road, to ascertain the necessity of taking the same, appraise the damage and fix the compensation therefor, according to the provisions of section two of article eighteen of the constitution of this State, and whenever such application shall be made as aforesaid; it shall be the duty of the said circuit court to appoint said commissioners for the purposes aforesaid, by an order to be entered upon the journals of said court, without delay or evasion.

Their duties

Sec. 15. It shall be the duty of the said last mentioned commissioners, after their appointment by the said court, to procure [proceed] without delay to ascertain the necessity of taking such private property as is claimed to be necessary by the first mentioned commissioners, and if by them deemed necessary to be taken, they shall appraise the damages and award the compensation therefor, as is provided by law in ordinary cases of laying out highways, and shall file such award in writing, signed by them, in the office of the township clerk of the township where the property taken may be, and the same, to-wit, the damages and the compensation therefor, shall become a legal charge against the said respective townships, as is provided in ordinary cases of laying out highways.

Am't awarded a legal charge against the township.

Compensation of last named commissioners.

Sec. 16. The compensation of the last mentioned commissioners appointed by the said circuit court, shall be one dollar and fifty cents per day for each day actually spent by them in the discharge of their duties under this act and the appointment aforesaid, which shall be allowed and paid in the same manner as in case of the first mentioned commissioners.

Sec. 17. All acts and parts of acts contravening the provisions of this act, are hereby repealed.

Sec. 18. This act shall take immediate effect.

Approved February 4, 1858.

[No. 29.]

AN ACT to amend an act entitled "an act to incorporate the Village of Allegan," approved March 20th, A. D. 1838, and to repeal an act amendatory thereto, approved April 28th, A. D. 1846.

SECTION 1. *The People of the State of Michigan enact,* That act No. 43, of the session laws of eighteen hundred and thirty-seven and eight, entitled an " act to incorporate the village of Allegan, be, and the same is hereby amended so as to read as follows:

SECTION 1. *The People of the State of Michigan enact,* Boundaries. That all that tract of land embraced in section twenty-eight, town two north, of range thirteen west, in which the county site of Allegan county was located, be and the same is hereby constituted a town corporate, and shall be hereafter known by the name or title of the village of Allegan.

Sec. 2. The male inhabitants of said village having the Elections. qualifications of electors under the constitution, shall meet at the "Old Court House," in said village, on the second Monday of March next, and on the second Monday of March, annually thereafter, at such place as shall be provided in the by-laws of said village, and then and there proceed by a plurality of votes to elect by ballot from among the qualified electors residing in said village, five trustees, two assessors, one president, one recorder and What officers to be one treasurer, who shall hold their offices for one year, and elected. until their successors are elected and qualified: *Provided,* That if an election of such officers shall not be made on

11

the day when pursuant to this act it ought to be made, the said corporation for that shall not be deemed to be dissolved, but it shall and may be lawful to hold such election at any time thereafter, pursuant to public notice to be given in the manner hereinafter described.

Sec. 3. At the first election to be holden under this act, there shall be chosen *viva voce*, by the electors present, two judges and a clerk of said election, each of whom shall take an oath or affirmation, to be administered by either of the others, faithfully and honestly to discharge the duties required of him as judge or clerk of said election, who shall form the board of election, and shall conduct the same, and certify the result in the same manner that the common council are required to do by this act: and subsequent elections shall be held in said village, and superintended by the president, recorder, and one or more of the trustees : and further, that at all elections the polls shall be opened between the hours of nine and ten o'clock in the forenoon, and continue open until three o'clock in the afternoon of the same day, and no longer; and that the name of each elector so voting at such election shall be written in a poll list, to be kept at such election by the officer or officers holding the same; after the close of the polls at such election, the said officer or officers shall proceed without delay, publicly to count the ballots, (unopened) and if the number of ballots so counted, shall exceed the number of electors contained in the poll list, the officer or officers holding said election shall draw out and destroy, unopened, so many of the ballots as shall amount to the excess; and if two or more ballots shall be found rolled or folded together, they shall not be estimated: and thereupon the officer or officers holding such election shall immediately proceed openly and publicly to canvass and estimate the votes given at such election, and shall complete the said canvass and estimate on the same day or on

Judges of election.

Opening and closing of the polls.

Ballots counted.

Canvass, when to be completed.

the next day, and shall thereupon certify and declare the number of votes given for each person voted for, and shall file such certificate in the office of the recorder of said village, before ten o'clock in the forenoon of the next day after said election; at which last period the common council shall proceed to canvass said returns, and shall declare the result of said election; and in case it shall at any time happen that two or more persons shall have an equal number of votes for the same office, the common council shall make as many strips of paper of equal size, as there are persons having an equal number of such votes, and write a ballot for each of such persons, one on each of said strips of paper, and shall then put said ballots together in a hat, and one of the members of said common council shall then draw from said hat one of said ballots, and the person whose name shall be upon the ballot so drawn, shall be declared elected.

Certificate of votes, when and where to be filed.

Common council to canvass returns.

Proceedings in case of a tie.

Sec. 4. It shall be the duty of the recorder of said village to give at least five days notice, in writing, by posting the same in at least three public places in said village, of the time and place of holding all elections, and as soon as practicable, and within five days thereafter, after closing the polls at any election, to notify the officers respectively of their election; and the said officers, so elected, and notified as aforesaid, shall, within ten days after receiving a copy of such notice, take and subscribe the oath of office prescribed by the constitution, before any person authorized to administer oaths, and file the same with the recorder of said village.

Notice of election.

Notice to persons elected.

Oath of officers.

Sec. 5. It shall be the duty of the president to preside at all meetings of the village council, and the recorder shall keep a fair and accurate record of the proceedings.

President & recorder.

Sec. 6. The president, recorder and trustee of said village shall be a body corporate and politic, with perpetual succession, to be known and designated by the name of

Body corporate.

Name, powers, &c.

the common council of the village of Allegan, and by that name they and their successors shall be known in law, and shall be capable of suing and being sued, of pleading and being impleaded, in all courts and places whatsoever, and may have a common seal and may alter and change the same at pleasure, and may purchase, hold and convey real and personal estate, for the use of such corporation.

May have seal, & hold real & personal estate.

Sec. 7. The inhabitants of said village shall be liable to the operation of any and all laws relating to the township government, except so far as relates to the laying out and construction of streets and highways, and the labor to be performed thereon, within the limits thereof.

Inhabitants liable to laws for townships.

Exception.

Sec. 8. The president, recorder and trustees, when assembled together and duly organized, shall constitute the common council of said village, and a majority of the whole shall be necessary to constitute a quorum for the transaction of business, (though a less number may adjourn from time to time;) and the said common council shall hold their meetings at such time and place as the president, or in his absence the recorder may appoint; and the common council shall have power to impose, levy and collect such fines as they may deem proper, for the non-attendance of the officers and members thereof, at any such meeting; and also to require the attendance of any officer by them appointed, and to impose and collect fines for non-attendance; *Provided*, No such fine shall exceed five dollars for one offence.

Who to constitute common council

Quorum.

Powers and duties.

Proviso.

Sec. 9. The board of common council may order a special election to fill any vacancy that may occur by the death, resignation, or removal of any of the officers elected by the electors of said village; but no special election shall be held until at least five days notice shall have been given, of the time and place of holding the same, as herein provided.

Common council may fill vacancy.

Sec. 10. The common council shall have power to re-

Removals.

move at pleasure, any of the officers by them appointed by virtue of this act, and to fill all vacancies that may happen in any of said offices, so often as the same may occur, by death, resignation, removal, or any other cause; and all officers so appointed shall be notified and qualified as aforesaid, and perform the duties of their respective offices.

Sec. 11. The treasurer and marshal shall, respectively, *Treasurer and marshal to give security.* before they enter upon the exercise of the duties of their respective offices, give such security for the faithful discharge of the trusts reposed in them, as the common council shall direct and require.

Sec. 12. The common council shall have full power and *Power of Council as to appointments.* authority to appoint a marshal, and all other officers necessary under the provisions of this act, for said village, whose election is not herein provided for, to make by-laws and ordinances relative to the duties, powers and fees of the marshal, treasurer, assessor, and other officers; relative to *Ordinances relative to the duties and powers of officers.* the time and manner of working upon the streets, commons, lanes and alleys; relative to the time and manner of assessing, levying and collecting all highway and other taxes in said village: relative to the prevention, removal and abate- *Nuisances.* ment of nuisances within the limits of said village; to construct sewers, cisterns and reservoirs; to license showmen; to suppress gaming; to compel the owners of buildings to *Gaming.* procure and keep fire buckets. relative to the protecting *Fire buckets* of the village from fires; relative to the calling of meetings of the electors of said village; relative to the keeping and sale of gun-powder in said village; relative to the re- *Gun powder* straining of swine, horses and other animals from running *Running at large of animals.* at large in the streets, commons, lanes and alleys in said village; to regulate and establish one or more pounds in said village; to suppress billiard and other gaming tables kept for hire, gain or reward, in said village; for the sup- *Riots.* pression of riots; for preventing and suppressing disor-

Disorderly houses.
derly houses or houses of ill fame in said village; for the apprehension and punishment of vagrants drunkards and idle persons in said village: to regulate the measuring of fire-wood and the weighing of hay in said village; to pre-

Stands for carts.
scribe stands for carts, drays, and for wood, hay and produce exposed for sale in said village; to prevent and punish immoderate drinking in any of the streets of said village; to prevent incumbering the streets, side-walks, alleys or public grounds, and to regulate all grave-yards and cemeteries within or belonging to said village; to preserve

Preservati'n of trees.
shade and ornamental trees in said village, and to make all such by-laws and ordinances as to them shall seem necessary for the safety and good government of said village and its inhabitants, and to impose all fines, penalties and forfeitures of all persons offending against such by-laws

Proviso.
and ordinances: *Provided always,* That such by-laws shall not be repugnant to the Constitution of the United States,

Proviso.
or the State of Michigan: *And provided also,* That no by-laws or ordinances of said corporation shall have any effect until the same shall have been published three weeks successively in a newspaper printed in said village, or by written notices posted up in three of the most public places in said village.

Streets, side walks, water courses, &c.
Sec. 13. The common council shall have authority to lay out and establish, open, make, and alter such streets, lanes, and alleys, sidewalks, highways and water courses, within the limits of said village, as they may deem necessary for the public convenience, and if they shall require the lands

Proceedings on taking private property for public use.
of any person for such purpose, they shall give notice thereof to the owner or parties interested, or his or their agent or representative, by personal service, or by written notice posted in at least three public places in said village, three weeks next preceding the meeting of the said common council for the purposes aforesaid, and the said common council are hereby authorized to contract for and pur-

chase such lands of such owner for the purposes aforesaid; and in case such owner or owners refuse to sell or convey such lands or premises for the purposes aforesaid, or the parties fail to agree, it shall and may be lawful for said common council to direct the recorder of said village to issue a venire facias to command the marshal of said village, or any constable of said county, to summon and return a jury of twelve disinterested freeholders, residing without the limits of said village, to appear before a justice of the peace in said village, at a time to be therein stated, to inquire into the necessity of using such ground or premises, and the just compensation to be made therefor to the owner or owners, or parties interested in such land and premises, which jury being duly sworn by such justice, faithfully and impartially to inquire into and determine the necessity of using such grounds or premises, and to ascertain and determine the just compensation to be made therefor, and after having reviewed the premises, if necessary, shall inquire and assess such damages and recompense as they may think proper to award to the owner or owners of such lands or premises, according to their respective estates or interests therein; and the said justice shall, upon the return of such assessment or verdict, enter judgment therefor, confirming the same, and such sum or sums so assessed, together with all costs, shall be paid or legally tendered, before such street, lane or alley, sidewalk or highway, shall be made, opened, established or altered, to the claimant or claimants thereof. It shall therefrom be lawful for the common council to cause the said lands and premises to be occupied and used for the purpose aforesaid: *Provided*, That any party Provise. claiming damages as aforesaid, may have the right to remove such proceedings, by appeal, to the circuit court for the county in which such proceedings were had, upon giving notice of his, her or their intention so to do, to said justice, in writing, within five days, or in case such party does not reside in said village, then within thirty days after the rendition of such verdict, and the judgment thereon as aforesaid, and upon filing a transcript of the proceedings aforesaid, duly certified by said justice, within forty days after the verdict and judgment as aforesaid, in the said circuit court, the same proceedings shall thereafter be had thereon as is prescribed by law in other cases of appeal :

Proviso.

Provided, That if the final judgment of said court shall not exceed the damages assessed before the said justice, at least five dollars, the party appealing shall pay the costs occasioned by such appeal.

Powers of justices of the peace of Allegan.

Sec. 14. Any justice of the peace of the township of Allegan, is hereby authorized and empowered to enquire, hear and determine all offences committed within the limits of said village, against any of the by-laws, ordinances and regulations of said common council, and to punish the offender or offenders as prescribed by such by-laws or ordinances:

Proviso.

Provided, That any person charged with violating any of said by-laws or ordinances, may demand and have a trial by jury as in other cases.

Compensation of certain officers.

Sec. 15. The marshal, recorder, assessors, and such other officers as may be appointed by the the common council, shall receive such compensation for their services as the by-laws and ordinances shall direct.

Annual statement of receipts and expenditures.

Sec. 16. The common council shall, at the expiration of each year, cause to be published a just and true statement of all the moneys received or expended by them, in their corporate capacity, during the year next preceding such publication, and also the disposition thereof; which statement shall contain in detail, all receipts and expenditures.

Citizens as jurors and witnesses.

Sec. 17. In all processes, prosecutions and other proceedings, wherein the common council of said village shall be a party, no citizen of said village shall be deemed an incompetent juror or witness, on account of the interest of such citizen in the event of such process or proceeding:

Provided, That such interest be only that which is in com- Proviso. mon with the citizens of said village.

Sec. 18. Process against such corporation may be served Process, on whom to be by leaving a copy of such process, attested by the proper served. officer, with the recorder or president of such corporation: *Provided*, That the first process shall be a summons served Proviso. at least ten days before the return day thereof.

Sec. 19. The common council shall have full power and Poll tax. authority to levy and collect a capitation or poll tax upon the legal voters of said village, and also taxes on all real and personal property [not exempt from taxation] within the limits of said village, necessary to defray the expenses thereof: *Provided*, The said taxes so assessed and collected shall not exceed in any one year, one half of one per centum upon the valuation of said real and personal property, and exclusive of the capitation or poll tax; and every as- Proviso. sessment of taxes lawfully imposed or laid by said common council, on any lands, tenements and hereditaments, or premises whatsoever in said village, shall be and remain a lien on such lands, tenements and hereditaments, from Taxes a lien. the time of making such assessment or imposing such tax, until paid; and the owner or occupants or parties in interest respectively in said real estate, shall be liable upon demand to pay every such assessment or tax to be made as aforesaid; and in default of such payment or any part thereof, it shall be lawful for the marshal of said village Sale of property for to sell personal estate, and for the want thereof to sell real taxes. estate, rendering the surplus, if any, after deducting the charges of such sale, to the person against whom the tax is levied: *Provided*, That whenever any real estate shall Proviso. be sold by said marshal, notice thereof shall be published in a newspaper printed in said county, and in each week for at least four weeks, or by posting written notices in three public places in said village, for at least four weeks previous to such sale; and the said marshal shall give to.

12

the said purchaser or purchasers of any such lands, a certificate in writing, describing the lands purchased, and the time when the purchaser will be entitled to a deed for said

land; and if the person claiming title to said land described in the sale, shall not within one year from the date thereof, pay to the treasurer of said village, for the use of the purchaser, his heirs or assigns, the sum mentioned in such certificate, together with the interest thereon at the rate of twenty per cent. per annum from the date of such certificate, the said marshal or his successor in office, shall,

at the expiration of the said one year, execute to the purchaser or purchasers, his or their heirs or assigns, a conveyance of the lands so sold, which conveyance shall vest in the person or persons to whom it shall be given, an absolute estate in fee simple, subject to all the claims the State shall have therein; and the said conveyance shall be *prima facie* evidence that the sale and all the proceedings therein, prior to such sale, were regular, according to the provisions of this act; and every such conveyance executed by the said marshal under his hand and seal, in the presence of two or more subscribing witnesses, and duly acknowledged and recorded in the usual form, may be given in evidence in the same manner and with like effect as a deed regularly executed and acknowledged by the owner, and duly recorded; and all personal estate so sold, shall be sold in such manner as the by-laws and regulations of the corporation shall direct.

Sec. 20. Whenever the assessors of said village shall have completed their assessment roll and valuation of the property, real and personal, in said village, it shall be their duty to give notice thereof by publishing in a newspaper printed in said village, by at least two insertions, or posting up the same in three of the most public places in said village, stating the place where the said roll is left, for the inspection of all persons interested, and of the time when, and the place where they will meet to hear the objections of any persons interested, to the valuations so made therein; and at the time so appointed the assessors shall meet, and on the application of any person considering himself aggrieved, may review and reduce the said valuation on sufficient cause being shown upon oath, to the satisfaction of said assessors; and if any person or persons Correction of roll. shall conceive himself or themselves aggrieved by the final decision of the said assessors, they shall have the right of appealing from such decision of the assessors, at any time within ten days thereafter, to the common council, Appeal. who are in like manner hereby authorized, upon sufficient cause being shown, as aforesaid, to reduce said valuation.

Sec. 21. It shall be the duty of the common council to Duplicate tax roll. make out a duplicate of the tax roll, charging each individual therein an amount of tax in proportion to the amount of real and personal estate of such individual within said village; which duplicate shall be signed by the president and recorder, and delivered to the marshal, whose duty it shall be to 'collect the same within such time and in such manner as the by-laws shall direct.

Sec. 22. All moneys received by the marshal shall be Moneys to be paid by the marshal to treasur'r. paid over to the treasurer of said village, as shall be prescribed by the ordinances of the common council.

Sec. 23. The common council shall have power to ap- Street commissioners, point one or more street commissions, or other officers, to superintend and direct the making, planking, paving, re- Their duties pairing and opening all streets, lanes, alleys, sidewalks or highways, within the limits of said corporation, in such manner as they may from time to time be directed by the common council: *Provided*, That the commissioners of Proviso. highways of the township of Allegan, shall possess the same powers, and are charged with the same duties within the corporate limits of said village, as to the maintanance of

bridges therein, as are now required of them by law; and
also for establishing the line upon which buildings may be
erected, and beyond which such buildings shall not extend;
Expense of grading,&c., how paid. and the common council shall cause the expenses of grading such side-walks to be assessed on lots or premises ad-
joining such improvements, or by general assessment, or
otherwise, as they may direct.

Fire companies. Sec. 24. The common council shall have authority to establish and organize fire companies, and hook and ladder
companies, and provide them with engines and other implements as shall be necessary to extinguish fires and preserve the property of the village from conflagrations, to
appoint from among the inhabitants of such village, such
number as may be deemed necessary to serve as firemen,
Their powers. and each fire company and hook and ladder company, shall
have power to elect their own officers, and establish rules
for the government of said companies, subject to the approval of the common council, and they may impose such
fines for the non-attendance or neglect of duty of any of
its members as they may deem necessary and proper; and
every member of such company may obtain from the recorder of said village, a certificate to that effect, which
shall be evidence thereof, and the members of such com-
Exemption of firemen. pany, during their continuance as such, shall be exempt
from serving on juries and working a poll tax on the
streets and highways of said village, and it shall be the
Duties of fire companies. duty of every fire company to keep in good repair and
condition, the fire engines, hose, ladders, and other instruments of such company, and they shall assemble at least
once in each month, or as often as may be directed by said
common council, for the purpose of working or examining
said engines and other instruments with a view to their
perfect order and repair.

Duties of marshal at fires. Sec. 25. Upon the breaking out of any fire in said village, the marshal shall immediately repair to the place of

such fire, and aid and assist as well in extinguishing such fire as in preventing any goods from being stolen, and also in removing and saving the same, and shall in all respects be obedient to the president, recorder and trustees, or either of them who may be present at the fire.

Sec. 26. That act No. eighty, of the session laws of eigh- Act repealteen hundred and fifty-[forty]-six, entitled "an act to amend an act entitled an act to incorporate the village of Allegan," approved March twentieth, eighteen hundred and thirty-eight, be, and the same is hereby repealed.

This act is ordered to take immediate effect. .

Approved February 4, 1858.

[No. 30.]

AN ACT to incorporate the city of Ypsilanti.

SECTION 1. *The People of the State of Michigan enact,* Boundaries. That so much of the township of Ypsilanti, in the county of Washtenaw, as is included in the following description, to wit: Beginning on the south bank of the Huron river, on the line between sections four and five in said township, thence south to the north-east corner of lot number eight of the sub-division of said section five ; thence west to the north-west corner of lot number six in said sub-division ; thence south to French claim six hundred and eighty, (680); thence east to the Huron river; thence down the west branch [bank] of said river to the south-east corner of the west half of the north-west fractional quarter of section fifteen in said township ; thence north to the north line of the southwest quarter of section three in said township ; thence west to the south bank of the Huron river ; thence up the said river to the place of beginning ; be and the same is hereby set off from the said township of Ypsilanti, and declared to be a city, by the name of "the city of Ypsilanti," by which name it shall hereafter be known.

Body corpo-   Sec. 2. The freemen of said city, from time to time, being
rate.
inhabitants thereof, shall be and continue a body corporate
and politic, to be known and distinguished by the name
Title.   and title of the city of Ypsilanti, and shall be and are here-
Powers.   by made capable of suing and being sued, of pleading and
being impleaded, of answering and being answered unto,
and of defending and being defended in all courts of law
and equity, and in all other places whatever ; and may
have a common seal, which they may alter and change at
pleasure, and by the same name shall be and are hereby
made capable of purchasing, holding, conveying and disposing of any real and personal estate for said city.
First ward.
Sec. 3. The said city shall be divided into five wards, to
Boundaries. wit : The first ward shall embrace all that portion of said
city included within the following boundaries, namely :
Beginning at the Huron river on the south line of Michigan
street projected eastward to said river, thence west to
the west line of Hamilton street, thence north to the south
line of the Chicago road, thence westerly along the south
line of the Chicago road to the west line of said city, thence
south to the south line of said city, thence east to the Huron river, thence up said river to the place of beginning.
Second ward The second ward shall embrace all that territory included
Boundaries. within the following boundaries : Beginning at the north-
east corner of said first ward, thence west along the north
line of said first ward to the west line of said city, thence
north to the south line of the Ann Arbor road, thence east
along the south line of the Ann Arbor road and Ellis street
projected eastwardly to the Huron river, thence down said
Third ward. river to the place of beginning.   The third ward shall embrace all that territory lying on the west side of the Huron
Fourth ward river and north of the said second ward.   The fourth ward
shall embrace all that territory north of a line drawn from
the Huron river along the south line of Cross street to the
east line of said city and east of the Huron river.   The

fifth ward shall embrace all that territory lying east of the Fifth ward.
Huron river and south of said fourth ward.

Sec. 4. The officers of said city shall be one mayor, Officers elected.
one supervisor, one treasurer, one clerk; and also one
justice of the peace and one constable in the first, second and third wards, and one justice of the peace and
one constable in the fourth and fifth wards of said city;
two aldermen in each ward of said city; two school inspectors, two directors of the poor, who shall be elected
at the annual city election by the qualified electors of the
whole city, or of the wards thereof respectively, by ballot
as hereinafter provided; also, one auditor, one marshal,
and watchmen not to exceed one for each ward, of whom Officers ap-
one shall be designated as captain of the watch, one health pointed.
physician, and so many fire wardens, common criers, pound
masters, inspectors of fire wood, weigh masters and auctioneers, as the common council shall from time to time
direct, to be appointed by the common council, and such
other officers as may be necessary to carry into effect the
powers granted by this act, whose powers and duties,
other than those defined in this act, shall be such as shall
be prescribed by ordinance of the common council.

Sec. 5. No person shall be eligible to either of said offi- Eligibility to office.
ces, unless he shall then be an elector and resident of said
city, nor shall he be eligible to any office for any ward or
district, unless he shall then be an elector and resident of
such ward or district, and when any officer elected or appointed for any ward or district, shall cease to reside in
said city, or if elected or appointed for any ward or district, (shall cease to reside in such ward or district,) his
office shall thereby become vacant.

Sec. 6. An election shall be held in each ward annually, Annual elec-
on the first Monday in April, at such place as the common tion.
council shall appoint by posting printed notices of the Notice of election.
holding of said election, in at least three of the most pub-

lic places in each ward, at least six days previous to said election.

Sec. 7. At the first annual election to be held in said city after the passage of this act, there shall be elected one mayor and one supervisor for said city, two aldermen in each ward, one for the term of one year, who shall enter upon the duties of his office immediately upon his qualification, in the year eighteen hundred and fifty-eight, and another for the term of two years, and the term for which the person voted for is intended, shall be designated on

the ballot; and at each annual election thereafter to be held, one alderman shall be elected in each ward, who shall hold his office for the term of two years; there shall be elected annually in the first, second and third wards, by the electors thereof, one constable, to hold his office for one year; and by the electors of the fourth and fifth wards, one constable, who shall hold his office for one year; and at the first annual election after the passage of this act, there shall be elected by the electors of the first, second

and third wards, one justice of the peace, and by the electors of the fourth and fifth wards, one justice of the peace, who shall hold their offices within the districts for

which they are elected, and for the term of four years from the time they enter upon the duties thereof, as hereinafter provided, and at every fourth annual election thereafter, unless a vacancy shall sooner occur, there shall be elected two justices of the peace, as aforesaid, who shall hold their office four years: *Provided,* That the persons already elected to the office of justice of the peace in said township, shall continue to hold their offices as justices of the peace for their unexpired terms; and there shall also be elected annually by the electors of the whole city,

voting in their respective wards, one mayor, one clerk, one treasurer, two directors of the poor, who shall hold their offices for the period of one year; at the first annual elec-

tion after the passage of this act, and at the annual elec- _{School inspector.}
tion every two years thereafter, there shall be elected in
said city by the electors thereof voting in their respective
wards, two school inspectors, to hold their office for the
term of two years: *Provided*, That the persons now holding said office of school inspector in said township, shall
continue to hold their office for the remainder of their unexpired term.

Sec. 8. The common council shall at the first meeting _{Commissioners of city cemetery.}
after their election, or as soon thereafter as may be, and as
often as any vacancy occurs in any of the offices in this
section named, appoint by ballot two commissioners for the
city cemetery (or cemeteries), one of whom shall hold his
office for the the term of two years, and one of them for
the term of one year, and the term of each shall be designated upon the ballot, and annually thereafter the said common council shall appoint one commissioner of the city
cemetery, who shall hold his office for two years; they _{Watchmen.}
may also appoint the watchmen for said city, not to exceed
one for each ward, of whom they shall designate one as
captain of the watch, to hold their respective offices during
the pleasure of said council; they shall appoint at their
first annual meeting after their election, or as soon there-
after as may be, one health physician, to hold his office one _{Physician.}
year, and so many firewardens, common criers, pound mas- _{Fire wardens.}
ters, weigh-masters, inspectors of fire-wood and auctioneers
as the common council shall deem necessary, each to hold
their offices during the pleasure of the common council;
the common council shall contract with a counsellor at law _{Attorney.}
to perform such services as may be required of him as at-
torney and counsellor at law for said city, for such period
not exceeding one year, and for such compensation not to _{Compensation of Attorney.}
exceed two hundred dollars for a year, and the same rate
for any less period, as the common council shall determine;
the person with whom such contract is made shall not be

entitled to receive during its continuance, [or for services rendered during its continuance,] any other fee or reward whatever which shall be paid out of, or withheld from the the treasury of the city.

Filling va-cancies. Sec. 9. When any vacancy occurs in any of the offices which are appointed by the common council, either by death, resignation or removal of the incumbent, the said council may fill such vacancies by appointment for the remainder of the unexpired term for which such officer was appointed.

Removals. Sec. 10. All officers appointed by the common council, by the provisions of this act, may each be removed from office by the common council, for official misconduct, or for the unfaithful or insufficient performance of the duties of his office, but notice of the charges against them, and an opportunity of being heard in their defence shall first be given.

Elections] Opening polls. Sec. 11. On the day of election, held by virtue of this act, the polls shall be opened in each ward, at the several places designated by the common council, at eight o'clock in the morning, and shall be kept open, without intermission or adjournment, until four o'clock in the afternoon, at which hour they shall be finally closed.

Closing polls

Who electors. Sec. 12. The inhabitants of the said city being electors under the constitution of the State of Michigan, and no others, are declared to be electors under this act, and qualified to vote at the elections held by virtue of this act; and each person offering to vote at any such election, if challenged by an elector of said city before his vote shall be received, shall take one of the oaths now provided by the laws of this State, approved June 27th, 1851, entitled an act to provide for holding general and special elections, which oath shall be administered to him by one of the inspectors of election, and if any person shall swear falsely, upon conviction thereof, he shall be liable to the pains and

Oaths of electors.

False swearing.

penalties of perjury, but the common council of said city
are hereby authorized and empowered to provide by general ordinance, from time to time, to so change the form of
the oath or oaths to be administered to such elector, (if
challenged,) as to conform to the constitution and laws of
the State which may from time to time be in force.

Sec. 13. The two aldermen of each ward shall constitute *Who to con-
the board of inspectors of elections, and such one of their *stitute the board of in-
number as they shall appoint shall be their chairman; said *spectors.
board shall also appoint two competent persons to be
clerks of election; each of said persons so appointed shall
take the constitutional oath of office, to be administered by
either inspector of said board, who are hereby authorized
to administer the same.

Sec. 14. Inspectors of election, as specified in the pre- *Inspectors,
ceding section, shall be inspectors of election held in said *&c., for State and Co. officers.
wards respectively, as well for the election of State, dis-
trict and county, as for the city and ward officers.

Sec. 15. The electors shall vote by ballot, and each per- *Manner of
son offering to vote shall deliver his ballot, so folded as to *voting.
conceal its contents, to one of the inspectors, in the presence of the board; the ballot shall be a paper ticket, which
shall contain, written or printed, or partly written and
partly printed, the names of the persons for whom the
elector intends to vote, and shall designate the office to
which each person so named is intended by him to be
chosen; but no ballot shall contain a greater number of
names of persons, designated for any office, than there are
persons to be chosen at the election to fill such office.

Sec. 16. The ballot shall contain the names of persons *Ballots.
designated as officers for the city; and as officers for a
ward. The common council shall provide two boxes for *Ballot boxes
each ward, with locks and keys, in which the two kinds
of votes shall be deposited separately.

Sec. 17. If at any annual election to be held in the said

Vacancies to
be named
on the bal-
lot.
city, there shall be one or more vacancies to be supplied in any office, and at the same time any person is to be elected for the full term of said office, the term for which each person voted for, for the said office, shall be designated on the ballot.

Canvass.
Sec. 18. Immediately after the closing of the polls, the inspectors of election, shall, without adjournment, publicly canvass the votes received by them, and declare the result; and shall, on the same, or on the next day, make a certificate stating the number of votes given for each person for each office, and shall file such statement and certificate on the day of election, or on the next day, with the clerk of the city.

Time of
making cer-
tificate.

Poll list.
Sec. 19. It shall be the duty of the inspectors of election, on receiving the vote, as specified in section fifteen, to cause the same, without being opened or inspected, to be deposited in the proper box provided by the common council for that purpose; the said board shall also write down or cause to be written down, the name of each elector voting at such election, in a poll list to be kept by said inspectors of election, or under their direction.

Method of
canvassing.
Sec. 20. The manner of canvassing said votes shall be as follows: the inspectors shall proceed to count the ballots, unopened, and if the number of ballots so counted shall exceed the number of names of electors contained in the poll list, one of the inspectors shall draw out and destroy as many as the number of ballots exceeds the number of electors contained in said poll list; and if two or more ballots are found rolled or folded up together, they shall not be counted; they shall then proceed to count and estimate said votes as provided in the preceding section:

Proviso.
Provided, however, That the first election held after the passage of this act, shall be conducted by the persons, at the time and places and in the manner to be designated for the first, second and third wards, by the common coun-

oil of the village of Ypsilanti; and for the fourth and fifth wards by the president and trustees of the village of East Ypsilanti, and the persons so elected shall be notified of their election, and file their oath of office, as the said bodies shall direct. *Notice of election. Oath of office.*

Sec. 21. The person receiving the greatest number of votes for any office in said city or ward, shall be deemed to have been duly elected to such office, and if any officer, except aldermen, shall not have been chosen by reason of two or more candidates having received an equal number of votes, the common council shall by ballot elect such officer from the two candidates having the highest number of votes. *Who to be deemed elected. Proceedings in case of tie*

Sec. 22. The common council of the village of Ypsilanti, and the president and trustees of the village of East Ypsilanti, shall convene on the Thursday next succeeding succeeding such election, at two o'clock in the afternoon, at their usual places of meeting; and shall determine and certify, in the manner provided by law, what persons are duly elected, at the said election, to the several offices respectively. Such certificate shall be made in triplicate, one of which shall be filed with the clerk of each of said villages, and the other with the clerk of the county of Washtenaw. The common council of the city, for the preceding year, shall convene on the Thursday next succeeding each annual election, at two o'clock in the afternoon, at their usual place of meeting, and shall determine and certify, in the manner provided by law, what persons are duly elected at the said election to the several offices, respectively; such certificate shall be made in duplicate, one of which shall be filed with the clerk of the city, and the other with the clerk of the county of Washtenaw. *Canvass by common council. Certificates of election. Duties of common council for preceding year. Certificate filed.*

All officers elected as hereinbefore provided shall enter upon the duties of their respective offices on the first Mon- *Terms of office, when to commence.*

day of May next following such election, unless otherwise herein provided.

Notifying officers of their election. Sec. 23. It shall be the duty of the clerk of said city, as soon as practicable, and within five days after the meeting of the common council, as provided in the preceding section, to notify the officers respectively of their election; and the said officers so elected and notified, as aforesaid, *Official oaths.* shall, within ten days after such notice, take the oath of office prescribed by the constitution of this State, before some officer authorized by law to administer oaths, and file the same with the clerk of said city.

Vacancy in office of aldermen; how filled. Sec. 24. Whenever a vacancy occurs in the office of alderman, by his refusal or neglect to take the oath of office within the time required by this act, by his resignation, death, ceasing to be an inhabitant of the city or ward for which he shall have been elected, removal from office, or by the decision of a competent tribunal declaring void his election, or for any other cause, the common council of said city shall immediately appoint a special election to be held in the ward for which such officer was chosen, at some suitable place therein, not less than five days nor more than fifteen days from the time of such appointment: *Provided,* *Proviso.* That in case any such vacancy shall occur in the said office of alderman within three months before the first Monday of April in any year, it shall be optional with the common council to order a special election or not, as they shall deem expedient.

Vacancies filled by appointment. Sec. 25. In case a vacancy shall occur in any of the offices in this act declared to be elective or appointive, except aldermen, the common council may, in their discretion, fill such vacancy by the appointment of a suitable person, who is an elector, and if appointed for a ward, who is also a resident of the ward for which he shall be appointed, and any *When to terminate.* officer appointed to fill a vacancy, if the office is elective, shall hold by virtue of such appointment only until the first

Monday of May next succeeding; if an elective office which shall have become vacant was one of that class whose terms of office continue after the next annual election, a successor for the unexpired term shall be elected at the next annual election.

Sec. 26. Whenever a special election is to be held, the common council shall cause to be delivered to the inspectors of election in the ward where such officer is to be chosen, a notice, signed by them, specifying the officer to be chosen, and the day and place at which such election is to be held, and the proceedings at such election shall be the same as at the annual or general election ; such notice shall also be published in a newspaper of the city, at least once before the day of such special election. Notice of special elections.

Sec. 27. Every person chosen or appointed by the common council, before he enters upon the duties of his office, and within five days after being notified of his appointment shall cause to be filed in the office of the city clerk, a notice in writing, signifying his acceptance of such office. Notice of acceptance.

Sec. 28. If any person elected or appointed under this title shall not take and subscribe the oath of office, and file the same as therein directed, or shall not cause a notice of acceptance to be filed as therein directed, or if required by the common council to execute an official bond or undertaking, shall neglect to execute and file the same, in the manner and within the time prescribed by the common council, such neglect shall be deemed a refusal to serve, unless before any step is taken to fill any such office by another incumbent, such oath shall be taken or such acceptance be signified as aforesaid. Neglect to signify acceptance deemed a refusal to serve.

Sec. 29. At the expiration of twenty days after any election or appointment of any officer or officers in the said city, the clerk of the said city shall deliver to the common council a list of the persons elected or appointed, and of the office to which they are chosen therein, specifying such as Clerk to deliver list of persons elected or appointed.

shall have filed with him the oath of office, or notice of acceptance required by this act, and such as shall have omitted to file the same within the time herein prescribed.

Mayor to report delinquents. Sec. 30. The mayor shall report to the common council the names of such officers as shall have neglected to give the bond and security required by the provisions of this act.

To whom resignation to be made. Sec. 31. Resignations by any officer authorized to be chosen or appointed by this act, shall be made to the common council, subject to their approval and acceptance.

Qualifications of electors. Sec. 32. At all city elections, every elector shall vote in the ward where he shall have resided ten days next preceding the day of election, otherwise he may vote in the ward **Proviso.** from which he removed: *Provided*, He shall have resided in such ward ten days prior to such removal. The residence of an elector under this act shall be the ward where he boards or takes his regular meals.

Vacancy in board of inspectors, how filled. Sec. 33. At any election held under this act, if, from any cause, either or all of the inspectors of election shall fail to attend any such election, at the appointed time and place, his or their place may be supplied for the time being by the electors present, who shall elect any of their number *viva voce*; who, when so elected, shall be duly sworn, by an officer authorized to administer oaths, to a faithful performance of their duteis.

Expenses of elections. Sec. 34. The expenses of any election to be held as provided by this act, shall be city charges, and defrayed in the same manner as the other contingent expenses of the city.

Officers to hold till successors qualified. Sec. 35. Any person elected to any office under this act, at the expiration of the term thereof, shall continue to hold the same until his successor shall be elected or appointed and qualified; and when a person is elected to fill a vacancy in any elective office, he shall hold the same only during the unexpired portion of the regular term limited

to such office, and until his successor shall be elected and
qualified.

Sec. 36. The mayor and aldermen of said city shall constitute the common council. They shall meet at such
times and places as they shall from time to time appoint;
and on special occasions, whenever the mayor or person
officiating as mayor, (in case of vacancy in the office of
mayor, or of his absence from the city, or inability to offi-
ciate,) shall, by written notice appoint, and which shall be
served on the members in such manner and for such time
as the common council may by ordinance direct.

*Who to con-
stitute com-
mon council*

*Times and
places of
meeting.*

Sec. 37. The mayor, when present, shall preside at the
meetings of the common council, and in his absence the
common council shall appoint one of their number, who
shall preside.

*Mayor to
preside.*

Sec. 38. No ordinance or resolution passed by the common council, shall have any force or effect, if, on the day
of its passage or on the next day thereafter, the mayor or
other officer legally discharging the duties of mayor, shall
lodge in the office of the city clerk, a notice in writing,
suspending the immediate operation of such ordinance or
resolution. If the mayor or other officer legally exercising
the office of mayor, shall, within twenty-four hours after the
passage of such ordinance or resolution, lodge in the office
of the city clerk his reasons in writing why the same should
not go into effect, the same shall not go into effect nor have
any legal operation, unless it shall, at a subsequent meeting of the common council, be passed by a majority of
two-thirds of all the members of the common council then
in office, exclusive of the mayor, or other officer legally
discharging the duties of mayor, and if so re-passed, shall
go into effect according to the terms thereof. If such reasons in writing shall not be lodged with the clerk as above
provided, such ordinance or resolution shall have the same
operation and effect as if no notice suspending the same

*Ordinances
may be sus-
pended by
mayor.*

*Veto power
lodged with
mayor.*

*Reconsider-
ation by
common
council.*

14

had been lodged with the city clerk, and no ordinance or resolution of the common council, for any of the purposes mentioned in this section, shall go into operation until after the expiration of twenty-four hours after its passage.

Duty of clerk. Sec. 39. It shall be the duty of the city clerk to communicate to the common council, at the next meeting of the board, any paper that may be lodged with him pursuant to the last preceding section.

Members to have one vote. Sec. 40. In the proceedings of the common council each member present shall have one vote, except the mayor or officer discharging the duties of mayor.

Sittings to be public. Sec. 41. The sittings of the common council shall be public, except when the public interests shall in their opinion require secrecy. The minutes of the proceedings shall be kept by the clerk, and the same shall be open at all times for public inspection.

Votes to be entered on the journal in certain cases. Sec. 42. Whenever required by two members, the votes of all the members of the common council, in relation to any act, proceeding or proposition, had at any meeting, shall be entered at large on the minutes; and such votes shall also be entered in relation to the adoption of any resolution, or ordinance, report of a committee, or other act, for taxing or assessing the citizens of said city, or involving the appropriation of public moneys.

Quorum. Sec. 43. A majority of the common council shall be a quorum for the transaction of business; but no tax or assessment shall be ordered, nor any appointment be made, except by a concurring vote of a majority of all the members of the common council: and the council shall prescribe the rules for its proceedings.

Rules.

Disabilities of members. Sec. 44. No member of the common council shall, during the period for which he was elected, be appointed to, or be competent to hold any office, of which the emoluments are paid from the city treasury, or paid by fees directed to be paid by any act or ordinance of the common

council, or be directly or indirectly interested in any contract, as principal, surety, or otherwise, the expenses or
consideration whereof are to be paid under any ordinance
of the common council; but this section shall not be con- Construction.
strued to prevent the mayor or clerk from receiving any
salary which may be fixed by the common council, nor
from holding any office, nor to deprive any alderman of any
emoluments or fees to which he may be entitled by virtue
of his office.

Sec. 45. The common council, in addition to the powers Powers of
and duties specially conferred upon them in this act, shall council.
have the management and control of the finances, rights
and interests, buildings, and all property, real and personal,
belonging to the city, and may make such orders and by-
laws relating to the same as they shall deem proper and
necessary; and further, that they shall have power within
said city to enact, make, continue, establish, modify, amend
and repeal such ordinances, by-laws, and regulations, as
they deem desirable within said city, for the following purposes:

1. To prevent vice and immorality, to preserve public Public
peace and good order, to regulate the police of the city, to peace.
prevent and quell riots, disturbances, and disorderly as-
semblages.

2. To restrain and prevent disorderly and gaming houses, Disorderly
and houses of ill fame, all instruments and devices used houses.
for gaming, and to prohibit all gaming and fraudulent de- Gaming.
vices, and regulate or restrain billiard tables, and bowling
alleys.

3. To forbid and prevent the vending or other disposi- Liquors.
tion of liquors and intoxicating drinks, in violation of the
laws of this State, and to forbid the selling or giving, to be
drank, any intoxicating liquors to any child or young person, without the consent of his or her parent or guardian,
and to prohibit, restrain and regulate the sale of all goods,.

wares and personal property at auction, except in cases of sales authorized by law, and to fix the fees to be paid by and to auctioneers.

Shows and exhibitions. 4. To prohibit, restrain, and regulate, all sports, exhibitions of natural or artificial curiosities, caravans of animals, theatrical exhibitions, circuses, or other public performances, and exhibitions for money:

Nuisances. 5. To abate or remove nuisances of every kind, and to compel the owner or occupant of any grocery, tallow-chandler shop, butcher's stall, soap factory, tannery, stable, privy, hog pen, sewer, or other offensive or unwholesome house or place; to cleanse, remove, or abate the same, from time to time, as often as they may deem necessary for the health comfort and convenience of the inhabitants of said city:

Slaughter houses, &c. 6. To direct the location of all slaughter houses, markets and buildings for storing gunpowder, or other combustible substances:

Gun powder and other dangerous articles. 7. Concerning the buying, carrying, selling and using gunpowder, fire-crackers, or fire-works, manufactured or prepared therefrom, or other combustible materials, and the exhibition of fire-works, and the discharge of fire-arms, and the lights in barns, stables and other buildings, and to restrain the making of bonfires in streets and yards:

Encumbrances in streets, &c. 8. To prevent the cumbering of streets, side-walks, cross walks, lanes, alleys, bridges, aqueducts, wharves, or slips, in any manner whatever:

Racing and immoderate driving. 9. To prevent and punish horse racing, and immoderate driving or riding in any street, or over any bridge, and to authorize the stopping and detaining any person who shall be guilty of immoderate driving or riding in any street, or over any bridge:

Railroads. 10. To determine and designate the route and grades of any railroad to be laid in said city, and to restrain and regulate the use of locomotives, engines and cars upon the railroads within the city:

11. To prohibit or regulate bathing in any public water, Bathing. and to provide for cleansing Huron river of drift wood and other obstructions:

12. To restrain and punish drunkards, vagrants, mendi- Drunkards and other cants, street beggars, and persons soliciting alms or sub- disorderly persons. scriptions for any purpose whatever:

13. To establish and regulate one or more pounds, and Pounds and running at to restrain and regulate the running at large of horses, cat- large of animals. tle, swine and other animals, geese and poultry, and to authorize the impounding and sale of the same for the penalty incurred, and the costs of keeping and impounding:

14. To regulate and prevent the running at large of dogs, Dogs. to impose taxes on the owners of dogs, and to prevent dog fights in the streets:

15. To prohibit any person from bringing and depositing Removing of putrid sub- within the limits of said city, any dead carcass or other un- stances. wholesome or offensive substances; and to require the removal or destruction thereof, if any person shall have on his premises such substances, or any putrid meats, fish, hides or skins of any kind, and on his default, to authorize the removal or destruction thereof by some officer of the city:

16. To compel all persons to keep side-walks in front of Clearing side-walks. premises owned or occupied by them, clear from snow, dirt, wood or obstructions:

17. To regulate the ringing of bells, and the crying of Ringing of bells. goods and other commodities for sale at auction, or other- Noises in the streets. wise; and to prevent disturbing noises in the streets:

18. To prescribe the powers and duties of watchmen, Regulate watchmen. and the fines and penalties for their delinquencies:

19. To regulate and establish the line upon which build- Building regulations. ings may be erected upon any street, lane or alley in said city, and to compel such buildings to be erected upon such line, by fine upon the owner or builder thereof, not to exceed five hundred dollars:

Burying the dead.   20. To regulate the burial of the dead, and to compel the keeping and return of bills of mortality:

Markets.   21. To establish, order and regulate the markets, to regulate the vending of wood, meats, vegetables, fruit, fish and provisions of all kinds, and prescribe the time and place for selling the same, and the fees to be paid by butchers *Proviso.* for license: *Provided,* That nothing herein contained shall authorize the common council to restrict in any way the sale of fresh and wholesome meats by the quarter within the limits of the city:

Water.   22. To establish, regulate and preserve public reservoirs, wells and pumps, and to prevent the waste of water;

Sextons, carmen, carts, &c.   23. To regulate sextons and undertakers for burying the dead, carmen and their carts, hackney carriages and their drivers, omnibuses and their drivers, scavengers, porters and chimney sweeps, and their fees and compensation, and the fees to be paid by them into the city treasury for license:

Prevent soliciting for passengers, &c.   24. To prevent runners, stage drivers and others, from soliciting passengers and others to travel or ride in any stage, omnibus, or upon any railroad, or to go to any hotel or otherwheres:

Lights and lamps.   25. Concerning the lighting of the streets and alleys, and the protection and safety of public lamps:

Hawking & peddling.   26. To regulate and restrain hawking and peddling in the streets, and to regulate pawn brokers:

Prescribe duties of appointed officers.   27. To prescribe the duties of all officers appointed by the common council, and their compensation, and the penalty or penalties for failing to perform such duties, and to prescribe the bonds and sureties to be given by the officers of the city for the discharge of their duties, and the time for executing the same, in cases not otherwise provided for by law:

Streams, low grounds, &c.   28. To preserve the salubrity of the waters of Huron river, or other streams within the limits of the said city;

to fill up all low grounds or lots covered or partially covered with water, or to drain the same as they may deem expedient:

29. To prescribe and designate the stands for carriages of all kinds which carry persons for hire, and for carts and carters, and to prescribe the rates of fare and charges, and the stand or stands for wood, hay and produce exposed for sale in said city. Stands for carts. Rates of fare, &c.

Sec. 46. The common council may ascertain, establish and settle the boundaries of all streets and alleys in the said city, and prevent and remove all encroachments thereon, and exercise all other powers conferred on them by this act, in relation to highways, common and other schools, the prevention of fires, the levying of taxes, the supplying of the city with water, and all other subjects of municipal regulation not herein expressly provided. Boundaries of streets. Powers and duties of common council.

Sec. 47. The common council shall also have power by ordinance or otherwise, to require the owners or occupants of any mill race within the said city, to cover the same with bridges or arches, to be constructed with such materials as the common council shall direct; or they may direct the same to be covered in the same manner that other public improvements are directed to be made. Owners of mill races may be required to cover the same.

Sec. 48. Whenever the owner or occupant of any mill race shall refuse or neglect within such time as the common council shall have appointed, to cover such mill race in the manner and with the materials by them directed, it shall be lawful for the common council to cause the same to be done at the expense of the city, and to recover the expenses thereof, with damages at the rate of ten per cent., with costs of suit, from such owner or occupant. Proceedings in case of refusal.

Sec. 49. Where, by the provisions of this act, the common council have authority to pass ordinances on any subject, they may prescribe a penalty not exceeding one hundred dollars, (unless the imposition of a greater penalty May impose penalties.

be herein otherwise provided,) for a violation thereof, and may provide that the offender, on failing to pay the penalty imposed, shall be imprisoned in the county jail of Washtenaw county, for any term not exceeding, ninety days, which penalties may be sued for and recovered, with costs, in the name of the city of Ypsilanti.

Ordinances imposing penalties; when to take effect. Sec. 50. No ordinance of the common council imposing a penalty shall take effect until after the expiration of at least three days after the first publication thereof in a newspaper published in said city.

Mode of introducing ordinances as evidence Sec. 51. A record or entry made by the clerk of the said city, or a copy of such record or entry duly certified by him, shall be prima facie evidence of the time of such first publication; and all laws, regulations and ordinances of the common council may be read in evidence in all courts of justice, and in all proceedings before any officer, body or board in which it shall be necessary to refer thereto; either,

1. From a copy certified by the clerk of the city, with the seal of the city of Ypsilanti affixed, or,

2. From the volume of ordinances printed by authority of the common council.

Mode of publication of ordinances, &c. Sec. 52. Whenever the common council are required by law to make publication of any notices, ordinances, or resolutions or proceedings, in one or more newspapers of said city, it shall be deemed sufficient to publish the same in any daily or weekly newspaper published in said city.

Cemeteries. Sec. 53. The common council shall have power to purchase and to hold a suitable lot or lots of land, within or without the corporation limits, for the purpose of a city cemetery or cemeteries; and they shall make such rules and regulations regarding the same as they may deem necessary; and may cause the same to be surveyed into suitable lots, and may dispose of the same to purchasers, and thereupon cause to be executed to such purchaser a good and sufficient deed, in the corporate name of said city which deed shall be signed by the mayor and clerk.

Sec. 54. The commissioners of the city cemetery, and the auditor, shall constitute a board of superintendents of the city cemetery, and the auditor shall be the treasurer of said board. Board of superintendents of city cemetery.

Sec. 55. The common council shall have power to purchase a Potter's field, within or without the city limits, for the burial of the city poor; and may make such rules and regulations concerning the same as they may deem necessary. Burial of city poor.

Sec. 56. The common council shall have power, whenever, in their opinion, the necessities of the city require, to construct a city watch house, city hall, and city market or markets, and to appoint the keepers, clerks, and necessary officers thereof, and may locate such city watch house, city hall, and city market or markets, within or without the city limits, and may make such regulations concerning the same as the common council may think proper. City buildings.

Sec. 57. 1. The common council shall have and exercise in and over said city the same powers in relation to the regulation of taverns, groceries, common victuallers, saloon keepers and others, as are now or may hereafter be conferred by the general laws of this State upon township boards, or upon the corporate authorities of cities and villages in relation to tavern keepers and common victuallers, and subject to the same conditions and limitations; and the general laws of this State now in force, or which may hereafter be enacted, in relation to the regulation of taverns, groceries and common victuallers, shall be deemed applicable to this city, unless otherwise limited. Council to have the same powers as township boards in certain cases.

2. No person shall engage in or exercise the business or occupation of tavern keeper, inn holder, common victualler, or saloon keeper, within the limits of said city, until he is first licensed as such by the common council; and Prohibition to taverns &c., without license.

15

Forfeiture for violat'n. any person who shall assume to exercise such business or occupation, without having first obtained such license, shall forfeit and pay, for every day he shall so exercise such occupation or business, the sum of two dollars, to be recovered by action of debt in the name of the city of Ypsilanti, before any justice of the peace of said city, together with the costs of prosecution.

Licenses granted by common council. 8. The common council shall have power to grant licenses to authorize persons to exercise the business of tavern keeper, inn holder, common victualler, or saloon keeper, within said city, and may impose such fees to be paid into the city treasury, on the granting of such license, as they may see fit.

Sealers of weights and measures. Sec. 58. The city clerk shall be the sealer of weights and measures of the said city, and shall perform all the duties of township clerk, so far as the same applies to the sealing of weights and measures; [and the laws of this State relating to the sealing of weights and measures].shall apply to the said city.

Annual settlement with city treasurer. Sec. 59. On the last Tuesday in the month of April, in each year, the common council shall audit and settle the accounts of the city treasurer, and the accounts of all other officers and persons having claims against the city or accounts with it; and shall make out a statement in detail of the receipts and expenditures of the corporation during the preceding year; in which statement shall be clearly and distinctly specified the several items of expenditure made by the common council, the objects and purposes for which the same were made, and the amount of money ex-*Items to be stated.* pended under each; the amount of taxes raised for the general contingent expenses; the amount raised for lighting and watching the city; the amount of highway taxes and assessments; the amount of assessments for opening, paving, planking, repairing, and altering streets, and building and repairing bridges; the amount borrowed on the credit of the city, and the terms on which the same was obtained; and such other information as shall be necessary to a full understanding of the financial concerns of the city.

Sec. 60. The said statement shall be signed by the mayor and clerk, and filed with the papers of the city; and the same shall be published by the clerk, at the expense of the city, in some newspaper thereof, to be designated by the common council, previous to the first day of May thereafter. *Statement by whom signed, &c.*

Sec. 61. It shall be the duty of the mayor to take care that the laws of the State, and the ordinances of the common council be faithfully executed; to exercise a constant supervision and control over the conduct of all subordinate officers, and to receive and examine into all complaints against them for neglect of duty; to recommend to the common council such measures as he shall deem expedient, to expedite such as shall be resolved upon by them, and, in general, to maintain the peace and good order, and advance the prosperity of the city. *General duties of mayor.*

Sec. 62. All official bonds of said city shall be deposited with the clerk of the city for safe keeping, and it shall be his duty to deliver the same to his successor in office. *Official bonds.*

Sec. 63. It shall be the duty of every alderman in said city to attend the regular and special meetings of the common council; to act upon committees when thereunto appointed by the mayor or common council; to order the arrest of all persons violating the laws of this State, or the ordinances, by-laws or police regulations; to report to the mayor all subordinate officers who are guilty of any official misconduct or neglect of duty; to maintain peace and good order, and to perform all other duties required of them by this act. *Duties of aldermen.*

Sec. 64. The mayor and aldermen, by virtue of their respective offices, shall be conservators of the public peace,

Mayor, re-corder and aldermen to be conserva-tors of pub-lic peace. and as such shall each have and exercise all the power and authority of justices of the peace in criminal cases, and in enforcing the laws of this State relating to the police thereof, but shall have no jurisdiction of civil cases, other than such as by this act shall be expressly conferred upon them, or either of them.

All accounts against city to be verif'd by affidavit. Sec. 65. The accounts and demands all of persons, against the city, shall be verified by affidavit, and shall set forth the items thereof in detail, which affidavits may be taken and certified by any member of said common council.

Duties of clerk. Sec. 66. The clerk shall keep the corporate seal, and all the papers and files belonging to said city as a corporation, not properly by this act in the custody of some other officer thereof, and shall make a record of the proceedings of the common council, whose meetings it shall be his duty to attend, and copies of all papers duly filed in his office and transcripts from the records of the proceedings of the common council, certified to by him under the corporate seal, shall be evidence in all places, when produced, of the matters therein contained; he shall countersign all licences granted for any purpose whatever by the mayor or common council, and shall enter in an appropriate book the name of every person to whom a license shall be granted, and the number of such license, and the date thereof, and the time during which it is to be continued in force, and the sum paid for such license. No license for any purpose granted shall be valid until thus countersigned by the clerk.

Clerk to publish or-dinances. Sec. 67. The clerk shall publish at least one week in a newspaper printed in the city, all the ordinances of the common council, for the violation of which any penalty may be imposed, and all votes, ordinances and resolutions, directing the payment of money, shall be published at least once in like manner, within eight days after the passage of such vote, ordinance or resolution; he shall also perform such other duties as this act shall direct, or which may be directed by ordinance of the common council.

Sec. 68. The treasurer shall receive all moneys belong- Treasurer to receive and keep moneys. ing to the city, and shall deposit and keep the same as directed by the common council, and shall keep an account of all receipts and expenditures in such manner as the common council shall direct; all moneys drawn from the trea- How money is to be drawn from the treasury sury shall be drawn in pursuance of an order of the common council, by warrant signed by the clerk, and countersigned by the audtior; such warrant shall specify for what purpose the amount named therein is to be paid; and the clerk shall keep an accurate account, under appropriate heads, of all expenditures, of all orders drawn upon the treasury, in a check book to be kept by him for that purpose; the books and accounts of the treasurer shall, at reasonable hours, be open to the inspection of any elector of said city; the treasurer shall exhibit to the common council, at the last regular meeting in the month of April, a full and fair account of the receipts and expenditures after the date of his or the last annual report, and also the state of the treasury, which account shall be refered to a committee for examination, and if found to be correct shall be filed.

Sec. 69. The attorney or counsellor of the city shall per- Duties of attorney and counsellor. form such duties and exercise such powers as shall be assigned to him by the common council, by an ordinance duly enacted.

Sec. 70. The city marshal shall be superintendent of the Duties of marshal. city, and it shall be his duty to superintend, under the general direction of the common council, all work to be done or performed, ordered or required to be done or performed upon or in relation to any of the public streets, walks, bridges, sewers or public pumps, reservoirs or grounds of said city; and to perform such other duties as by this act or the ordinances or resolutions of the common council shall be required.

Oaths of office of justices of the peace.

Jurisdiction

Sec. 71. The justices of the peace of said city shall file their oaths of office in the office of the clerk of the county of Washtenaw, and shall have, in addition to the jurisdiction conferred by this act on them, the same jurisdiction, powers and duties conferred on justices of the peace in townships. *And provided further,* That all actions within the jurisdiction of justices of the peace, may be commenced and prosecuted in said justices' courts when the plaintiff or defendant or one of the plaintiffs or defendants reside in the township next adjoining the township of Ypsilanti.

Proviso.

Duties of justices.

Sec. 72. It shall be the duty of the justices of the peace of said city to keep their offices in said city, and attend to all complaints of a criminal nature which may properly come before them, and they shall receive for their services when engaged in cases for the violation of the ordinances of said city, such fees as the common council shall by ordinance prescribe.

Penalties & forfeitures to be paid into city treasury.

Report of justices.

Sec. 73. All fines, penalties or forfeitures, recovered before any of said justices, for violation of any city ordinance, shall, when collected, be paid into the city treasury and each of said justices shall report on oath to the common council, at the first regular meeting thereof, in each month during the term for which he shall perform the duties of such justice, the number and name of every person against whom judgment shall have been rendered for such fine, penalty or forfeiture, and all moneys by him received for or on account thereof, which moneys, so received, or which may be in his hands, collected on such fine, penalty or forfeiture, shall be paid into the said city treasury on the first Monday of each and every month during the time such justice shall exercise the duties of said office;

and for any neglect in this particular, he may be suspended or removed, as hereinafter provided.

Sec. 74. In addition to the security now required by law to be given by justices of the peace, [each of the justices of the peace] shall, before entering upon the duties of his office, execute a bond to the city of Ypsilanti, with one or more sufficient sureties, to be approved by the mayor or recorder of said city; which approval shall be endorsed on said bond, in the penalty of one thousand dollars, conditioned for the faithful performance of his duties as a police justice of said city, and to pay over the moneys so collected, and make his report as in this act required; which bond shall be filed in the office of the treasurer of said city.

Sec. 75. It shall be the duty of each justice of the peace, at the first regular meeting of the common council in each of the months of August, November, February and May, in every year, to account on oath, before the common council, for all such moneys, goods, wares and merchandise, seized as stolen property, as shall then remain unclaimed in the offices of either of said justices of the peace, and immediately thereafter to give notice, for four weeks, in one of the public newspapers printed in the said city, to all persons interested or claiming such property: *Provided, always,* That if any goods, wares, merchandise, or chattels of a perishable nature, or which shall be expensive to keep, shall at any time remain unclaimed in the offices of either of said justices, it shall be lawful for such justice to sell the same at public auction, at such time, and after such notice, as to him and the said common council shall seem proper.

Sec. 76. It shall be the duty of each of the justices of the peace aforesaid, who may recover or obtain possession of any stolen property, on his receiving satisfactory proof of property from the owner, to deliver such property to the owner thereof, on his paying all necessary and reason-

able expenses, which may have been incurred in the re-
covering, preservation or sustenance of such property,
and the expenses of advertising the same.

Sale of un-
claimed pro-
perty.   Sec. 77. It shall be the duty of each of the justices of
the peace aforesaid to cause all property unclaimed after
the expiration of the notice specified in the last preceding
section but one of this act, money excepted, to be sold at
public auction to the highest bidder, unless the prosecuting attorney of the county of Washtenaw shall direct that
it shall remain unsold for a longer period, to be used as
evidence in the administration of justice, and the proceeds
thereof forthwith to pay to the treasurer of the said city,
together with all money, if any, which shall remain in his
hands after such notice as aforesaid, first deducting the
charges of said notice of sale.

Fees of con-
stables.
Powers and   Sec. 78. The constables of said city shall have and re-
duties   ceive the same fees, and have the like powers and authority in matters of civil and criminal nature, as is conferred
by law upon constables in the several towns of this State,
and shall, if required by the common council, give like security.

Duties of
constables.   Sec. 79. The city constables shall obey the orders of the
mayor and aldermen, or of any person legally exercising
the criminal jurisdiction of a justice of the peace in said
city, in enforcing the laws of the State or the ordinances of
said city, and in case of refusal or neglect so to do, he or
they shall be subject to a penalty of not less than one nor
more than twenty-five dollars.

Expenses in
criminal ca-
ses, how
paid.   Sec. 80. The expenses of apprehending, examining and
committing offenders against any law of this State, in the
said city, and of their confinement, shall be audited, allowed and paid by the supervisors of the county of Washtenaw, in the same manner as if such expenses had been incurred in any town of the said county.

Sec. 81. The city auditor, previous to entering upon the

duties of his office, shall take ,and subscribe an oath for City auditor to take oath and give bond. the faithful performance of the same, and he shall also enter into a bond in such sum and with such sureties as the common council shall fix and approve in writing endorsed thereon, which bond shall be filed with the city clerk. Said auditor shall countersign all orders for the payment of money out of the city treasury, and shall perform such other duties as the common council shall by ordinance prescribe, and such other duties as are prescribed in this act.

Sec. 82. The superintendents of the city cemetery or Duties of superinten- dents of city cemetery. cemetaries shall have care of the city cemetery or cemeteries, and all the grounds and other property belong- ing thereto, subject to the ordinances and direction of the common council ; they shall make such improve- ments upon the property as they shall think expedient, but shall not expend in any one year more than one hun- dred dollars, without the consent of the common council previously obtained, and they shall receive no pecuniary compensation for their services; and said superintendents shall report quarterly to the common council the amount expended by them in the improvement of said property.

Sec. 83. The auditor shall, as treasurer of the board of To receive moneys for cemetery lots. superintendents, receive all moneys for lots which shall be sold in said city cemetery or cemeteries, and also all pen- alties collected for violation of city ordinances in relation to such cemetery or cemeteries, and shall pay, upon reso- lution of the board, for improvements made upon the grounds of the said cemetery or cemeteries, and also the incidental expenses of the board, where the accounts for said incidental expenses shall have been audited and al- lowed by the common council.

Sec. 84. The auditor shall pay over to the city treasurer To pay the same to city treasurer. all moneys which shall come into his hands as treasurer of the board of superintendents of the city cemetery, which are not by this act appropriated.

16

Annual report of superintendents.

Sec. 85. It shall be the duty of said board of superintendents to publish an annual report in relation to the matters committed to their charge, in one of the newspapers printed in said city, between the first and fifteenth days of February in each year.

School inspectors and poor directors.

Sec. 86. The school inspectors and directors of the poor shall continue to perform such duties as are required of them by law.

Duties of certain other officers.

Sec. 87. The health physician, fire wardens, common criers, pound master, inspectors of fire wood and weigh masters, shall perform such duties, and if required, shall file such securities as the common council shall by ordinance direct.

Common council to fix salaries of officers.

Sec. 88. The common council shall annually determine the salary or compensation to be paid to the several officers of said city, within the limitations hereinafter prescribed, and which shall be as follows, to-wit: to the city clerk, in addition to his fees and perquisites prescribed by law, a sum not exceeding one hundred dollars per annum; to the city treasurer, a sum not exceeding one hundred dollars per annum; to the city marshal, as superintendent of streets and highways, a sum not exceeding one dollar and fifty cents per day, and at that rate for any part of a day, for every day by him actually spent in the performance of such duties; to each alderman of said city [as such] a sum not exceeding one dollar per annum; to the city auditor, a sum not exceeding one hundred dollars; to the city attorney, a sum not exceeding two hundred dollars per annum; and they may also establish the fee or salary to be paid to all other officers appointed by them, whose fees are not prescribed by law, and whose compensation for services is required to be paid from the city treasury.

Common council to audit accounts.

Sec. 89. The common council shall examine, settle, and allow all accounts and demands properly chargeable against said city, as well of its officers as other persons, and shall have authority to provide means for the payment of the same, and for defraying the contingent expenses of the said city, subject only to the limitations and restrictions in this act contained.

Sec. 90. For the purpose of defraying the expenses and all liabilities incurred by said city, and paying the same, the common council may raise annually, by tax levied upon the real and personal property within said city, such sum as they may deem necessary, not exceeding one half of one per cent. on the valuation of such real and personal estate within the limits of said city, according to the valuation thereof, taken from the assessment roll of the year preceding the levying of such tax, and the sum or sums so to be raised shall be apportioned between the several wards of said city, in the manner in this act provided. *Power of common council to levy taxes.*

Sec. 91. The treasurer of said city shall collect all taxes levied or assessed in said city, and for that purpose, such treasurer shall give bond to said city, in such sum and with such surety or sureties as the common council shall require and approve; and such treasurer shall also give to the treasurer of the county of Washtenaw such further security as is or may hereafter be required by law of the several township treasurers of the several townships of this State; and for the purposes of the collection and return of all such taxes, and the return of property delinquent for the non-payment of taxes, the said treasurer, on giving the bonds or surety so required, shall possess all the powers, and perform all the duties, of the several township treasurers of this State, as prescribed by law, and shall also perform such other duties, respecting the collection and return of taxes, as this act imposes. *Treasurer to collect taxes. To give bond. To give security to Co. treasurer.*

Sec. 92. The supervisor shall represent the city in the board of supervisors of the county, and shall be entitled to all the rights, privileges and powers, and shall be subject to all the obligations of supervisors of townships. *Supervisor.*

His powers and duties. Sec. 93. The supervisor of said city shall complete the tax roll and deliver the same, with his warrant thereto attached, to the treasurer, within the time prescribed by law for the completion and delivery of the township tax rolls to **Proviso.** the respective township treasurers of this State: *Provided,* Security has been given by such treasurer, as required by law, or in this act provided; but if such security shall not have been given by such treasurer, in the manner and within the time required, the common council shall immediately appoint some suitable person, who will give the requisite security, to collect such tax roll; and the person so appointed shall thereupon be entitled to receive said tax roll, and shall collect and pay over such taxes, and make return of his doings thereon, in the same manner, and shall have all the powers, and shall perform all the duties, and shall be subject to the same liabilities, in this act conferred upon the treasurer, for the purpose of the collection and return and paying over such taxes.

Per centage for collecting taxes. Sec. 94. For the collection of all such taxes, the treasurer, or other person appointed to collect the same, shall be entitled to receive such percentage as shall be prescribed by the common council by ordinance, not exceeding two per cent. upon the sum to be collected; which sum shall be added in the computation of the taxes on said tax rolls of the respective wards of said city.

Supervisors to make assessment rolls. Sec. 95. The supervisor of said city, shall, in each and every year, make and complete the assessment of all the real and personal property within each ward of said city, separately, in the same manner and within the same time as required by law for the assessment of property in the several townships of this State, and in so doing shall conform to the provisions of law governing the action of the supervisors of the several townships of this State, performing like services; and in all other respects, within said city shall, unless when otherwise in this act provided, conform to the provisions of law governing the action of supervisors in the several townships of this State, in the assessment of property, the levying of taxes, and the issuing of warrants for the collection and return thereof; and shall, also, in each year, within thirty days after the time required by law for completing the assessment rolls in the several townships of this State, make and file with the city clerk of said city, a true and certified copy of the assessment roll for such year, and such city clerk shall receive and file the same in his office.

To file copies with city clerk.

Sec. 96, It shall be the duty of the common council of said city, on or before the last Saturday preceding the first day of October in each year, to determine by resolution the amount necessary to be raised by tax for city purposes within said city for such year; and it shall be the duty of the city clerk to certify the amount so to be raised, to the supervisor of said city, on or before the first Monday in october in each year; and it is hereby made the duty of the supervisor to apportion the same so to be raised among the several wards of said city, according to the valuation of the property appearing upon the assessment roll of said several wards for such year; as equalized by the board of supervisors for such year; and also to notify each of the aldermen of the several wards of said city, of the amount so apportioned to their respective wards, within five days after the board of supervisors of said county of Washtenaw shall have completed the equalization of the valuation of the property in the said city and said townships of said county for such year; and it is hereby made the duty of the supervisor of said city, to levy the sum so apportioned, and such other taxes as may be required by law, upon the taxable property of such ward in the same manner as taxes for township purposes are required by law to be levied by the supervisors of the townships of this State.

Duties of common council as to amount to be raised by tax.

Duties of city clerk.

Apportionment made by supervisor.

Notice to aldermen.

Aldermen to
report am't
to common
council.

Sec. 97. Within five days after the aldermen of each
ward shall have been notified, as directed in the last preceding section, of the amount of general tax to be raised in
their respective wards, they shall report to the common
council and supervisor the sum required to be raised in
their several wards, for local improvements, and such sum
shall be levied and assessed by the supervisor upon the taxable property of such ward, in addition to the general tax;
shall be collected by the treasurer and expended by the
the city marshal, under the direction of the common council, for the local improvements in such ward for which it
was so raised.

Amount to
be assessed
by supervi-
sor.

Collected by
treasurer.

Taxes to be
a lien.

Sec. 98. The taxes so levied for city purposes shall be
and remain a lien upon the property on which the same
was levied in the same cases, to the same extent, and in
like manner as taxes required by law to be levied on property in the several townships of this State, are liens upon
such property, and all provisions of law respecting the return and sale of property for the non-payment of taxes for
State, county and township purposes, shall apply to the return and sale of property for the non-payment of such city
taxes, except as herein otherwise provided.

Net pro-
ceeds of
sales to be
paid by Co.
treasurer to
city treasu-
rer.

Sec. 99. The net proceeds of the sales of all property
delinquent for non-payment of city taxes, shall be paid to
the treasurer of said city by the treasurer of the county of
Washtenaw, whenever required by the city treasurer, and
the net proceeds of all sums paid to the treasurer of the
county of Washtenaw, before sale on account of property
within said city returned delinquent for non-payment of city
taxes, shall in like manner be paid to said city treasurer.

Common
council may
borrow mo.
ney to im-
prove ceme-
tery.

Sec. 100. For the purchase and improvement of a city
cemetery or cemeteries, the common council may borrow
on the faith of the city, a sum not exceeding three thousand dollars, for a term not exceeding twenty years, at a
rate of interest not exceeding seven per cent. per annum,

payable annually, and for that purpose may issue the _{May issue bonds.} bonds of the city, signed by the mayor and clerk, and countersigned by the auditor, and in such form and in such sums (not exceeding in the aggregate the said sum of three thousand dollars,) as the said common council shall direct, and such bonds shall be disposed of under the direction of the common council of said city, upon such terms as they shall deem advisable, but not for less than their par value, and the avails shall be applied in the purchase and improvement of a city cemetery or cemeteries, and the necessary appurtenances, and for no other purpose whatsoever.

Sec. 101. It shall not be lawful for the common council _{Limitation of powers of common council in borrowing money, &c.} (except as herein otherwise provided) to borrow any money or authorize the creation of any liability or indebtedness against said city in any one year exceeding in the aggregate the amount which by this act may be raised by tax for such year, and in case any sum or sums of money shall be borrowed by said common council in any one year, or the said common council, or any officer thereof, shall enter into any contract or contracts for the payment of money binding upon said city, the same shall be paid out of the sums raised by tax for such year, if the payment thereof is not otherwise provided, and all sums of money borrowed by said city shall be applied to the purposes for which the same was borrowed, and for no other purpose whatsoever, but nothing in this act contained shall be construed to prohibit said common council from making assessments and levying and collecting taxes for the purpose of local improvements.

Sec. 102. All sums of money directed to be raised by _{Money directed to be assessed upon property.} the common council, except as in this act otherwise provided, shall be assessed upon all the real and personal estate in the said city, according to the valuation of the same as from the valuation thereof by the last preceding assessment roll filed in the office of the city clerk; but no real or personal property which shall be exempt from taxation by the general laws of this State, nor any public square, park, or other public ground, shall be assessed for the ordinary city or county taxes.

Sec. 103. Whenever by the provisions of this act the common council shall be authorized to issue city bonds for the payment of any sum or sums of money, the said common council shall thereupon have the power to create a sinking fund for the payment of the interest as it falls due, and the extinguishment of the principal at the expiration of the time limited for the payment thereof, which fund shall be raised by a direct tax, which shall not exceed in any one year one mill on the dollar on the valuation of the real and personal property within said city, and which shall be levied and collected in the same manner as the ordinary city taxes of said city are levied and collected, and when so collected the same shall be applied to the credit of said sinking fund, for the purpose of paying off the principal and interest of the debt so created as the same becomes due.

No. 104. No money shall be drawn from the city treasury unless it shall have been previously appropriated to the purpose for which it shall be drawn; and all ordinances, resolutions and orders directing the payment of money, shall specify the object and purposes of such payment, which shall be certified by the clerk, and countersigned by the auditor, before the same shall be paid by the treasurer.

Sec. 105. The treasurer shall, at the first regular meeting of the common council in each month, make report of the finances of said city, showing what appropriations and payments have been made out of each of the several funds of said city since his last preceding report, and of the state of each of said funds.

Sec. 106. The common council of the city of Ypsilanti shall have full power to lay out, establish, open, extend, widen, straighten, alter, close, fill in or grade, vacate or abolish any highways, streets, avenues, lanes, alleys, public grounds or spaces in said city, whenever they shall deem it a necessary public improvement, and private property may be taken therefor; but the necessity for using such property, the just compensation to be made for the same, and the damages arising to any person from the making of said improvements, shall be ascertained by a jury of twelve freeholders residing in said city. *Powers of common council in relation to streets.* *Taking private property.*

Sec. 107. Whenever the common council shall deem any such improvements necessary, they shall so declare by resolution, which shall be drawn by the attorney of the corporation, and in said resolution shall describe the contemplated improvement; and if they intend to take private property therefor, they shall declare such intention and describe such property in said resolution with particularity sufficient for an ordinary conveyance thereof, and further declare that they will, on some day to be named in said resolution, apply to any justice's court of said city, for the drawing of a jury to ascertain the necessity for using the property intended to be taken, if it be intended to take any for such improvement, to ascertain the just damages and compensation which any person may be entitled to if such intended improvement be made, and to apportion and assess such damages and compensation to and upon all lots, premises and sub-divisions thereof which will be benefited by such improvement, and the time to be named for applying to said court shall be on a day subsequent to the required publication of said resolution. *Resolution that improvement is necessary* *Proceedings when private property is intended to be taken.*

Sec. 108. The common council shall give notice of the intended improvement, and of the intended application to said court, by causing a copy of said resolution, certified by the clerk of the city, to be published for four successive *Common council to give notice of intended improvement.*

17

Notice, how given. weeks in some newspaper published in said city, and the marshal shall also give notice of said resolution by delivering a notice thereof, with a copy of the same annexed, to the owner or owners of any private property intended to be taken, if they can be found in said city, which notice shall be directed to them; or if they cannot be found in said city, by leaving the same at their place of residence in said city with some person of proper age; if they or their place of residence cannot be found, and such property be occupied, said notice and copy of said resolution shall be served by delivering the same to the occupant or occupants, or by leaving the same at their place of residence within said city with some person of proper age; but if the owner or owners of such property, or their place of residence cannot be found, and it be not occupied, or, if it be occupied, but they, their place of residence and that of the occupant or occupants, cannot be found, or if the owner or owners, occupant or occupants, cannot be found, or if the owner or owners, occupant or occupants, be unknown or non-residents of said city, then, in either of such cases, notice of said resolution may be given by posting the same, with a copy of said resolution, in some conspicuous place upon the

Marshal to make return of service. property intended to be taken; the marshal shall give notice of said resolution as above directed, and make return of his doings and of the manner of giving said notice as soon as practicable after the passage thereof, which return shall be made to the said court at least six days before the day appointed in said resolution for the hearing of said application, and all persons interested therein, after notice given in the manner aforesaid, shall take notice of and be bound by all subsequent proceedings without any further notices except as herein otherwise provided.

Duties of clerk. Sec. 109. The clerk of said city shall deliver to the attorney of the corporation a certified copy of said resolution of the common council, whose duty it shall be to appear in said court and make the application therein referred to, and conduct all further proceedings thereon in behalf of the common council.

Sec. 110. Upon the day designated in said resolution, or Jury. on some other day to be appointed by the court, and on filing a copy of said resolution and an affidavit showing the required publication thereof, the marshal shall attend said court and write down the names of twenty-four disinterested freeholders residing in said city, and who shall be approved by the court as such disinterested freeholders and residents, and qualified to serve.

Sec. 111. Said court shall then issue a summons com- Summons to manding the marshal to summons said twenty-four persons jurors. to be and appear in said court to serve as jurors, on some day to be named therein, which shall not be less than seven days after the issuing thereof; the marshal shall serve Service. such summons at least three days before the return day thereof, and make return in the same manner as in the case of an ordinary venire for jurors for said court; and the persons thus summoned shall be bound to attend said court and serve until discharged, and said court shall impose upon Fine. them a fine not exceeding five dollars for each day's nonattendance in court or neglect to serve; but they may be exempted and excused by the court from serving for the same reasons for which jurors in the circuit court may be exempted or excused.

Sec. 112. The names of the jurors in attendance and who Drawing of do not claim to be exempted or excused from serving, shall jurors. then be written by the clerk of the court on separate slips of paper of equal size and appearance, as near as practicable, and be deposited by him in a box having a lid or cover; he shall then shake said box so as thoroughly to mix said slips of paper, and shall then draw impartially, openly, and in the presence of the court, so many of the slips of paper or ballots containing names written thereon, one after another, as shall be sufficient to form a jury.

Deficiency, how made up. Sec. 113. If, in consequence of jurors being exempted, excused or set aside, there shall not be in the box any slips or ballots, or not a sufficient number of ballots from which to draw the jury, the marshal [shall] forthwith, under the order of the court, summons such number of persons as the court shall deem necessary, and may order them to be and appear in said court to serve as jurors, and the persons thus summoned shall be returned, be bound to attend said court and serve, and be competent to form the jury in the same manner and to the same effect as those first summoned.

First 12 persons to constitute jury. Sec. 114. The first twelve persons who shall appear as their names are drawn and called by the clerk, or who are called by him when all the ballots have been drawn from the jury box, and shall be approved by the court as quali-**Jury to be sworn.** fied, shall be the jury, and shall be sworn to discharge the duties imposed on them by this title, faithfully, impartially, and according to the best of their abilities; said court **Instructions to jury.** shall then instruct said jury as to their duties and the law applicable to the case, and deliver to them a copy of the resolution of the common council as filed in said court, certified by the clerk thereof.

Jury to view Sec. 115. Each of said jurors shall go to the place of the intended improvement, and upon or as near as practicable to any property intended to be taken and described in said resolution, or as the case may be, which will be damaged or benefitted if the intended improvement be made.

Jury to ascertain necessity for taking property & assess damages. Sec. 116. Said jury shall then ascertain the necessity for using the property intended to be taken, if it be intended to take any for such improvement, the just damages and compensation to be paid to the owner or owners of any property intended to be taken for or that may be damaged by the intended improvement, and award to the owner or

owners thereof such damages and compensation as they
shall deem just. If such property shall be subject to a Apportion
damages in
valid mortgage, lease, lien, levy or agreement, or to either, case of incumbrance.
then said jury shall apportion and award to the owner or
owners of such property, the parties in interest to such
mortgage, lease, lien, levy or agreement, or to either of
them, such portion of the damage and compensation as
they shall deem just.

Sec. 117. Said jury shall apportion and assess the to-Jury to assess total
tal damages and compensation to be paid in any case to damages.
and upon all lots of land, premises, or subdivisions thereof,
which will be benefitted if the intended improvement be
made, apportioning and assessing to and upon each, such
portion of said total damages and compensation as they
shall deem just: *Provided, however,* That if the total Proviso.
damages and compensation to be awarded to any person
or persons as above shall exceed the total benefits to be
apportioned to and assessed upon any property for the
benefit of such property will receive, then such excess
shall be apportioned and assessed to the city of Ypsilanti.

Sec. 118. Said jury shall then make in writing, and each Jury to
make re-
shall sign, a report to said court of their doings, enclose port.
the same in a sealed envelope, and file it in said court,
within thirty days after they were sworn.

Sec. 119. Said jury shall state in their report the just Contents of
report.
damages and compensation ascertained and awarded by
them to the owner of any private property, or to any person claiming an interest therein by virtue of any mortgage,
lease, lien, levy, or agreement, or either, to which such
property may be subject, together with the name of such
owner or claimant, if known, and a description of the
property intended to be taken. In case any damage and
compensation be awarded to any person claiming an interest in such property by virtue of any valid mortgage,
lease, lien, levy, or agreement, or either, to which such

property may be subject, it shall be sufficient to state further, in such case, the name of such interested party, the date of such mortgage, lease, lien, levy, or agreement, or assignment thereof, if there be any, by virtue of which such interested party has an interest in the property intended to be taken.

Ib.

Sec. 120. Said jury shall also state in the their report what portions in amount of the total ascertained damages and compensation they have apportioned to and assessed upon any lot, premises, or subdivision thereof, which will be benefited by the intended improvement, together with the names of the owners thereof, if known, and a description of the same, and also what portion, if any, of the ascertained damages and compensation they have apportioned and assessed to the city of Ypsilanti, in the case above provided for.

Confirmation of re-
report.

Sec. 121. Said report may be confirmed by said court at any time when said court may be regularly in session; and the said court shall appoint some day when it will

Objections,
when heard.

consider said report, and objections against the confirmation thereof on the part of all persons interested therein, whereof the city attorney shall give notice by publishing the same in some newspaper published in said city for one week, and he shall file in said court an affidavit of such publication before the time appointed for considering said

Objections
to be filed.

report; said objection shall be filed with the clerk in writing, but may be argued, and the consideration of said report and objections may be adjourned from time to time until said report be confirmed or otherwise disposed of, as herein provided.

What may
be enquired
into.

Sec. 122. Said report shall not be annulled for objections as to matters of form; all objections shall be objections of law, and to matters of substance; but the damages and compensation to be paid to any person, or the portions thereof, apportioned to and assessed upon any lot of land, premises, or subdivision thereof, may be enquired into if objected to as being excessively large or small.

Sec. 123. If no objections be filed, said report shall be confirmed; but if objections be filed, said court, after considering the same, and after argument thereon, shall, in its discretion, confirm or annul said report, or may refer it back to the same jury, for the purpose of reviewing all matters and correcting all errors therein contained, and making any alterations thereof which said court may direct or said jury may deem just or necessary; and thereon said jury shall review, correct, or alter, said report, in manner aforesaid, and shall retnrn and file the same with said court, within five days after said report was referred back to them as aforesaid; and thereupon said court shall confirm or annul said report. *Court may confirm, annul or refer back to jury*

Sec. 124. If said report be annulled, or the jury cannot agree, or from death, sickness, or any other cause, shall fail to make a report within the thirty days required above, the court may, on the application of the attorney, designate some day when another jury may be had, and such jury shall be obtained, drawn summoned, returned, bound to attend and serve, have the same qualifications, be sworn, and when sworn have the same powers and duties as the first jury; the same proceedings, after they are sworn, shall be had by them, and by and in said court, as provided for above, after the first jury is sworn. *New jury.*

Sec. 125. If any juror after being sworn shall die, or from sickness be unable to discharge his duties, the court may appoint another person to serve in his place, who shall be sworn, and shall have the like qualifications, powers and duties as those already sworn. *Vacancy in jury, how filled.*

Sec. 126. Any person to whom damages and compensation may be awarded for any of his property intended to be taken, or on account of the intended improvement, or to and upon whose property any portion of such damages and *Grievances, how redressed.*

Appeal.   compensation may be apportioned and assessed, considering himself aggrieved, may appeal from the judgment of
the court confirming the report of the jury to the supreme
Notice.   count, by filing in writing with the said court a notice of such
appeal and specification of the errors complained of, within
five days after the confirmation, and serving within the
same time a copy of said notice and specification of errors
Bond.   on the attorney of the corporation, and filing a bond in said
court, to be, approved by the said justice, conditioned for
the prosecution of said appeal, and the payment of all costs
that may be awarded against the appellant in case the
judgment of confirmation of the justice's court be affirmed.

Duty of cl'rk   Sec. 127. In case of appeal as above, it shall be the duty
of the court.   of the court forthwith, or as soon as practicable, to transmit to the supreme court a certified copy of all the proceedings in the case, which may be filed in said court.

Duties and   Sec. 128. The supreme court at any term thereof shall,
powers of
supreme   with the least practicable delay, hear and try the matter of
court.   said appeal, and may affirm or revise [reverse] the judgment
of the justice court confirming the report of the jury, but
the same shall not be reversed for matter of form, nor for any
errors except errors of law, and only in regard to the appellant or appellants. The court shall give judgment for
reasonable costs and expenses in the matter of said appeal
and proceedings thereon, to be taxed, and all costs and expenses awarded to the city in case of affirmation, shall be
applied on and deducted from the damages and compensation, if any, to be paid to the appellant or appellants.

Case may be   Sec. 129. If there be a reversal for any errors which it
remanded
for correc-   is practicable for the court or said jury to correct with due
tion.   regard to the public interest and rights of individuals, the
proceedings shall be remanded to said court with direction
that such errors be corrected. Said court or (as the case
may be) said jury, under the direction of said court, shall
correct such error, and thereupon the report of the jury

shall be confirmed by said court, without any further right
of appeal.

Sec. 130. In case of every annulment of the report of the Powers of common
jury by the court, or reversal by the supreme court, the council in relation to
common council, in behalf of said city, may by resolution damages.
elect to pay the damages and compensation claimed by, or
the assessment made upon the property of the objector, appellant or appellants, on filing a certified copy of said resolution in the said court, within twenty days after the annulment or reversal, the report of said jury shall be reviewed and confirmed by said court as to all persons interested
therein, except the objector, appellant or appellants, and
without further right of appeal. If the common council do
not elect as above provided, all the proceedings shall be
null and void, and no further proceedings shall be had except in a case of reversal, when the proceedings may have
been remanded to the court for the correction of certain errors, in which case such errors shall be corrected, and the
report of the jury confirmed as above provided.

Sec. 131. If the report of the jury be confirmed by the Confirma-
court in any case above provided for, or if the judgment of tion to be final.
confirmation be affirmed on appeal to the supreme court,
such confirmation shall be final and conclusive as to all persons interested therein; and the damages and compensation
apportioned to and assessed upon any lot of land, premises
or sub-division thereof, according to said report as confirmed, shall be a lien thereon from the time of the aforesaid
confirmation until they are paid and satisfied.

Sec. 132. When the report of the jury shall have been Certified co-
thus finally confirmed, or the judgment of confirmation af- py of report to be filed
firmed by the supreme court, the court shall prepare a cer- with city clerk.
tified copy of the report of the jury as confirmed by the
court, and of the order of the court confirming the same,
and shall file said certified copy in the office of the clerk of
the city, who shall record the same in a book to be provi-
18

ded, used and known as a book of street records. Such certified copy, such record, or a like copy made and certified by the court, shall in all courts and places be presumptive evidence of the matters therein contained, and of the regularity of all proceedings from the commencement thereof to and including the order of the court confirming the report of the jury.

Amount paid to city treasurer. Sec. 133. The amounts apportioned to and assessed upon all lots of land, premises or sub-divisions thereof, for the benefits they will receive, shall be paid to the treasurer of said city, in case of confirmation of the report of the jury as above provided, or in case the judgment of confirmation **Warrant issued by supervisor.** be affirmed by the supreme court, and warrant or warrants authorizing the collection thereof shall be issued, as soon as practicable, under the hand of the supervisor of the city, directed to the treasurer thereof, and in the collection of **Treasurer to collect.** such assessments the said treasurer shall proceed in the same manner, and shall levy, collect, make return to the city clerk of the sums remaining uncollected, with a description of the lots, premises or sub-divisions, or parts or portions thereof, upon which such tax was assessed, and which remains unpaid as aforesaid, and the city clerk shall **Provision for collecting unpaid assessments.** report the same to the supervisor, and the supervisor shall assess the same upon his assessment and tax roll upon such premises, and the same shall be thereupon collected and returned, and the same proceedings had for the collection and return thereof, and for the sale of such premises for the non-payment of such assessment and the charges accruing thereon, as is provided by this act in the case of the collection of assessments made for public improvements in said city.

Common council to pay or tender amount. Sec. 134. Within three months after the confirmation of the report of the jury, or after the judgment of confirmation shall, on appeal, be affirmed, the common council shall pay or tender to the respective persons the several amounts

of damages and compensation awarded to them, according
to the report of the jury as confirmed, or elected, as above
provided for, to be paid by the common council; and in
case any such person shall refuse the same, be unknown,
or a non-resident of said city, or for any reason incapacita-
ted from receiving his or her amount, or the right thereto
be disputed or doubtful, the common council may deposit Amount to be deposited in city treasury in certain cases.
the amount awarded in such case, or elected to be paid by
the common council, in the treasury of the city, to the
credit of any person entitled thereto, and shall, on demand,
pay the same over to any person or persons competent and
entitled to receive it, and the treasurer shall take receipt
and voucher therefor.

Sec. 135. Upon such payment, tender, or deposit in the When title to vest in city.
city treasury, the fee and ownership of the land and prop-
erty to be taken, with its appurtenances, shall be fully vested
in the said city and the common council may enter upon
take possession of, and convert the same to the uses and
purposes for which it has been taken. A certificate of the Certificate to be evidence.
city treasurer of such tender, payment, or deposit, or
record thereof in the book of street records, or certified
copy of such record, shall in all courts and places, be presumptive evidence of the facts therein stated, of the vest-
ing of the fee of the property taken in the city and of the
right of the common council to take possession of and convert the same to the uses for which it has been taken.

Sec. 136. In all cases where any real estate, subject to Leases on agreements to be void after final confirmation.
any lease or agreement, shall be taken as aforesaid, all the
covenants and stipulations contained therein shall cease,
determine, and be discharged, upon the final confirmation
of the report of the jury, or upon the affirmation, by the
supreme court, of the judgment of confirmation. If a part
only of such real estate be taken, said covenants and stipulations shall cease, determine and be discharged, only as
to such part ; and the court, on application of any party.

·in interest to such lease or agreement, and after a notice thereof of eight days, in writing to the other parties in interest, may appoint three disinterested residents and freeholders of said city, commissioners, to determine the rents and payments to be thereafter paid, and the covenants, stipulations or conditions thereafter to be performed under the lease or agreement, in respect to the residue or part of such real estate not taken. Said commissioners shall, before entering on their duties, take and subscribe an oath, to be administered by the court, faithfully to discharge their duties, which oath shall be filed in said court. Said three commissioners shall make and sign a report, in writing of their doings to said court, which shall be filed therein within thirty days after their appointment; and said report, on being confirmed by the court, shall be binding and conclusive on the parties in interest to such lease or agreement, and the fees and expenses of proceedings under this section shall be borne in whole or in part by the parties to such lease or agreement, or either of them, or by the city in the discretion of the common council.

Sec. 137. The duties above to be performed by the marshal of said city, in case of the inability of such marshal, whether by absence, sickness, or interest in the subject matter of the proceedings, may be performed by either of the constables of said city.

Sec. 138. The common council shall pay said jury such compensation for their services as they may deem just, and they shall have power to abandon or discontinue proceedings under this chapter in said court, at any time before the final confirmation of the report of the jury.

Sec. 139. The common council shall be commissioners of highways for said city, and shall have the care and supervision of the highways, streets, bridges, lanes, alleys, parks, and public grounds therein; and it shall be their duty to

give directions for the repairing, preserving, improv- Duties as
ing, cleansing and securing of such highways, bridges, such.
lanes, alleys, parks and public grounds, and to cause the
same to be repaired, cleansed, improved and secured, from
time to time, as may be necessary; to regulate the
roads, streets, highways, lanes, parks and alleys already laid out, or which may hereafter be laid out, and
to alter such of them as they shall deem inconvenient, subject to the restrictions contained in this title; to cause such
of the streets and highways in said city as shall have been
used for six years or more as public highways and streets,
and which are not sufficiently described, or have not been
duly recorded, to be ascertained, described, and recorded
in the office of the city clerk of said city, in the book of
street records; and the recording of such highways, streets,
lanes, alleys or public grounds, so ascertained and described, or which shall hereafter be laid out and established
by the said common council, and recorded in the book of
street records, in the office of the clerk, by order of the
common council, shall be presumptive evidence of the existence of such highway, street, lane, alley, or public ground
therein described; to divide said city from time to time,
into so many highway districts as they shall deem expedient, by an ordinance or resolution, entered in their
minutes; to appoint and assign to each of such districts.
so many inspectors of streets as they shall from time to.
time deem proper, and such inspectors shall in all cases,
when required by the common council, give such securities.
as said council shall require, for the faithful performance
of their duties; and the council may assign to such inspectors such duties in relation to the opening, laying out,
making, repairing and preserving the streets, highways,.
lanes, alleys, parks, squares and public grounds of said
city, as they may deem expedient; and the said inspectors.
shall possess all the powers, and be subject to all the

liabilities, of overseers of highways in the several townships of the State, so far as the same may be applicable to said 'city under the provisions of this act.

Powers of common council as to sewers, drains, &c.

Sec. 140. The common council shall have power to cause common sewers, drains and vaults, arches and bridges, wells, pumps and reservoirs to built in any part of said city; to cause the grading, raising, levelling, repairing, amending, paving or covering with broken or pounded stone, plank or other material, any street, lane, alley, highway, public ground or side-walk of said city.

Streets, highways, &c.

Sec. 141. The common council shall have the same power in relation to discontinuing any street, highway, lane or alley in said city, which the commissioners of highways in townships have or may hereafter receive in relation to town highways, and they may adopt the same proceedings to effect such object as near as may be as the commissioners of highways in townships are or may be by law required to adopt, and appeals may be taken to the circuit court for the county of Washtenaw in like manner as far as practicable as appeals are now or may hereafter by law be taken from the decisions of highway commissioners in townships, and the said circuit court is hereby authorized and empowered to hear and determine such appeals.

Duties of common council in relation to certain improvements

Sec. 142. Whenever the common council shall determine that the whole or any part of the expense of any public improvement not requiring the taking of any land by the said city, shall be defrayed by an assessment on the owners or occupants of houses and lands to be benefited thereby, they shall declare the same by an entry in their minutes, and after ascertaining, as they may think proper, the estimated expense of such improvement, they shall declare by an entry in their minutes whether the whole or what portion thereof shall be assessed to such owners and occupants, specifying the sum to be assessed, and the portion of the city which they deem to be benefited by such improvement; the costs and expenses of making the estimates, plans and assessments incidental thereto, shall be included in the estimated expenses of such improvement.

Sec. 143. The common council shall thereupon make an Ib. order reciting the public improvement so as aforesaid intended to be made, the amount of expense to be assessed as aforesaid, and the portion or part of the city on which the same is to be assessed, designating and directing three resident freeholders of said city not interested in any of the property so benefited, nor of kin to any person interested, to make an assessment upon all the owners or occupants of lands and houses within the portion or part so designated, of the amount of expense in proportion as nearly as may be to the advantage which each shall be deemed to acquire by making of such improvements; which order shall be certified by the clerk of the city and delivered to one of said commissioners, together with a map or profile of the proposed improvement in cases where the same is practicable.

Sec. 144. It shall be the duty of said commissioners so Duties of commission-designated and appointed by the common council, to meet ers. together at such time and place as the common council shall appoint, or in case said council do not so appoint, as said commissioners shall themselves agree upon, and thereupon said commissioners shall severally take and subscribe an oath before some officer by law authorized to administer the same, that they are not interested in the premises described in said order, and not of kin to any person so interested, and that they will faithfully and impartially discharge the duty imposed upon them by said order, which said oath shall forthwith be returned and filed with the city clerk. In case any such commissioner shall not be able to take such oath, the city clerk shall forthwith return that fact to the common council, and the said council shall thereupon appoint one or more commissioners not interested and not of kin as aforesaid, to make the number three, and proceed in like manner until three commissioners are sworn as aforesaid.

Ib.

Sec. 145. The commissioners thus sworn shall proceed to make an assessment according to the said order, and shall make out an assessment roll, in which shall be entered the names of the persons assessed, the value of the property for which they are assessed, the amount assessed to each of them respectively, and in case any lots or parts of lots shall be unoccupied, belonging to any person residing in the said city, such person shall be assessed for the same, and his name entered accordingly; and in case such lots or parts of lots shall belong to a non-resident or owner or owners unknown, the same shall be entered accordingly, with a description of such lots or premises, as is required by law in assessment rolls made by supervisors of towns, with the value thereof and the amount assessed thereon, which assessment shall be subscribed by them, or a majority of them, who acted in the premises, and returned as speedily as may be to the common council of the said city.

Compensation of commissioners.

Sec. 146. The said commissioners shall receive such compensation for their services as shall be allowed them by the common council, to be paid out of the contingent fund of the said city, not exceeding two dollars per day for each.

Notice.

Sec. 147. Upon such return being made and filed, the clerk of the city shall cause notice of the names being returned to his office to be published in a newspaper of the said city for at least ten days, and that the common council will, on such day as they shall appoint, proceed to hear any appeals from the said assessment.

Hearing of appeals.

Sec. 148. At the day appointed for that purpose, and such other days as the hearing shall be adjourned to, the common council shall hear the allegations and proofs of all persons who may complain of such assessment, and may rectify and amend the said assessment list in whole or in part, or may set the same aside and direct a new assessment, either by the same persons,. or by such other persons as the common council shall appoint for that purpose ; and in such case the same proceedings shall be had as are herein provided upon the first order of the assessment, or the said common council may ratify and confirm such assessment without any corrections, or with such corrections therein as they may think proper.

Sec. 149. Every assessment so ratified and confirmed by the common council, as aforesaid, shall be final and conclusive, and the same shall remain and continue a lien upon the premises assessed for such tax. Within ten days after such assessment shall have been so ratified, the supervisor shall affix to such assessment and tax roll his warrant for the collection thereof ; which warrant shall direct the treasurer to collect the same within the time prescribed by the resolution of the common council; and the said assessment and tax roll, with the warrant of the supervisor annexed, shall be delivered to said treasurer, within the ten days aforesaid, who shall thereupon be authorized to levy and collect the same by distress and sale of any personal property upon such premises, or in possession of the person chargeable with such tax ; and in case sufficient personal property cannot be found whereon to levy and collect such tax, the treasurer shall, within five days after the time prescribed by his said warrant for the collection thereof has expired, make a report to the city clerk of the sums so remaining unpaid, which he was unable, for want of such personal property, to levy and collect .of the same, together with the description of the premises assessed for such unpaid taxes ; and the city clerk, within five days thereafter, shall in like manner notify the supervisor of the amount of such taxes and the description of the premises assessed and chargeable with such tax, who shall assess such unpaid

Assessments conclusive & to be a lien.

Warrant issued by supervisor.

Tax collected by treasurer.

taxes on such premises in the tax roll of such ward next thereafter to be made, and such tax shall then be levied, collected and returned, and the said premises may be sold for non-payment thereof, as provided by law for the non-payment of the ordinary city taxes.

Owner or landlord to pay tax. Sec. 150. In cases where there is no agreement to the contrary the owner or landlord, and not the occupant or tenant, shall be deemed in law the person who ought to bear and pay every such assessment, made for the expense of any public improvement in the said city.

Person paying may recover of person who ought to pay. Sec. 151. Where any such assessment shall be made upon or paid by any person, when by agreement or by law the same ought to be borne or paid by any other person, it shall be lawful for the one so paying to sue for and recover of the person bound to pay the same the amount so paid, with interest.

Sec. 152. Nothing herein contained shall impair, or in any way affect, any agreement between any landlord and tenant, or other persons, respecting the payment of any such assessments.

Excess to be apportioned and paid to tax payer. Sec. 153. If, upon completion of any such improvement for which such assessment shall have been made, it shall appear that a greater amount has been assessed and collected than is necessary to defray the expenses thereof, the common council shall apportion such excess among the persons and property assessed, in proportion to the amount collected of them, and shall pay the same to such persons and the owner of such property entitled thereto, on demand.

Deficit may be assessed. Sec. 154. If it shall appear that a greater sum of money has been expended in the completion of such improvement than was estimated as aforesaid, the common council may direct the assessment of the same on the owners and occupants of houses and lands benefited by such improvements, in the same manner as herein above directed, and the same proceedings in all respects shall be had thereon, and the common council may enlarge the territory to be assessed for such improvements.

Sec. 155. Every tax or assessment for public improve- Taxes a lien. ments, or for other purposes authorized by this act, except as herein otherwise provided, assessed upon any lands, tenements, or real estate, or upon the owners or occupants thereof, shall be and remain a lien upon such lands, tenements and real estate, on which, or in respect to which the same shall be made, from the time of filing the roll containing the same with the city clerk, until the same shall be paid or satisfied.

Sec. 156. Whenever the common council shall deem it Common council may expedient to construct any sidewalk or pavement, or plank require owners to any street within the said city, they may, by ordinance or construct otherwise, require the owner or occupant of any lot or sidewalks. house adjoining such street to lay such sidewalk, or construct such pavement, or plank such street, to the middle of the said street, in front of his or her lot or house; or they may direct such sidewalks and pavements, and such streets, to be planked, to be made according to the provisions of this act. The common council may, in like manner, by ordinance or otherwise, under such penalty or penalties as they may prescribe, require the owners and occupants, or either, of land in said city, or in any specified part thereof, to repair, maintain and re-construct sidewalks, pavements and street improvements adjoining their respective premises, to the middle of the street or alley, in such manner as the common council, by ordinance or otherwise, may direct; the expense to which any occupant or tenant may be thus subjected, may be collected by him from the owner of the premises, unless otherwise agreed, or unless such tenant or occupant be bound to bear such expense by the terms or nature of the agreement under which he holds the premises.

Sec. 157. Whenever the owner or occupant of any lot or house shall refuse or neglect, within such time as the common council shall have appointed, to conform to any regulation made by the said council for widening streets, or for any other purpose, it shall be lawful for the said common council to cause such regulations to be enforced at the expense of the city, and to recover the amount of such expenses with damages, at the rate of ten per cent. with costs of suit, from the owner or occupant of such lot or house, whose duty it was to conform to such regulation.

Sec. 158. The common council are authorized to assess the lands of non-residents of said city, their just proportion of the expenses of cleaning and repairing streets and sidewalks, and removing nuisances, and the said expenses shall be assessed in the same manner, and the amount so assessed shall be collected in the same manner, and the same proceedings shall be had in case of the non-payment of the same, as in relation to the assessments for public improvements in said city; except as the common council
may otherwise determine or direct. It shall in all cases be the duty of the owner of every lot or parcel of land in said city, to keep the sidewalk adjoining his lot or piece of land in good repair, and also to remove and clear away all snow and ice and other obstructions from the sidewalk. If any owner, after notice so to do shall have been posted on the premises, or otherwise given, served or published, as the common council may direct by ordinance, resolution or otherwise, shall fail or neglect so to do, for such time
not less than twenty-four hours, as the common council by a general or special ordinance, resolution or otherwise may fix, the common council may cause the same to be done at the expense of the city, and may add such expense (not exceeding ten dollars on any lot or piece of land in any year) to the amount of the general city tax on such

land, in the next general assessment rolls of said city, and such amount so added shall be a lien on' the premises in the same manner as the tax to which it is added, and may be collected and enforced, and (if not paid or collected) the land sold therefor, in the same manner as for general city taxes.

Sec. 159. Every person owning or occupying land or tenements in the said city, and every male inhabitant thereof over the age of twenty-one years and under the age of fifty, except as hereinafter provided, residing in said city, shall be assessed for highway taxes in said city; and the lands and tenements of non-residents situated in said city shall be assessed for highway taxes as hereinafter provided. Persons lia-
ble for high-
way, taxes.

Sec. 160. The aldermen of each ward of said city, shall, on or before the fifteenth of May in each year, furnish the common council with a list subscribed by them, of the names of all the inhabitants of his ward who are liable to be assessed for highway taxes. List to be
furnished.

Sec. 161. The common council shall, in the month of May in each year, make out from the assessment rolls in said city a separate list and statement of the value of all the taxable personal property, and a description of all lots or parcels of land within each highway district in said city, inserting in a separate part of said list descriptions of lands and tenements owned by non-residents of the city, with the value of each lot or parcel set down opposite to such description, as the same shall appear on the assessment roll; and if such lot or tract was not separately described in such roll, then in proportion to the valuation which shall have been affixed to the whole tract of which such lot or parcel forms a part. Annual
statement
of common
council.

Sec. 162. In making the estimate and assessment of highway taxes, the common council shall proceed as follows: Estimate,
how made.

1. Every male inhabitant in each ward, being above the

age of twenty-one and under fifty, except paupers, idiots and lunatics, and other persons exempt by law from taxation for highway purposes, shall be assessed fifty cents;

2. The residue of the highway taxes shall be assessed, not exceeding ten cents upon every one hundred dollars of the valuation, shall be apportioned upon the estate, real and personal, of every inhabitant in each highway district in said city, and upon each of the tracts or parcels of land in the respective highway districts of which the owners are non-residents, as the same shall appear from the assessment roll;

3. The common council shall affix to the name of each person named in the list furnished by the supervisors, and not assessed upon the assessment roll, and also to each valuation of property within the several highway districts, the amount of which such person or property shall be assessed for highway taxes, adding fifty cents to the assessment of each person between the age of twenty-one and fifty years, liable to such assessment upon the city assessment roll.

Sec. 163. The said tax list shall be made in duplicates and signed by the mayor, one of which shall be filed with the city clerk, and the other shall be put into the hands of the treasurer for collection, who shall, before receiving the same, give such security as the common council may require for the faithful discharge of his duties.

Tax list to be made in duplicates.

Sec. 164. Whenever the said tax list shall have been delivered to the treasurer with the warrant of the supervisor annexed for collection, he shall give like notice, and proceed in like manner, as near as may be, to collect said tax as hereinbefore provided for the collection of the ordinary taxes of said city.

Treasurer to give notice.

Sec. 165. The taxes assessed and collected in each ward shall be kept separate, and when collected the treasurer shall enter the respective amounts so paid in a book to be

Taxes in each ward to be kept separate.

kept by him for that purpose, to the credit of the ward from which they were collected.

Sec. 166. The moneys so collected and paid into the treasury as aforesaid shall constitute the highway fund of said ward districts in said city, and shall be applied as follows: *Highway fund, how applied;*

1. The street inspectors of the several ward districts, under the general supervision of the marshal, shall at all times keep the streets, bridges, culverts and drains allotted to them to oversee, in thorough repair and free from obstructions; they shall report on oath to the common council, once in each month, which report shall contain an accurate statement of the amount of labor performed and the expense necessarily incurred for material, and the streets upon which the same was performed, or expense incurred, and their charges for the same; *Monthly report of street inspectors.*

2. The common council shall examine such report, and if satisfied of its correctness, and that the charges therein made are just and reasonable, they shall accept it and order it filed, but if they are satisfied that it is incorrect, or that the charges therein are unreasonable, they shall alter the same as they think proper, and shall allow such charges as they shall deem just and equitable; they shall then let said report lay upon the table one week, and if not withdrawn by the inspector by filing a notice in writing to that effect with the city clerk in that time, they shall accept it and order it filed as corrected by them; *Examined by common council and filed.*

3. When any such report is filed the mayor shall draw an order upon the highway fund of the district in which the repairs were made, to the amount of such charge in said report, payable to said inspector, which order shall be countersigned by the auditor, and upon presentment, the city treasurer shall pay from the funds of such district, if there be any money in the treasury belonging to such dis- *Order on highway fund drawn by mayor.*

trict, and enter the same to the debit of the fund of such district, in a book to be kept by him for that purpose.

Money of each ward, &c.

4. No money belonging to one ward district, shall be applied in payment for repairs made in any other ward district.

Books open to inspection.

Sec. 167. The books kept by the city treasurer in which the debts and credits of the highway funds are entered, shall be open at all reasonable hours to the inspection of members of the common council.

Assessm'nts on cellars and drains.

Sec. 168. The common council shall have full power to assess and collect of each individual using or being benefited by any public sewer or drain, as follows, to wit: The sum of one dollar and fifty cents annually for each cellar drained directly or indirectly by a drain, into any public drain or sewer, which assessment shall be taken to include all other drainage of the premises to which said cellar especially belongs; and the sum of fifty cents annually for each lot, or sub-division of lot, being without a cellar, drained as aforesaid into any public drain or sewer; and such sums as may be fixed by the common council for all establishments requiring an unusual or extraordinary amount of drainage, drained as aforesaid; which sums, when collected, shall constitute the sewer fund, and shall be expended exclusively for the repair and construction of sewers, and the collection of the charges to individuals for drainage in this section provided, shall be enforced in such manner as the common council may by ordinance direct.

All assessments a lien

Sec. 169. When any assessment for public improvements, or for any local improvements or expenses upon any ward district, street, lane, alley, public sewer, or other improvement shall have been made, as in this act provided, and the tax roll for the same shall have been delivered to the treasurer for collection, the same shall be a lien upon the premises upon which the same was assessed, and the treasurer collecting such tax, shall levy and collect the same of any personal property found on the premises so assessed, or in possession of that person chargeable with such tax, and in case sufficient personal property shall not be found to levy and collect the same, the treasurer shall make return to the city clerk of the sums so remaining uncollected by him with a description of the lots or parcels upon which such tax was assessed, and which remains unpaid as aforesaid, and thereupon the city clerk shall report the same to the supervisor, who shall assess the same upon his assessment and [tax roll upon such premises, and the same shall be thereupon collected and returned, and the same proceedings had for the collection and return thereof, and for the sale of such premises for the non-payment of such tax, as is provided by law for the collection, return and sale of premises for non-payment of the ordinary city taxes. *Collection.*

Sec. 170. When the treasurer shall have levied upon any personal property for the non-payment of any tax or assessment in this act provided, he shall proceed to advertise and sell the same, in the same manner and upon like notice, as required by law in the levy and sale of personal property for non-payment of taxes by township treasurers. *Sale of personal property.*

Sec. 171. For the purpose of guarding against the calamities of fire the common council may from time to time, by ordinance, designate such portions and parts of the said city as they shall think proper, within which no buildings of wood shall be erected; and may regulate and direct the erection of buildings within such portions and parts, and the size and materials thereof, and the size of the chimneys therein; and every person who shall violate any such ordinance or regulation shall forfeit to the city the sum of one hundred dollars; and every building erected contrary to such ordinance is hereby declared to *Common council may prevent erection of wooden buildings.*

be a common nuisance, and may be abated and removed by such common council.

May require owners of buildings to have scuttles, &c.

Sec. 172. The common council may, by ordinance, require the owners and occupants of houses and other buildings to have scuttles on the roofs of such houses and buildings, and stairs or ladders leading to the same; and whenever any penalty shall have been recovered against the owner or occupant of any house or other building for not complying with such ordinance, the common council may at the expiration of twenty days after such recovery, cause such scuttles and stairs or ladders to be constructed, and may recover the expense thereof, with ten per cent. in addition, of the owner or occupant whose duty it was to comply with such ordinance.

Fire buckets

Sec. 173. The common council may, by ordinance, require the inhabitants of the city to provide such and so many fire buckets for each house or tenement therein, and within such time as they shall prescribe, and may require such buckets to be produced at every fire.

Ashes, stoves and pipes, flues, &c.

Sec. 174. The common council may regulate and direct the construction of safe deposits for ashes, and may compel the clearing of chimneys, flues, stovepipes, and all other conductors of smoke, and upon the neglect of the owner or occupant of any house, tenement, or building of any description, having therein any chimneys, flues, stovepipes, or other conductors of smoke, to clean the same, as shall have been directed by any ordinance, the common council may cause the same to be cleansed, and may collect the expenses thereof, and ten per cent. in addition, from the owner or occupant whose duty it was to have the same cleaned.

Other safeguards against fires

Sec. 175. The common council may regulate the use of lights and candles in livery stables and other buildings in which combustible articles may be deposited, and may prescribe the use of lanterns or safety lamps in such buildings, and may regulate the transporting, keeping and deposit of gunpowder or other dangerous or combustible materials, and may prevent or regulate the carrying on of manufactories dangerous in causing or promoting fires, and may authorize and direct the removal of any hearth, fireplace, stovepipe, flue, chimney, or other conductor of smoke, or any other apparatus or device in which any fire may be used, or to which fire may be applied, that shall be considered dangerous, and liable to cause and promote fires, and generally may adopt such other regulations for the prevention and suppression of fires as they may deem necessary,

Sec. 176. For the purpose of enforcing such regulations, May cause dwellings to be examined. the common council may authorize any of the officers of the said city, and may appoint persons at all reasonable times, to enter into and examine all dwelling houses, buildings and tenements of every description, and all lots, yards and enclosures, and to cause such as are dangerous to be put in safe condition: and may authorize such officers and persons to inspect all hearths, fireplaces, stoves, pipes, flues, chimneys, or other conductor of smoke, or any apparatus or device in which fire may be used, or to which fire may be applied, and remove and make the same safe, at the expense of the owners or occupants of the buildings in which the same may be, and to ascertain the number and condition of the fire buckets, and the situation of any building in respect to its exposure to fire, and whether scuttles and ladders thereto have been provided, and generally, with such powers and duties as the common council shall deem necessary to guard the city from the calamities of fire.

Sec. 177. The common council may procure, own, build, Fire engines, engine houses, &c. erect, and keep in repair, such and so many fire engines, with their hose and other apparatus, engine houses, ladders, fire hooks and fire buckets, and other implements and conveniences for the extinguishment of fires, and to prevent injuries by fire, and such and so many public cisterns, wells, reservoirs of water, as they from time to time shall judge necessary.

Fire districts.

Sec. 178. The common council shall have power to organize said city into so many fire districts as they may deem necessary, and may organize and maintain a fire department for said city, to consist of one chief engineer, two assistant engineers, twice as many wardens as there are wards in the said city, a proper number of firemen, not exceeding fifty to each engine, such number of hook and ladder men, and such number of tub and hose men as may be appointed by the said common council; all to have privileges and exemptions of firemen, and to hold their appointment during the pleasure of the common council.

Fire companies.

Sec. 179. The common council may make rules and regulations for the government of the said engineers, wardens, firemen, hook and ladder men, and tub and hose men; may prescribe their respective duties in case of fire or alarms of fire; may direct the dresses and badges of authority to be worn by them; may prescribe and regulate the time and manner of their exercise, and may impose reasonable fines for the breach of any such regulations.

Powers and duties of engineers and fire wardens

Sec. 180. The engineers and fire wardens, under the direction of the common council, shall have the custody and general superintendence of the fire engines, engine houses, hooks, ladders, hose, public cisterns, and other conveniences for the extinguishment and prevention of fires, and it shall be their duty to see that the same are kept in order, and to see that the laws and ordinances relative to the prevention and extinguishment of fires are duly executed, and to make detailed and particular reports of the state of their department, and of the conduct of the firemen, hook and ladder men, tub and hose men, to the common council, at stated periods, to be prescribed by the common council, and to make such reports to the mayor whenever required by him; the certificate of the city clerk that a person is or has been a fireman shall be evidence of the facts in all courts and places, on proof of the genuineness of such certificate.

Sec. 181. The common council may, by ordinance, direct **Fire bells.** the manner in which the bells in the city shall be tolled or rung in cases of fire or alarms of fire, and may impose penalties for ringing or tolling of such bells in such manner at any other time than during a fire or alarm of fire.

Sec. 182. The common council may provide suitable **Compensation to injured firemen.** compensation for any injury that any fireman, hook-and-ladder man, or tub-and-hose man may receive, in his person or property, in consequence of his exertions at any fire.

Sec. 183. The common council may by ordinance : **General powers of council in relation to fires.**

1. Prescribe the duties and powers of the engineers and wardens at fires and in cases of alarms of fire, and may vest in them such powers as shall be deemed necessary to preserve property from being stolen, and to extinguish and prevent fires ;

2. Prescribe the powers and duties of the mayor and aldermen at such fires and in cases of alarm; but in no case shall the mayor or any alderman control or direct the chief engineer or his assistants, during any fire ;

3. Provide for the removal and keeping away from such fires of all idle, disorderly or suspicious persons, and may confer powers for that purpose on the engineers, fire wardens or officers of the city ;

4. Provide for compelling persons to bring their fire buckets to any place of fire, and to aid in the extinguishment thereof by forming lines or ranks for the purpose of carrying water, and by all proper means to aid in the preservation, removal and securing of property exposed to danger by fire ;

5. To compel the marshal, constables and watchmen of

the city to be present at such fires, and to perform such duties as the said common council shall prescribe.

Sec. 184. Whenever any person shall refuse to obey any lawful order of any engineer, fire warden, mayor or alderman, at any fire, it shall be lawful for the officer giving such order, to arrest, or to direct orally a constable, watchman, or any citizen. to arrest such person and confine him temporarily in any safe place, until such fire shall be extinguished, and in the same manner such officers, or any of them, may arrest or direct the arrest and confinement of any person at such fire, who shall be intoxicated or disorderly.

Sec. 185. Whenever any building in said city shall be on fire, it shall be the duty, and be lawful for the chief engineer, with the consent of the mayor, or any alderman, or of any two aldermen, to order and direct such building, or any other building which they may deem hazardous, and likely to communicate fire to other buildings, or any part of such building, to be pulled down and destroyed, and no action shall be maintained against any person or against the said city therefor; but any person interested in any such building so destroyed or injured, may, within three months thereafter, apply to the common council to assess and pay the damages he has sustained. At the expiration of the three months, if any such application shall have been made in writing, the common council shall either pay to the said claimant such sum as shall be agreed upon by them and the said claimant for such damages, or if no such agreement shall be effected, shall proceed to ascertain the amount of such damages, and shall provide for the appraisal, assessment, collection and payment of the same in the same manner as is provided by this act, for the ascertainment, assessment, collection and payment of damages sustained by the taking of lands for purposes of public improvement.

[Margin notes: Arrest of person disobeying orders at fires.]

[Margin notes: Buildings may be destroyed to prevent spread of fires.]

[Margin notes: Damages, how paid.]

Sec. 186. The commissioners appointed to appraise and assess the damages incurred by the said claimant by the pulling down or destruction of such building by the direction of the said officers of the city, as above provided, shall take into account the probability of the same having been destroyed or injured by fire if it had not been so pulled down and destroyed, and may report that no damage should be equitably allowed to such claimant. Whenever a report shall be made and finally confirmed, in the said proceedings for appraising and assessing the damages, a compliance with the terms thereof by the common council shall be deemed a full satisfaction of all said damages of the said claimant. *Duties of commissioners.*

Sec. 187. The directors of the poor elected in said city, as hereinbefore provided, shall be directors of the poor of said city, and shall possess all the powers and authority of directors of the poor of towns in this State, in relation to the support and relief of indigent persons, the binding out of children who shall solicit alms, or who, or whose parents, shall become chargeable to the said city, or to the county of Washtenaw, in said city; the safe keeping and care of lunatics; the care of habitual drunkards; the binding out and contracting for the service of disorderly persons; the support of bastards; and all such other powers as are conferred on directors of the poor in the respective towns, and shall be subject to the same duties, obligations and liabilities. *Powers and duties of city poor directors.*

Sec. 188. Until provisions shall otherwise be made as hereinafter authorized, the indigent persons, and such others as shall be entitled to relief under the laws of this State, who are or shall become chargeable to the said city, being in the said city, shall continue to be supported and relieved in the manner provided by law in respect to the county of Wastenaw. *Temporary support of poor.*

Sec. 189. All money that shall be raised in the said city

License mo-
ney to be
applied to
support of
poor.

by licenses to grocers, tavern keepers or common victualers, and for penalties for the violation of any city ordinances regulating the retailing of any spirituous liquors,
shall be paid into the city treasury, and shall belong to and
constitute a part of the fund of the city for the support of
the poor therein, and shall be deposited for safe keeping
by the treasurer as other moneys under his care ; and
accounts thereof shall be kept, and the same shall be
drawn, in the manner hereinbefore prescribed in relation
to the funds of of said city.

Justices'
courts.

Jurisdiction
in civil cases

Sec. 190. The jurisdiction of the justice's court of said
city shall extend to, and said court shall have original jurisdiction, and shall have power to hear, try and determine
all civil actions arising in said city, wherein said city, in its
corporate capacity, shall be a party, or any city or ward officer, in his official character, shall be a party; all charges,
complaints, actions and prosecutions for the recovery of any
and all forfeitures and penalties for alleged violations or
infringements of the acts of the legislature of this State incorporating said city except in cases where jurisdiction is
especially given to some other court; all actions for alleged
breaches or violations of any of the by-laws or ordinances
of said city, except in cases where, by such by-law or ordinance, jurisdiction is especially given to some other court,
and all actions for encroachments upon or injury to any of
the streets, lanes, alleys, bridges, parks, or other public
improvements of said city; which courts shall proceed according to, and be governed by, the general laws and rules
of practice of this State, applicable to courts of justices of
the peace.

Courts may
imprison
offenders in
county jail.

Sec. 191. Until the common council shall have provided
a city watch house, as hereinbefore provided, the courts of
justice in said city shall have power to imprison in the jail
of the county of Washtenaw, and it is hereby made the
duty of the keeper of said jail to receive such persons as

are brought to his custody by authority of any of said courts, or of the common council, or any officer of said city authorized so to commit such person, in the same manner as any court of record of this State, or other competent authority, is authorized to commit to said jail.

Sec. 192. The justices of the peace in the said city exercising civil jurisdiction, shall be deemed justices of the peace of the county of Washtenaw, and shall be subject to the general laws of the State in relation to civil causes before justices of the peace, and appeals from their judgment may be made to the circuit court for the county of Washtenaw, in the same manner as appeals from justice's judgments in towns are made.

Sec. 193. The justices of the peace of said city shall have all the authority of justices of the peace in towns in criminal matters, and shall have all the authority and perform all the duties hereinbefore provided and required of them, and shall hold a session of court daily, if necessary.

Sec. 194. All suits which shall be brought to recover any penalty or forfeiture for the violation of any ordinance of the common council, shall be brought in the name of the city of Ypsilanti, under the direction of the common council, or of the attorney of said city, and no person being an inhabitant, freeman or freeholder of the said city, shall be disqualified for that cause from acting as a judge, justice or juror in the trial or other proceeding, in any suit brought to recover a forfeiture or penalty for the violation of any provision of this act, or for the violation of any ordinance of the common council, nor from serving any process or summoning a jury in such suit, or from acting in any such capacity, or being a witness on the trial of any issue, or upon the taking or making any inquisition or assessment, or any judicial investigation of facts, to which issue, inquest or investigation the said city, or any city or ward officer, is a party, or in which said city or such officer is in-

21

terested; nor shall any judge of any court be disqualified
to hear and adjudicate on an appeal in any matter origina-
ting in said city, because he is an inhabitant thereof.

Judgments against city may be appealed. Sec. 195. If any judgment in any action shall be rendered against the city by any justice of the peace, such
judgment may be removed by appeal to the circuit court
for the county of Washtenaw, in the same manner and
with the same effect as though the city were a natural
person, except that no bond or recognizance, to the adverse party, shall be necessary to be executed by or on
behalf of the said city.

Executions to issue immediately in certain cases. Sec. 196. Every execution for any penalty or forfeiture
recovered for the violation of any of the provisions of this
act, or for the violation of any by-law or ordinance of the
said city, may be issued immediately on the rendition of
the judgment, and shall command the amount to be made
of the property of the defendant, if any such can be found,
and if not, then to commit the defendant to the county
jail, for such time as shall have been directed by the ordinance of the common council.

Powers of common council as to fines. Sec. 197. The common council may direct any moneys
that may have been recovered for penalties or forfeitures,
under said city ordinances, to be applied to the payment of
any extra expenses that may have been incurred in apprehending offenders or in subpœnaing or defraying the expenses of witnesses in any suit for such penalties or forfeitures, or in conducting such suits.

Who to be deemed vagrants. Sec. 198. All persons being habitual drunkards, destitute,
and without any visible means of support, or who being
such habitual drunkards, shall abandon, neglect or refuse
to aid in the support of their families, being complained
of by such families; all able bodied and sturdy beggars
who may apply for alms or solicit charity; all persons
wandering abroad, lodging in watch houses, out houses,
market places, sheds, stables or uninhabited dwellings, or

in the open air, and not giving a good account of themselves; all common brawlers and disturbers of the public quiet; all persons wandering abroad and begging, or who go about from door to door, or place themselves in streets, highways, passages or other public places, or beg or receive alms within the said city, shall be deemed vagrants, and may upon conviction before any justice of the peace Their punishment of said city, be sentenced to confinement in the county jail of said county for any time not exceeding sixty days.

Sec. 199. All persons who shall have actually aban-Who to be deemed disorderly persons. doned their wives or children in the city of Ypsilanti, or who may neglect to provide according to their means for their wives or children, are hereby declared to be disorderly persons within the meaning of chapter thirty-nine of title nine of the revised statutes of eighteen hundred and forty-six, and may be proceeded against as such, in the manner directed by said title; and it shall be the duty of the magistrate before whom any such person may be brought for examination, to judge and determine from the facts and circumstances of the case whether the conduct of such person amounts to such desertion or neglect to provide for his wife or children.

Sec. 200. It shall be the duty of the common council of Board of health. said city to appoint a board of health once in each year for said city, to consist of not less than three nor more than seven persons, and a competent physician to be the health officer thereof.

Sec. 201. The said board of health shall have power, and Powers and duties. it shall be their duty, to take such measures as they shall deem effectual to prevent the entrance of any pestilential or infectious disease into the city; to stop, detain and examine, for that purpose, every person coming from any place infected, or believed to be infected, with such a disease; to establish, maintain and regulate a pest-house or hospital, at some place within the city, or not exceeding

three miles beyond its bounds; to cause any person not
being a resident of the city, or if a resident of the city, who
is not an inhabitant of this State, and who shall be, or be
suspected of being, infected with any such disease, to be
sent to such pest-house or hospital; to cause any resident
of the city, infected with any such disease, to be removed
to such pest-house or hospital, if the health physician and
two other physicians of the city, including the attending
physician of the sick person, if he have one, shall certify
that the removal of such resident is necessary for the preservation of the public health; to remove from the city or
destroy any furniture, wearing apparel, goods, wares or
merchandise, or other articles or property of any kind,
which shall be suspected of being tainted or infected with
any pestilence, or which shall be, or be likely to pass into
such a state as to generate and propagate disease; to abate
all nuisances of every description which are or may be in-
jurious to the public health, in any way and in any manner
they may deem expedient; and from time to time to do all
acts, make all regulations, and pass all ordinances which
they shall deem necessary or expedient for the preservation of health and the suppression of disease in the city,
and to carry into effect and execute the powers hereby
granted.

Duties of persons having charge of public conveyance to report sick persons

Sec. 202. The owner, driver, conductor, or person in
charge of any stage-coach, railroad car, or other public conveyance, which shall enter the city, having on board any
person sick of a malignant fever or pestilential or infectious disease, shall, within two hours after the arrival of
such sick person, report in writing the fact, with the name
of such person, and the house or place where he was put
down in the city, to the mayor, or some member or officer
of the board of health; and any and every neglect to comply with these provisions or any of them, shall be a misdemeanor, punishable with fine and imprisonment.

Séc. 203. Any person who shall knowingly bring or pro- *Bringing certain articles into city a misdemeanor.* cure or cause to be brought into the city any property of any kind, tainted or infected with any malignant fever or pestilential or infectious disease, shall be guilty of misdemeanor, punishable by fine and imprisonment.

Sec. 204. Every keeper of an inn or boarding house or *Inn keepers, boarding house keepers & physicians to report persons sick with infectious diseases.* lodging house in the city, who shall have in his house at any time any sick traveler, boatman or sailor, shall report the fact, and the name of the person, in writing, within six hours after he came to the house or was taken sick therein, to the mayor, or some officer or member of the board of health; every physician in the city shall report under his hand to one of the officers above named, the name, residence and disease of every patient whom he shall have, sick of any infectious or pestilential disease, within six hours after he shall have visited such patient. A violation of either of the provisions of this section, or of any part of either of them, shall be a misdemeanor, punishable by fine and imprisonment; the fine not to exceed one hundred dollars, nor the imprisonment six months.

Sec. 205. All fines imposed under the last five sections *Certain fines, how devoted at.* shall belong to the city, and when collected shall be paid into the city treasury, and be devoted to the maintenance and support of the pest-house or of any hospital that may hereafter be established by the city.

Sec. 206. The common council shall have power to pass *Powers of common council as to preserving health and cleanliness of city.* and enact such by-laws and ordinances as they from time to time shall deem necessary and proper, for the filling up, draining, cleansing, cleaning and regulating any grounds, yards, basins, slips or cellars within the said city, that shall be sunken, damp, foul, incumbered with filth and rubbish, or unwholesome, and for filling or altering and amending all sinks and privies within the said city, and for directing the mode of constructing them in future, and to cause all such work as may be necessary for the purpose aforesaid, and for the preservation of the public health and the cleanliness of the city, to be executed and done at the expense of the city corporation, on account of the persons respectively upon whom the same may be assessed, and for that purpose to cause the expenses thereof to be estimated, assessed and collected, and the lands charged therewith to be sold in case of non-payment, in the same manner as is provided by law with respect to other public improvements within said city; and in all cases where the said by-laws or ordinances shall require anything to be done in respect to the property of several persons, the expenses thereof may be included in one assessment, and the several houses and lots in respect to which such expenses shall have been incurred, shall be briefly described in the manner required by law in the assessment roll for the general expenses of the city, and the sum of money assessed to each owner or occupant of any such house or lot shall be the amount of money expended in making such improvement upon such premises, together with a ratable proportion of the expenses of assessing and collecting the moneys expended in making such improvements.

Buildings, walls, &c., liable to fall, may be removed. Sec. 207. Whenever, in the opinion of the common council, any building, fence, or other erection of any kind, or any part thereof, is liable to fall down, and persons or property may thereby be endangered, they may order any owner or occupant of the premises on which such building, fence, or other erection stands, to take down the same, or any part thereof, within a reasonable time to be fixed by the order, or immediately, as the case may require, or may immediately, or in case the order is not complied with, cause the same to be taken down at the expense of the city, on account of the owner of the premises, and assess the expense on the land on which it stood. The order, if not immediate in its terms, may be served on any occupant of the premises, or be published in the city paper, as the common council shall direct.

Sec. 208. The said board of health shall have power to appoint a clerk, whose duty it shall be to attend the meetings thereof, and to keep a record of its proceedings, and such record, or a duly certified copy of the same, or of any part thereof, shall be prima facie evidence of the facts therein contained in any court, or before any officer. The compensation of the clerk of said board of health shall be fixed by said board of health, by and with the consent of the common council, and such compensation shall be paid in the same manner as the other expenses of said board. *Clerk of board of health. His duty and compensation.*

Sec. 209. The members of said board of health shall receive such compensation for their services as the common council shall deem reasonable, to be paid from the general contingent fund of said city. *Comp'ead'n of board of health.*

Sec. 210. The common council, or the mayor or other officer whose duty it shall be to judge of the sufficiency of the proposed sureties of any officer of whom a bond or instrument in writing may be required under the provisions of this act, shall examine into the sufficiency of such sureties, and shall require them to submit to an examination under oath as to their property; such oath may be administered by the mayor or any alderman of said city. The deposition of the surety shall be reduced to writing, be signed by him, certified by the person taking the same, and annexed to and filed with the bond or instrument in writing to which it relates. *Sureties may be examined on oath.*

Sec. 211. The mayor or chairman of any committee or special committee of the common council, shall have power to administer any oath or take any affidavit in respect to any matter pending before the common council or such committee. *Who may take affidavit, &c.*

Sec. 212. Any person who may be required to take any necessary oath or affirmation under or by virtue of any provision of this act, who shall, under such oath or affirmation, in any statement, or affidavit, or otherwise, wilfully swear falsely as to any material fact or matter, shall be guilty of perjury.

Double costs may be recovered in certain cases. Sec. 213. If any suit shall be commenced against any person elected or appointed under this act to any office, for any act done or omitted to be done under such election or appointment, or against any person having done any thing or act by the command of any such officer, and if final judgment be rendered in such suit whereby any such defendant shall be entitled to costs, he shall recover double costs in the manner defined by law.

Process against city; how to run; how served. Sec. 214. All process issued against said city shall run against said city in the corporate name thereof, and such process shall be served by leaving a true and attested copy of such process with the mayor or clerk of said city, at least ten days before the day of appearance mentioned therein.

Bridges over Huron river Sec. 215. For the purposes of building, maintaining and repairing the bridges over the Huron river, within said city, the township of Ypsilanti and the said city shall be deemed the township of Ypsilanti, as the said township existed before the passage of this act, and shall be subject to all the provisions of the general laws of this State relative to the building, maintaining and keeping in repair such bridges.

School inspectors. Sec. 216. The school inspectors to be elected under this act, together with the city clerk, who shall be *ex-officio* school inspector, shall perform all the duties and be in every way subject to the general laws of this State applicable to school inspectors.

Sec. 217. This act shall be deemed a public act.

When this act is to take effect. Sec. 218. This act shall take effect and be in force whenever the common council of the village of Ypsilanti and the president and trustees of the village of East Ypsilanti shall carry out the provisions and requirements of section twenty of this act, and immediately thereafter all former acts and parts of acts relating to the villages of Ypsilanti and East Ypsilanti, or either of them, so far as the same affect said villages, or either of them, and all organizations under any general laws of this State for the incorporation of villages, so far as the same relate to or affect the said villages, or either of them, shall be and the same are hereby repealed; but nothing herein contained shall be construed to destroy, impair, or take away any right or remedy acquired or given by any act hereby repealed, and all proceedings commenced under any such former act shall be carried out and completed, and all prosecutions for any offence committed, or penalty or forfeiture incurred, shall be enforced in the same manner in all respects, and with the same effect, as if this act had not been passed; but nothing in this section contained shall be so construed as to annul or impair or affect any ordinance, by-law, or resolution of said villages, or either of them, not inconsistent with the provisions of this act, but the same shall continue and be in force until the same are amended or repealed, as fully as though this act had not been enacted.

Certain acts repealed.

Enacting clause.

This act is ordered to take immediate effect.

Approved February 4, 1858.

[No. 31.]

AN ACT to provide for the sale of the swamp lands, and the reclamation thereof, and to secure the pre-emption claims of settlers thereon.

SECTION 1. *The People of the State of Michigan enact,* That the swamp lands granted to said State by act of Congress, approved September twenty-eighth, one thousand eight hundred and fifty, shall continue under the supervision of the Commissioner of the State Land Office, and subject to sale by him, as hereinafter provided; but none of

Commissioner to have control of swamp lands.

22

said lands shall be offered for sale prior to the issue of patents to the State therefor.

Sec. 2. Said lands shall first be offered at public sale, by auction, but shall not be sold at a less price than one dollar and twenty-five cents per acre, which shall be the minimum price therefor, and shall be subject to entry at private sale at such minimum price, after being offered at public auction, as in this act provided, and such lands shall be sold at public and private sale in the smallest legal subdivisions required by purchasers.

Sec. 3. Before any such sale at auction shall be made, the said Commissioner shall forward to at least one weekly newspaper in each county of the State where a paper is published and established at the time of the passage of this act, a full description, by legal divisions, of the lands to be sold, and a notice of the time and place of such sale, to be published once in each week for four successive weeks prior to such sale, and one copy of each and every paper containing such advertisement, shall be forwarded, prepaid, to the treasurer of every county in which are situated any of the said swamp lands thus offered for sale: *Provided*,

That the whole expense of such advertising shall not exceed fifteen thousand dollars.

Sec. 4. The sales of said lands at public auction shall be made at Lansing, and if deemed practicable by the Commissioner, at Saginaw City, Lexington, Newaygo, Ontonagon, Mackinaw, Grand Haven, and such other places as said Commissioner shall deem proper; and the said Commissioner, in his notice of sale at public auction, shall name the counties in which the lands are situated that he shall

offer for sale at each of the places designated. The Commissioner, or any person whom he may duly authorize to sell said lands at public auction, may, in his discretion, adjourn said sale from time to time. The purchaser at such public

sale shall pay on the day of sale the purchase money to the

State Treasurer, or any person who shall be duly authorized by him to receive the same, and who shall attend the said sale, and he shall give official receipts for the money so received; and if the said purchaser shall refuse or neglect to make such payment, his bid shall be void, and the tract shall again be offered at public sale, and such person shall be liable to pay to the people of the State the difference between his bid and the price at which the said land shall be sold, (if less than his bid,) with double costs, and may be arrested therefor, and if a recovery be had, imprisoned, as in cases where it is competent to proceed against the body.

Sec. 5. All moneys heretofore received and all moneys hereafter received from the sales of said swamp lands, donated by the aforesaid act of Congress, after deducting the expenses of sales, fifty per cent. shall be denominated a primary school fund, and the interest thereof, at five per centum per annum, shall be appropriated and distributed in like manner as the primary school fund of this State; and fifty per cent. shall be denominated a swamp land fund, and the interest thereof, at five per centum, shall be paid over annually to the order of the board of supervisors of the several counties, in the proportion in which the same is received from the sales in said counties respectively, to be used as said board shall direct, in draining and reclaiming swamp lands in said county, and all the moneys received on such sales as aforesaid, after deducting the expenses as aforesaid, shall be used and applied to the payment of the outstanding indebtedness of the State, in the order in which the same shall fall due.

Sec. 6. Purchasers of said lands, whether at public or private sale, shall be entitled to receive from the Commissioner of the State Land Office, a certificate of purchase, in which he shall certify the date of such purchase, the name of the purchaser, description of the land sold, and the price for which the same was sold; which purchase money shall be paid to the State Treasurer, or his agent, or other person duly authorized, and endorsed by him upon said certificate of purchase, and countersigned by the Auditor General, in the form now in use in the

What certificate is to state. certificates of purchase of State lands. Said certificate shall also state that such purchaser, his heirs or assigns, shall be entitled to a patent for said land, to be executed by the Governor, and upon the presentation and surrender

Purchaser entitled to patent. of such certificate to the Secretary of State, a patent shall issue to such purchaser or his assigns, as in cases now provided by law for the issue of patents; but no purchaser receiving such certificate or patent shall, by reason of such purchase, have any claims against the State for drainage, reclamation or other improvements of such land, which condition shall be inserted in all certificates of purchase,

Drainage. and all such sales shall be made subject to drainage and reclamation by the purchaser, in accordance with the act of Congress granting such land to the State.

Statement of receipts to be published. Sec. 7. The Commissioner of the State Land Office shall publish, with his annual report, as now required by law, a statement of the receipts from sales of the swamp lands, exhibiting the amounts of sales in each county, together with the expenditures and disbursements under the provisions of this act.

Provision in relation to actual settlers. Sec. 8. Any person over twenty-one years of age, who shall, at the time of purchase, either at public or private sale, make affidavit before said Commissioner of his or her intention to become an actual and *bona fide* settler upon said lands so purchased, and furnishing satisfactory evidence to said Commissioner that said land is valuable mainly for agricultural purposes, shall be allowed to pur-

Amount to be paid at the time of purchase. chase the same by paying at the time of such purchase twenty-five per cent. of the purchase price, and the balance of principal, at the option of the purchaser, any time

within ten years thereafter, and paying interest annually
on said balance of principal; and said Commissioner shall,
upon the payment of said twenty-five per cent., issue to
said purchaser a certificate agreeable to the terms of said
sale, which certificate shall be void if said purchaser or
his assigns shall not, within one year thereafter, settle
upon and become an actual and permanent resident thereon and cultivate and improve the same.

Sec. 9. Every settler or occupant of said lands at the Occupants of swamp lands authorized to purchase.
time of the passage of this act, and who shall have
been a settler thereon on the first day of December, one
thousand eight hundred and fifty-seven, and which lands
are valuable mainly as agricultural lands, is authorized to
enter with the Commissioner of the Land Office, by legal
subdivisions, any number of acres not above one-quarter Amount limited.
section, in one body, to include his improvements; and
any person owning and occupying lands adjoining any Owners of adjoining lands.
swamp lands on the first day of December, one thousand
eight hundred and fifty-seven, valuable mainly for agricultural purposes, is also authorized to enter with the
Commissioner of the Land Office, by legal sub-divisions,
any number of acres not to exceed one hundred and sixty
acres, including the land and improvements so owned and
occupied by said claimant.

Sec. 10. If two or more persons are settled upon and Conflicting claims, how adjusted.
claim the same quarter section, the said quarter section
shall be divided between the first two settlers, if by a line
east and west, or north and south, the improvements of
each can be included on a half-quarter section; and in
such case each of said persons shall be entitled to enter a
half-quarter section elsewhere on said lands.

Sec. 11. Any person claiming pre-emption under this Proof of settlement, &c.
act, shall make proof of settlement within sixty days from within sixty days.
the passage of this act, to the Commissioner, to his satisfaction, in such manner as hereinafter directed, and agree-

able to such rules and regulations as shall be from time to time prescribed by such Commissioner; and shall also, within the same time, make proof of the character and quality of said land claimed, and said Commissioner shall make entry in a book kept for that purpose, that said land is claimed.

Redemption rights defined.

Sec. 12. No person shall be entitled to more than one pre-emption right by virtue of this act, nor shall any person be entitled to any rights of pre-emption under this act, who is at the same time the proprietor of a half-quarter section of land in any State or Territory of the United States, and no section or fraction of sections included within the limits of any incorporated village or city, and no part of a lot settled and occupied for purposes of trade and not for agriculture; and no lands on which are known salines or mines shall be liable to entry by pre-emption by virtue of this act.

What affidavit is to state.

Sec. 13. Before any person shall be entitled to enter any lands by pre-emption under the provisions of this act, such person shall make proof to the Commissioner of the State Land Office, by his affidavit and other testimony, in such manner as said Commissioner shall direct, that said land is valuable mainly as farming land, and not for timber; that he has resided upon the same since the first day of December, eighteen hundred and fifty-seven; that he or she has never had the benefit of any pre-emption under this act; that he or she is not the owner of a half-quarter section of land in any State or territory of the United States, and that he or she has not abandoned a residence on other lands still owned by him or her to reside upon said land claimed under this act; and if any such person shall swear falsely in the premises, they shall be liable to all the pains and penalties of perjury.

Penalty for false swearing.

Payment, when made.

Sec. 14. Any person pre-empting under this act, shall, within one year from the passage of this act, pay to the State Treasurer twenty-five per cent. of the minimum price of said land, and the Commissioner of the Land Office shall issue to him, upon the payment of said twenty-five per cent., a certificate requiring the payment of the balance of principal at any time, at the option of the purchaser, not exceeding ten years from the date of said certificate, and the payment of interest annually, and said certificate shall be void, and all payments thereon forfeited, if default be made thereon.

Sec. 15. The part paid swamp lands heretofore sold, and Taxation. which shall hereafter be sold, shall be assessed in the same manner, and the taxes thereon shall be collected in the same manner, in all respects, as part paid primary school lands.

Sec. 16. All of said swamp lands situate in the townships Disposition of Lansing and Meridian, in the county of Ingham, and in swamp lands in the townships of DeWitt and Bath, county of Clinton, ex-Clinton and Ingham cept such as have been occupied by persons entitled to counties. pre-emption under this act at least thirty days next previous to the passage of this act, shall be reserved from sale by said Commissioner, and possession of the same shall be immediately delivered over to the Agricultural College for its use, and for the purposes of drainage and reclamation, in accordance with the provisions of the act of Congress donating the same to the State.

Sec. 17. All the provisions of law now in force, not incon-Existing laws to apsistent with this act and applicable to the public lands of ply to swamp this State, shall be held to apply to the said swamp lands, lands. and all powers and duties prescribed to any public officer, or court, or prosecuting attorney, relative to the public lands, shall, if not inconsistent with this act, be exercised and performed in relation to said swamp lands.

Sec. 18. The provisions of act number 106, approved February 14th, 1857, except the tenth and eleventh sec-Repeal. tions thereof, are hereby repealed.

Sec. 19. This act is ordered to take immediate effect.
Approved, February 4, 1858.

[No. 32.]

AN ACT to amend an act entitled an act to provide for assessing property at its true value, and for levying and collecting taxes thereon, approved February 14th, 1853, and an act amendatory thereto, approved February 12th, 1855.

Sections amended

SECTION 1. *The People of the State of Michigan enact,* That sections eight, eleven, eighteen, twenty, twenty-three, twenty-four, twenty-five, twenty-six, twenty-seven, twenty-nine, thirty-three, thirty-eight, forty, forty-three, fifty-three, sixty-one, sixty-eight, eighty, eighty-eight, eighty-nine, ninety-one, ninety-nine, one hundred and one, one hundred and two, one hundred and three, one hundred and ten, one hundred and twenty-four, one hundred and thirty, one hundred and thirty-three, one hundred and thirty-five, one hundred and forty-two, one hundred and fifty-four, one hundred and fifty-five, and one hundred and fifty-six of said acts are hereby amended so as to read as follows:

Cases excepted.

Sec. 8. The excepted cases referred to in the preceding section, and not included in said section three, are the following:

1st. All goods, wares and merchandise, or stock in trade, including stock employed in the business of the mechanic arts, in any township other than where the owners reside, shall be taxed in the township where the same may be, if the owner hire or occupy a store, shop or warehouse therein, and shall not be taxable where the owner resides.

2. All horses, mules, neat cattle, sheep and swine, kept throughout the year in any township other than where the owner resides, shall be assessed to such owner in the township where they are kept.

3. All personal property belonging to minors under guardianship, shall be assessed to the guardian in the township where he is an inhabitant, and the personal

property of every other person under guardianship, shall be assessed to the guardian in the township of which the ward is an inhabitant.

4. All personal property held in trust by any executor, administrator or trustee, the income of which is to be paid to any maried woman or other person, shall be assessed to the person having possession or charge of such property, in the township of which he is an inhabitant, whether such married woman or other person reside within or without this State.

5. Personal property placed in the hands of any corporation as an accumulating fund, for the future benefit of heirs or other persons, shall be assessed to the persons for whose benefit the same is accumulating, if within this State; otherwise to the person so placing it, or his executors or administrators, until a trustee shall be appointed to take charge of such property, or of the income thereof.

6. The personal estate of persons deceased, which shall be in the hands of executors or administrators, shall be assessed to the executors or administrators in the township where the deceased last dwelt, until they shall give notice to the supervisor that the estate has been distributed and paid over to the parties interested.

7. All property held by any religious society as a ministerial fund, shall be assessed to the treasurer of such society; and if such property consists of real estate, it shall be taxed in the township where such property lies; if it consists of personal property, it shall be taxed in the township where such society usually holds its meetings.

Sec. 11. Any person holding a part paid certificate of purchase of university, primary school, State building, swamp or salt spring lands, or occupying the same, shall be liable to be assessed therefor, as if he were the actual owner thereof: *Provided however,* That the same shall be assessed as personal property and not as real estate, and the

23

tax thereon shall be collected in the manner hereinafter prescribed.

Supervisor to furnish blank forms. Sec. 18. It shall be the duty of each supervisor, on or before the second Monday in May, to call upon each taxable person in his township, at their residence, boarding place, or usual place of business, at which time he shall furnish each taxable person a blank form for the statements required by the fifteenth section of this act; and thereupon **Taxable person to make and deliver statem't to supervisor.** said taxable person shall forthwith make and deliver to said supervisor a full and true statement of the taxable property in his possession, according to the provisions of this act; **Supervisor to ascertain & set down true value thereof.** and immediately thereafter, the said supervisor shall proceed to examine said property, and estimate, and set down the true value thereof, deducting from the moneys at interest and other credits of such person, the amount of money upon which he or she pays interest, together with his other bona fide indebtedness, as set forth in said statement.

When assessment to be received and completed. Sec. 20. On the third Monday of May, it shall be the duty of the supervisors of the several townships to be present at their respective offices, from eight o'clock in the forenoon until twelve, noon, and from one o'clock in the afternoon till five o'clock in the afternoon, for the purpose of reviewing their assessments, and so on the two next following days, in case they shall have any matter before them for their action under this section; and on the request of any person, his agent or attorney, considering himself aggrieved, on sufficient cause being shown to the satisfaction of the supervisor, he shall alter the assessment as to **May alter assessment as to valuation.** the valuation thereof, and he shall also, upon sufficient cause being shown by any credible person on behalf of any other person whose property is assessed, alter the assessment in such manner as shall to him appear just and equal; **Supervisor may administer oath.** and to this end he may in either case examine on oath the person making the application, or any other person present, touching the matter, which oath the supervisor is hereby authorized to administer.

Sec. 23. The description of real estate may be as follows: Real estate, how described.

1. If the lands to be assessed be an entire section, it may be described by the number of the section, township and range;

2. If the tract be a sub-division of a section authorized by the United States for the sale of the public lands, it may be described by a designation of such sub-division, with the number of the section, township and range;

3. If the tract be less or other than such sub-division, it may be described by a designation of the number of the lot or other lands by which it is bounded, or in some way by which it may be known;

4. In case of lands surveyed or laid out as a town, city or village, and a plat thereof recorded in the register's office of the county, if the tract to be assessed be a whole lot or block, it shall be described by a designation of the number thereof; if it be a part of a lot or block, it may be described by its boundaries, or some other way by which it may be known, and it shall not be necessary to insert the quantity of such land in the assessment roll. When any lands have been, or hereafter shall be laid out as a town, city or village, or as an addition of any town, city or village, and the same has not been duly recorded in the register's office of the county, and any one or more of the lots have been or may be sold by the numbers thereof, according to the plat of said town, city or village, or addition thereto, such land, laid out as aforesaid, may, in the discretion of the supervisor, be assessed in whole or in part, according to the sub-division as represented on the plat of said town, city or village, or in some other way by which it may be known; and if such sub-division or parcel be a whole lot or block, it shall be described by a designation of the number thereof; if it be a part of a lot or block, such part shall be

defined, or it shall be described by its boundaries, or in some other way by which it may be known; and it shall not be necessary to insert the quantity or contents of such land in the assessment roll;

5. If the land to be assessed be a tract of which the sub-division is not known to the supervisor, it shall be entered upon the roll by the boundaries thereof, or in some other way by which it may be known;

Undivided shares.
6. Undivided shares or interests in lands shall be assessed to the owner thereof, if such ownership is known to the supervisor, and no tract in the same section known to the supervisor to have been originally entered as one parcel, shall be sub-divided in assessing, unless the fact of a subdivision having been made known to the supervisor;

7. It shall be sufficient to describe lands to be assessed or sold for taxes in the manner heretofore in use by initials, letters, abbreviations and figures.

Non-resident lands.
Sec. 24. All lands unoccupied and not claimed to be owned by any resident of the township where they are situated and not exempt from taxation, may be assessed as non-resident lands or to the person supposed by the supervisor to be the owner thereof, and it shall be the duty of the supervisor to enter the same on a part of the roll separate from that upon which the estates of residents are entered, and when real estate is occupied it may be assessed to the occupant or supposed owner or person exercising **Property held in trust, &c.** control over the same. When a person is assessed as a trustee, guardian, executor, or administrator, a designation of his representative character may be added to his name, and such assessment shall be entered on a separate line from his individual assessment.

Certificate to be att'ch-ed, to roll.
Sec. 25. When the supervisor has reviewed and completed the assessment roll, it shall be his duty to attach thereto, signed by him, a certificate which may be in the following form: "I do hereby certify that I have set down in the

above assessment roll, all the real estate in the township of —————— liable to be taxed, according to my best information, and that I have estimated the same at what I believe to be the true cash value thereof ; that the said assessment roll contains a true statement of the aggregate valuation of the taxable personal estate of each and every person named in said roll, and that I have estimated the same at its true cash value, according to my best information and belief."

Sec. 26. It shall be the duty of the township clerk of each township, on or before the second Monday of October of each year, to deliver to the supervisor of his township a statement of the money to be raised therein for township purposes, and the amount voted for the maintenance and support of common schools, and the township library, stating the amount of each as well as the aggregate amount. The board of supervisors in each county shall, at their session in October in each year, examine the assessment roll of the several townships, and ascertain whether the relative valuation of the real estate in the respective townships has been equally and uniformly estimated. The supervisor and assessors shall be allowed for their services in assessing property and copying the tax rolls, and for extending the taxes thereon, at the rate of one dollar and fifty cents for each day actually and necessarily spent in perfecting the same, which shall be verified, audited and paid in the townships in the same manner provided by law for the payment of other township officers, and they shall receive payment from no other source.

Sec. 27. If, on such examination, they shall deem such valuation to be relatively unequal, they shall equalize the same, by adding to or deducting from the valuation of the taxable property in the township or townships, such an amount as in their judgment will produce relatively an equal and uniform valuation of the real estate in the county, and the amount added to or deducted from the valuation in each township shall be entered upon the records.

Corrected
roll to be
certified and
delivered to
supervisor.

Sec. 29. After the assessment shall have been equalized, and the descriptions corrected, as provided in the two last preceding sections, it shall be the duty of the chairman of the board to make and sign a certificate upon, or appended to the roll of each township, which certificate may be in the following form, to wit :

"I do hereby certify that the board of supervisors have equalized and corrected the within roll, by adding to or deducting from the valuation of the real estate made by the supervisor thereon, or without adding to or deducting from the valuation of the real estate made by the supervisor, as the case may be, and have determined the aggregate value of the taxable property in the township of ———— to be ———— dollars and ———— cents, for the year eighteen hundred ————;" which assessment roll, certified as aforesaid, shall be delivered to the supervisor of the proper township, whose duty it shall be to file and keep the same in his office.

How taxes
assessed by
supervisor.

Sec. 33. The supervisor of each township shall proceed to assess taxes for the amount specified in such certificate, together with a tax for the amount of money to be raised by his township, adding thereto, and to all other taxes re-

Collecting
expense not
to be more
than four
nor less
than two
per cent.

quired by law to be assessed by him, not more than four nor less than two per cent., as shall be determined by the electors at their annual meeting, at the same time and in the same manner that overseers of highways are elected, for collecting expenses, upon the taxable property in the township, according and in proportion to the individual and particular estimate and valuation specified in the as-

May add to
amount to
be raised to
avoid frac-
tions in ex-
cess.

sessment roll of the township for the year, and for the purpose of avoiding fractions in excess in said tax, may add to the several amounts to be raised, on a sum not exceeding one hundred dollars, five per cent. or under, on a sum over one hundred dollars and not exceeding four hundred dollars, three and a half per cent. or under, on a sum not exceeding one thousand dollars and over four hundred dollars, two per cent. or under, and on any sum exceeding one thousand dollars, not over one per cent.; said excess, more or less, to be paid into and to belong to the contingent fund of the township or ward where assessed.

Sec. 38. The taxes assessed upon any real estate of any resident or non-resident, and all legal charges made thereon, shall be a charge against the person owning the same on the second Monday of April, and shall be a lien on said real estate from the fifteenth day of November of the year in which such real estate was assessed.
Taxes to be a charge against the owner of real estate on 2d Monday of April. When taxes to be a lien on real estate.

Sec. 40. In case any person shall refuse or neglect to pay the tax imposed on personal or real estate belonging to him, the treasurer shall levy the same by distress and sale of the goods and chattels of said person, whenever the same may be found within his township.
Proceedings in case of refusal to pay.

Sec. 43. If the property distrained shall be sold for more than the amount of the tax and collection fees, the surplus shall be returned to the person in whose possession said property was when the distress was made.
Surplus, how disposed of.

Sec. 53. Upon making an affidavit to be annexed to such statement before the county treasurer or his deputy duly appointed, or before any officer authorized to administer oaths, that the sums mentioned in such statement remain unpaid, and that he has not upon diligent inquiry been able to discover any goods or chattels belonging to the person charged with or liable to pay such sums, where-upon he could levy the same, the township treasurer shall be credited by the county treasurer with the amount thereof, and for making the return aforesaid, he shall be entitled to recover [receive] one dollar and fifty cents, and six cents per mile, traveling fee one way, to be allowed and paid to him by the county treasurer, together with
Affidavit of town treasurer at time of making return. Compensation for making return.

two per cent. on all taxes returned as delinquent; but no such treasurer shall be allowed more than ten dollars, including said two per cent. for making his return.

Collecting officer to give receipt on payment of taxes.

Sec. 61. The township treasurer or other collecting officer, on receipt of any tax, shall give a receipt for the same, and shall note on his tax roll the payment thereof, and if any such treasurer or other collecting officer shall wilfully return to the county treasurer as unpaid any taxes which have been paid to him, except when the same have been doubly assessed, he shall be deemed guilty of a mis-

Penalty for wrongfully returning lands.

demeanor, and shall, on conviction thereof, be punished by imprisonment in the county jail not exceeding one year, or by fine not exceeding five hundred dollars, or both, in the discretion of the court, and be liable, together with the surety in his bond, to any person injured by such false return to the full amount of any loss sustained thereby.

Real estate assessed to residents; proceedings on return of

Sec. 68. If the taxes on any real estate, assessed to a resident or owner thereof, shall be returned unpaid, the same proceedings shall be had thereon in all respects as in cases of lands assessed as non-resident, and with like effect.

Cost of printing.

Sec. 80. The cost of printing and publishing such statement shall not exceed forty (40) cents for each description of land so advertised, and no printer shall be paid for publishing any such statement, who shall not forward to the Auditor General within (20) twenty days after the last publication thereof an affidavit made by some person to whom the facts are known, stating such publications, and also that he has transmitted to each county treasurer, by mail, copies of the two first numbers of his paper containing such statement, immediately after their publication :

Where statem'nt to be publish'd

Provided however, That such statement shall be published in a newspaper in the county in which the sale takes place, if there be one; and if no newspaper be printed in such county, then such statement shall be published in an adjoining county, or in a newspaper published in the next nearest county to the county in which such sale takes place.

Sec. 88. At the sale aforesaid the respective county *Certificate of sale, &c.* treasurers shall give to the purchasers, on the payment of their bids, a certificate in writing, describing the lands purchased, and the amount paid therefor, and such certificate shall be regularly numbered and a copy of each forwarded by the county treasurers to the Auditor General in such manner as he shall direct.

Sec. 89. On presentation of such certificate of sale to *Deed to purchaser.* the Auditor General after the expiration of the time provided by law for the redemption of land sold as aforesaid, he shall execute to the purchaser, his heirs, or assigns, a deed of the land therein described, unless he shall have discovered that the taxes for which said lands were sold had been paid according to law, which deed shall be *prima facie* evidence of the regularity of all the proceedings from the valuation of the lands by the assessors to the date of the deed inclusive, and of title (in fee) in the purchaser, and every such deed when witnessed and acknowledged in the manner prescribed by law for witnessing and acknowledging deeds in other cases, and after it shall have been on record two years in the office of the register of deeds of the county in which the lands therein described are situated shall, except:

First. When the same shall be annulled according to law;

Second. When the land sold was not subject to taxation at the date of the assessment of the taxes for which it was sold;

Third. When the taxes have been paid to the proper officer within the time limited by law for the payment or redemption thereof; or

Fourth. When a certificate that no taxes were charged against the land has been given by the proper officer within

24

the time limited by law for the payment or redemption thereof;

Be positive evidence that the lands therein described were by such deed conveyed in fee simple to the grantee therein named and his heirs and assigns, and no suit of ejectment shall be commenced to recover said lands, or title thereto sustained thereafter by any person claiming or holding possession or title through any other source.

How lands may be redeemed from sale.

Sec. 91. Any person owning any of the lands, sold as aforesaid, or any interest therein, may, at any time within one year next succeeding such sale, redeem any parcel of said lands, or any part or interest in said lands, by showing to the satisfaction of the Auditor General or county treasurer that he owns only that part or interest in the same which he proposes to redeem, and by paying at his option, into the State treasury, or to the treasurer of the county where such land is situated, the amount for which such parcel was sold, or such portion thereof as the part or interest redeemed shall amount to, with interest thereon at the rate of twenty-five per cent. per annum; of which interest twenty per cent. shall be paid by the State Treasurer to the purchaser, and five per cent. shall belong to the State and be passed to the credit of the general fund.

Proceedings in case of irregularity.

Sec. 99. If the Auditor General shall discover before the sale, or before the conveyance of any lands, as aforesaid, that the same were not subject to taxation at the date of the assessment of the taxes, or that the taxes have been paid, he shall forbear to cause the same to be sold, or withhold a conveyance after sale, as the case may be; and in such case, if a sale has been made, he shall, on demand, cause the money paid therefor to be refunded, with seven per cent. interest thereon.

Sec. 101. Any person having an interest in any lands sold as aforesaid by the Auditor General, other than such as hold or claim to hold under a tax title, whether in his own right, or in trust, or as executor, administrator, guardian or trustee, may, at any time within two years from the date of the deed, and in cases of sales at any time heretofore made, within two years from the time this act shall take effect, and not after that period, present a petition to a circuit court commissioner of the county in which the land or a part thereof is situated, setting forth that the taxes have been paid, or that he had [has] good ground to believe and does believe that there are irregularities in the assessment or other proceedings, affecting the rights of such party in interest, and especially setting forth each and all the objections and alleged errors on which he relies, and the names and residences of all persons having any interest in the lands under the tax sale and deed, which petition shall be verified by the affidavit of the person presenting the same, or by his agent or attorney, to be attached to such petition: *Provided,* That he may present such petition at any time:

1st. When the land sold was not subject to taxation at the date of the assessment of the taxes for which it was sold ;

2d. When the taxes have been paid to the proper officer within the time limited by law for the payment or redemption thereof ;

3d. When a certificate that no taxes were charged against the land has been given by the proper officer, within the time limited by law for the payment or redemption thereof.

On the presentation of such petition, such commissioner shall make and endorse thereon an order for receiving evidence, and for taking the examination of witnesses on the part of the parties to said petition, before him, in the matter of said petition; and shall in said order fix the time, not less than twenty days from the presentation of the petition, and the place in his county when and where he will proceed to take such evidence or examination of witnesses. A copy of such petition, affidavit and order, shall be served upon the person or persons holding such tax title, or claiming any interest therein in law or equity, if residing in the county, and in the same manner prescribed for the service of a summons from the circuit court, at least twenty days before the commissioner shall take such evidence or examination. If such person or persons reside in any other county in this State, the commissioner shall allow such further reasonable time for making such service, and the appearance of such parties, as shall be just; and after the first time fixed for the hearing, the commissioner shall, upon the application of any party to the petition, and upon good cause shown, continue the hearing from time to time for the purpose of taking the evidence. In case any party entitled to such service is not a resident of this State, and cannot be served as aforesaid, on filing an affidavit of that fact with the commissioner, the petitioner shall be entitled to an order of the commissioner for the appearance of such party, such as is or may be authorized by law for the appearance of such parties in suits in chancery in the circuit courts, which order shall be published as required by law in such suits; or in case of failure of appearance in accordance with such order, the commissioner may proceed *ex parte* to take the evidence and examination, and the same shall be binding on the parties failing to appear. All statutes and rules of the circuit court sitting in chancery, in force during the pending of such petition before the commissioner, touching infants and persons under guardianship, as parties to a suit, shall, so far as may be, apply to the proceeding before the commissioner, and he shall apply the same. The commissioner shall have power to administer oaths to all such witnesses, who may be examined and cross-examined, and who shall subscribe to their respective depositions; and the commissioner may take all affidavits requisite in the matter, and may issue subpœnas, which may be served on witnesses in any part of the State. And when the evidence and the examination of witnesses shall be completed, the commissioner shall certify them; [and,] thereupon, and within four days thereafter, render his decision thereon, and within ten days after the rendition of said decision or judgment, either party, or any person interested in such proceeding, may appeal therefrom to the circuit court for the county in which such proceedings may be had, by giving notice in writing of his intention to appeal, and such commissioner shall within ten days after receiving notice of such appeal, file the petition, certified copies of all his orders, the originals of all proofs of service and depositions taken by him, together with his decision, in the office of the clerk of the circuit court of his county, and shall in his return set forth, briefly, all objections taken before him, to any portion of the evidence, to the competency thereof, or to any order made by him. And upon such filing, the circuit court shall have jurisdiction of the matter, and full power and authority to determine all questions of law or fact therein, and to render judgment annulling or affirming the title in controversy, which judgment shall be rendered and recorded like other judgments in said court, subject to be reviewed on writ of *certiorari*, by the supreme court, at any time within two years: *Provided however*, That on the application of any party to said petition, to the circuit court, he or they shall be entitled to have any issue of fact arising in the matter, tried by a jury, in which case the court shall, by order, cause the issue to be made up and tried, as in other cases of trial of issues of fact.

Sec. 102. Whenever any judge of the circuit court shall have annulled, for any of the reasons enumerated in the preceding section, the title to any description of land conveyed in any deed executed by the Auditor General as aforesaid, or any part thereof, the clerk of the circuit court of the county in which the land is situated, shall, on application of either party, and the payment of fifty cents, make and deliver to such party, a certified copy of such judgment. And whenever such copy of judgment shall be presented to the register of deeds of said county, where said deed shall have been recorded, the register shall record the same, and make a short written memorandum on the margin or face of the deed of the description of the land, and that the title has been annulled or affirmed, as the case may be, and the date of the judgment, and of the recording thereof.

Register to record, &c.,

Aud. Gen'l to certify to county treasurers. Sec. 103. In all cases where lands sold for taxes have been conveyed by deed, and the title has been annulled pursuant to law, the Auditor General shall, on presentation of a copy of the judgment annulling the same, refund to the holder of said title the purchase money and interest thereon, as the law requires, and certify the fact to the proper county treasurer.

Co. treasurer to lay statement before board of supervisors. Sec. 110. The county treasurer receiving such certificate of the Auditor General, shall lay the same before the board of supervisors at their next session thereafter, and if such taxes shall have been rejected or charged back by the Auditor General for any error or informality, excepting an insufficient description of the land, or for the reason that it was not subject to taxation, the board of supervisors shall cause the same to be re-assessed upon the same land, and collected with the taxes of the then current year, and in the same manner.

Aud. Gen'l to execute deed for St. tax land. Sec. 124. The Auditor General shall, on the presentation and surrender of the State tax land certificate of sale at his office, or as soon thereafter as may be, (except in cases where the land has been previously sold at the Auditor General's office, or redeemed, when the purchase money only shall be refunded) execute a deed of the land to the purchaser or his assigns, which shall convey all the right acquired by the State under the original sale or sales. And such deed shall be *prima facie* evidence of the legality of all the proceedings to the date of the deed, and of the title in fee, in the grantee therein named; and when duly acknowledged, may be recorded and admitted as evidence in the same manner as other deeds of conveyance; and every such deed, when witnessed and acknowledged in the manner prescribed by law for witnessing and acknowledging deeds in other cases, and after it shall have been recorded for two years in the office of the register of deeds, in the county in which the land therein described is situated, shall, except:

First. When the same has been annulled according to law;

Second. When the land sold was not subject to taxation at the date of the assessment of the taxes for which it was sold;

Third. When the taxes have been paid to the proper officer within the time limited by law for the payment or redemption thereof; or

Fourth. When a certificate that no taxes were charged against the land has been given by the proper officer within the time limited by law for the payment or redemption thereof;

Be conclusive evidence that the land therein described was by such deed conveyed in fee simple to the grantee therein named, and his heirs and assigns; and no suit of ejectment or other suit for the recovery of possession shall be thereafter commenced to recover said lands, nor the title thereto [sustained] by any person claiming or holding possession or title through any other source.

Sec. 130. All the provisions of this act relative to deeds executed by the Auditor General, on the surrender of certificates of sale of State tax lands, issued by the several *What provisions applicable to State tax land deeds.*

county treasurers, shall be applicable to deeds executed by him for lands purchased at his office pursuant to the provisions of this act.

Who to be made defendant in case of prosecution of ejectment.

Sec. 133. In case it shall become necessary in the prosecution of an action of ejectment by any person holding an adverse claim to any land bid in for the State, as provided in this chapter, the Auditor General may be defendant, and in all cases in the prosecution or defence of an action of ejectment or tresspass, by any person holding or claiming land, under any deed or deeds or other conveyance of land bid off or purchased for delinquent or unpaid taxes, the party so claiming, under and by virtue of such purchase for unpaid taxes as aforesaid, may show his title to said land and premises, whether the same was derived under one or more purchases or sales for taxes or otherwise, and may give in evidence any and all deeds of conveyance or other evidence of such purchase as aforesaid, which he may at any one or more different times have received on sales for taxes, and may claim title under any or all of them.

When State acquires absolute title to tax lands.

Sec. 135. Any description of land bid off to the State at the annual sales, which shall have remained undisposed of for five years from the date when it was so bid off, shall vest in the State an absolute title in fee simple, and no suit of ejectment shall be commenced to recover said lands or title thereto, [or be] sustained thereafter by any person claiming or holding possession or title through any other source; but such lands shall be subject to sale at any time by payment in like manner as other State tax lands, the amount of taxes due thereon and interest at the rate of ten

When lands to be struck from assessment roll.

per cent; and after the expiration of five years, as aforesaid, said lands shall be stricken from the assessment roll, but shall be restored thereto after the same shall have been sold.

Sec. 142. If any township clerk or supervisor shall wilfully neglect or refuse to perform any of the duties required of him by the provisions of this chapter, he shall forfeit and pay a sum not exceeding five hundred dollars to any person injured by each [case of] such neglect, but such sum shall not exceed the injury sustained.

Penalty for neglect of duty by certain town officers.

Sec. 154. In all cases of sales of land for taxes, if the purchaser or his assigns shall die before a deed shall be executed on such sale, the deed may be executed by the Auditor General to and in the name of such deceased person, if such person being still alive would be entitled to the same; which deed shall vest the tax title in the heirs or devisees of such deceased person in the same manner and liable to like claims of creditors and other persons as if the same had been executed to such deceased person immediately previous to his death; or the deed may issue to the assignee of said deceased person, [his] executors or administrators; and in like cases which have heretofore occurred, the same rules shall apply, and [to] all deeds heretofore issued in the name of any deceased person, who, if living at the time of the execution thereof, would have been entitled to said deed as above provided.

In case of death of purchaser or assignee.

Sec. 155. The supervisor of every township in which there shall be assessed the interest of any purchaser of university, primary school, State building, normal school, asylum, swamp or salt spring lands, as personal property, shall, on or before the first day of November, in the year when the same was so assessed, transmit to the treasurer of his county a list of all such] lands, containing a full description thereof, together with the names of the persons to whom the same was so assessed.

University, pri school, St. building, normal school, asylum, swamp and salt spring land to be returned, &c.

Sec. 156. That the several county treasurers shall at the same time and in the same manner they are now required to return to the office of the Auditor General, lands delinquent for taxes in their respective counties, return to the State land office a statement of all university, primary school, State building, normal school, asylum, swamp and

Co. treasurers to return to St. land office.

salt spring lands, upon which, from returns made to them
by the township treasurer, it appears the taxes assessed
have not been paid and cannot be collected.

Improvements made by purchasers under this act to be paid for. Sec. 157. If any person dispossessed of lands purchased
in pursuance of the provisions of this act shall have made
valuable improvements thereon, he shall be entitled to
receive what such improvements are reasonably worth,
to be assessed on the trial of said cause, and the same so
assessed shall be a lien on said land till paid.

Sec. 158. This act is ordered to take effect fifty days after its approval.

Approved February 4, 1858.

JOINT RESOLUTIONS.

[No. 1.]

JOINT RESOLUTION relative to an appropriation of a grant of land for the endowment of the Michigan Agricultural College.

Whereas, A memorial has been presented to Congress by the Board of Education, and the president and faculty of the "Michigan Agricultural College," praying for a grant of land as an endowment of said Michigan Agricultural College; and,

Whereas, We believe that the practical working of the Michigan Agricultural College fully vindicates the feasibility and correctness of the principles upon which it is founded; therefore,

Resolved, That our Senators in Congress be instructed, and our Representatives requested ·to use all honorable means to secure the passage of a law in accordance with the memorial.

Resolved, That the Governor be requested to forward copies of the foregoing preamble and resolutions to each of our Senators and Representatives in Congress.

Approved January 29, 1858.

[No. 2.]

JOINT RESOLUTION relative to the protection and permanent security of the St. Mary's Falls Ship Canal.

Whereas, It appears by the report of the Superintendent of the St. Mary's Falls ship canal, that during the past season, owing to the unavoidable action of frost upon the embankments, leaks have occurred in various portions of the same, and in two instances breaks of a serious and alarming character;

And whereas, It appears that some further expense is necessary in securing the said embankment, and in the erection of an additional set of gates to facilitate the navigation of said canal; therefore,

Resolved, That our Senators in Congress be instructed, and our Representatives in that body be requested to use all proper means, to secure by Congress, such appropriation as may be necessary to render the above work permanent and secure.

Resolved, That the Governor be requested to transmit copies of the foregoing preamble and resolution, together with copies of the report of the late Superintendent of the canal, to each of our Senators and Representatives in Congress.

Approved, January 30, 1858.

[No. 3.]

JOINT RESOLUTION relative to a Northern Pacific Rail Road.

Whereas, an immense commerce has within a few years grown up on our Pacific coast, which is continually increasing in importance, and the benefits of which commerce is increasing and accruing to other countries, in consequence of the difficulties, delays and dangers attending travel and transportation to and from our eastern and western ocean ports, by the long, dangerous and fatiguing route of the oceans, gulfs and isthmus;

And whereas, A vast domain, lying between our western States and the Pacific, remains and must ever remain waste and undeveloped, without some safe, easy and commodious means of conveyance through our western territories;

And whereas, Such means of conveyance would not only facilitate the settlement and cultivation of a region that can never be improved without it, but would open the heart of a continent to the poor but enterprising working men of the older States—substitute for worthless wilds, cultivated fields, the great source of all wealth, and open to us a commerce of the greatest magnitude;

And whereas, The cost of providing such means of conveyance would be more than returned by the increased value of our now waste and unproductive lands, and is scarcely worthy a moment's consideration in view of the immediate and lasting benefits which would necessarily accrue, upon furnishing such means of intercommunication from ocean to ocean through our entire domain which must ultimately revolutionize the commerce of the world and centralize the trade of Europe and Asia from opposite directions, with the productions of every clime, in the "New Republic" of America; therefore,

Resolved, That our Senators and Representatives in Congress be requested to urge the passage of a law granting public lands to aid in the construction of a railroad from the Mississippi river to the Pacific ocean, upon or near the line known as the "Stevens" or "Northern Pacific Railroad" route; and also for the passage of a law granting public lands in the State of Michigan to aid the construction of a railroad to aid in forming a connection between said Northern Pacific Railroad and the eastern States, on the line of the Grand Trunk and Great Western Railways, to commence at Port Huron, in the State of Michigan, and terminate at some point on the Montreal River, on the western boundary of the Upper Peninsula of the State of Michigan.

Resolved, That the Governor of this State be requested

to transmit, as soon as the same can be done, to each of
the Senators and Representatives in Congress from this
State, a copy of the foregoing preamble and resolution.
Approved January 30, 1838.

[No. 4.]

JOINT RESOLUTION in relation to granting the public
    lands of the United States to actual settlers.

Whereas, There is a bill now pending before Congress
granting to actual settlers a homestead, free of cost; therefore,

Be it resolved by the Senate and House of Representatives,
That in the name and by the authority of the people of the
State of Michigan, we respectfully demand of our Senators
and earnestly ask of our Representatives in Congress, to
use their best exertions to secure the immediate passage of
the homestead bill.

Resolved, That the Governor be requested to forward
copies of the foregoing preamble and resolution to our
Senators and Representatives in Congress.

Approved, February 2, 1858.

[No. 5.]

JOINT RESOLUTION of Instruction to our Senators and
    Representatives in Congress, urging the passage of an
    act of Congress making appropriations for the improve-
    ment of certain harbors.

Whereas, By the ordinance of 1787, the inland waters of
the States and Territories of the United States are declared to be common highways, forever free to the citizens
of said States and Territories and therefore necessarily
beyond the care and control of local legislation, but essen-
tially within the province of the General Government.

And whereas, The immense commercial interest involved in the successful navigation of said waters, as well as the great floating capital invested in commerce, wherein citizens of the Union at large are more or less concerned, and the security, wealth and prosperity of the union are eminently concerned;

And whereas, The protection of such varied and general interests, is necessarily dependant upon safe and accessible harbors, into which shipping may repair for safety from the frequent storms which vex and imperil its security; the removal of obstructions to navigation, and the improvement of harbors for the free ingress and egress of such shipping interest, are absolutely essential to the maintenance of commerce, and the necessary legislation and protection thereof, inevitably national in their character, as repeatedly recognized by appropriations from the Federal Government. Therefore, be it

Resolved by the Senate and House of Representatives of the State of Michigan, That our Senators in Congress be instructed, and our Representatives requested to use every honorable exertion to procure the passage of an act of Congress making suitable appropriations for the improvement of the following harbors, to wit: New Buffalo, St. Joseph, Kalamazoo, Black Lake, Grand River, Muskegon, White River, Pere Marquette, Manistee, Saginaw Bay, Monroe, Thunder Bay, Marquette, Ontonagon, Mackinac and Cheboygan.

Resolved, That the Governor be requested to forward copies of the foregoing preamble and resolution to our Senators and Representatives in Congress.

Approved February 3, 1858.

[No. 6.]

JOINT RESOLUTION relative to the extension of slavery.

Whereas, The people of the State of Michigan have shown an unyielding hostility to the further extension of slavery, by a large majority, at every election since eighteen hundred and fifty-four, (1854,) when their will could be expressed in reference to that subject;

And whereas, The Legislature of the State of Michigan have on two several occasions instructed their Senators and requested their Representatives to act in accordance with the above expressed sentiment, in Congress, which instructions have been by some of those thus instructed, wholly disregarded; therefore,

Resolved by the Senate and House of Representatives of the State of Michigan, That our Senators be instructed and our Representatives requested to use all proper means to prevent the further extension of slavery in the territories of the United States, or the admission of any more slave States into the Union; to oppose the admission of Kansas into the Union under the Lecompton constitution, or any constitution maintaining slavery therein;

Resolved, That the Governor be requested to forward copies of the foregoing preamble and resolution to our Senators and Representatives in Congress.

Approved, February 3, 1858.

[No. 7.]

JOINT RESOLUTION relative to the indebtedness of the county of Washtenaw to the State.

Resolved by the Senate and House of Representatives of the State of Michigan, That the Auditor General is hereby authorized to settle with the county of Washtenaw upon just and equitable terms, as shall appear for the best interest of the State and county of Washtenaw.

This resolution shall take immediate effect.

Approved, February 3, 1858.

[No. 8.]

JOINT RESOLUTION providing for the distribution of Highway Laws to certain Township Officers.

Resolved by the Senate and House of Representatives of the State of Michigan, That the Secretary of State be and he is hereby instructed to procure to be printed in pamphlet form, the laws passed during this session of the Legislature relative to highways and the duties of commissioners of highways, and that he forward to each of the county clerks a sufficient number of copies of said laws to furnish one copy to each township clerk and highway commissioner in each organized township.

This resolution is ordered to take immediate effect.

Approved, February 3, 1958.

[No. 9.]

JOINT RESOLUTION relative to the distribution of the Session Laws, Journals and Documents of the Legislature of the year 1858.

Resolved by the Senate and House of Representatives of the State of Michigan, That the members and officers of the present legislature be and they are hereby entitled to one copy of the session laws passed in the year eighteen hundred and fifty-eight; also, the journals and documents of the legislature of said year; and the Secretary of State is hereby authorized and directed to forward one copy of each to the several members and officers of this legislature by forwarding the same to the county clerk of the several counties of this State, in which the members and officers reside, as soon as the same are printed, bound and ready for delivery.

This resolution is ordered to take immediate effect.

Approved February 3, 1858.

[No. 10.]

JOINT RESOLUTION relative to the Saginaw and Cheboygan [State] road.

Whereas, The northern portion of our Peninsula is now, and has always been inaccessible for the want of wagon roads, which cause has retarded emigration to that part of the State, rich in agricultural and mineral resources, and abounding in the finest forests in the world;

And whereas, The opening of roads into those regions would induce immediate emigration and settlement upon the public lands belonging to the State and to the United States;

And whereas, A military road was laid out and established by act of Congress, in the year 1832, which road was never opened or worked, nor any appropriations made therefor;

And whereas, An act providing for laying out a State road from Saginaw to Cheboygan has been passed by the present session of the Legislature; therefore,

Resolved, That our Senators and Representatives in Congress be requested to use all honorable means to secure a grant of lands from Congress for said road.

Resolved, That His Excellency, the Governor, be requested to forward a copy of this joint resolution to each of our Senators and Representatives in Congress.

Approved, February 4, 1858.

Note.—The words and sentences enclosed in brackets in the foregoing pages, were in the engrossed bills as reported by the Legislature, but are not in the enrolled copies.

APPENDIX:

CONTAINING

CERTIFIED STATEMENTS OF BOARDS OF SUPERVISORS,

RELATIVE TO

THE ERECTION OF NEW TOWNSHIPS: ALSO,

STATE TREASURER'S ANNUAL REPORT

FOR THE YEAR 1857.

APPENDIX.

ALLEGAN COUNTY.

In the matter of the application of Cornelius I. Voorhorst and others for the erection and organization of a new township.

It being made to appear to the Board of Supervisors that application has been made and that notice thereof has been signed, posted up and published, as in the manner required by law, and having duly considered the matter of said application, the board order and enact, that the territory described in said application, bounded and described as follows, to wit: Township number four north of range fourteen west, in the said county of Allegan, at present attached to the township of Fillmore, be and the same is hereby erected into a township, to be called and known by the township of "Overisal." The first annual township meeting shall be held at the school house, in school district number four, on the first Monday of April, A. D. 1857, at nine o'clock A. M., and at said meeting, Cornelius I. Voorhorst, Hendrick Browers and Jan Boers, three electors of said township, shall be the persons whose duty it shall be to preside at such meeting, appoint a clerk, open and keep the polls, and exercise the same powers as the inspectors of election at any township meeting, as the law provides. And it is further ordered, that the next annual meeting in the township of "Fillmore," be held on the first Monday of April, A. D. 1857, at the school house in school district No. one, and Isaac Fairbanks, Anton Schormo and Martenus Van Tubbergen, are hereby appointed to act as inspectors at the said election.

E. B. BASSETT,
Chairman.
JAMES B. PORTER,
Clerk.

State of Michigan, County of Allegan, ss.:

I, James B. Porter, clerk of the county aforesaid and of the board of supervisors thereof, do hereby certify that I have carefully compared the foregoing copy of an order of said board with the record thereof in my office, as clerk of said board, and the copy thereto attached of the map or survey of the new township of Overisal, in my office, and furnished said board on the application for the erection and organization of said township, and that said copies are true copies. And I further certify that the foregoing order of said board was passed by them at their meeting held at Allegan, in said county, on the 15th day of October, 1856, as appears by their record.

In testimony whereof, I have hereunto set my [L. S.] hand and affixed the seal of the circuit court of said county this 16th day of October, A. D. 1856.　　　　JAMES B. PORTER,

Clerk.

GRAND TRAVERSE COUNTY.

In the matter of application of John E. Fisher, C. C. McCarty, L. S. Campbell, John Dorsey, Geo. Ray, Erasmus Nutt, John Larue, Frederick Werner, Carston Barfiend, H. N. Merrill, Wm. D. Burdick, W. L. Aikin, Joseph Oliver, P. P. Smith, Wm. Coggshell, and H. Decker, for the erection and organization of a new township.

It appearing to the board of supervisors that application has been made, and that notice thereof has been signed, posted up and published as in the manner required by law, and having duly considered the matter of said application, the board order and enact that the territory described in said application, bounded as follows, to wit: Commencing on the shore of Lake Michigan at the point where the dividing line between the township number twenty-nine (29) north, range thirteen (13) west, and twenty-nine (29) north, range twelve (12) west, intersects said shore, thence running up the shore of said lake to the division line between the counties of Leelanaw and Manistee, thence east on said line to the south-east corner of township number twenty-five (25) north, range thirteen (13) west, thence north on east line of said township range thirteen (13) to the place of beginning, be and the same is hereby erected into a new township by the name of the township of Glen Arbor; the first annual township meeting thereof shall be held at the Mill House of Nutt & Ray, on the first Monday of April next, the usual time for holding township meetings; and at said meeting, John E. Fisher, John Larue and Erasmus Nutt, three electors of said township, shall be the persons whose duty it shall be to preside at such meeting, appoint a clerk, open and keep the polls, and exercise the same powers as the inspectors of election at any township meeting, as the law provides; and Geo. Ray be and is hereby appointed to post up notices according to law of the time and place of such meeting in the newly organized township of Glen Arbor.

Dated, Traverse City, October 15, A. D. 1857.

State of Michigan, County of Grand Traverse, ss:

I, Theron Bostwick, clerk of the county aforesaid and of the board of supervisors thereof, do hereby certify that I have carefully compared the foregoing copy of an order of said board with the record thereof, in my office as clerk of said board, and the copy thereto attached of the map or survey of the new township of Glen Arbor, in my office, and furnished to said board on the application for the erection and organization of said township, and that said copies are true copies. And I further certify that the foregoing order of said board was passed by them at their meeting, held at Traverse City, in said county, on the fifteenth day of October, A. D. 1857, as appears by their record.

In testimony whereof, I have hereunto set my [L. S.] hand and affixed the seal of the Circuit Court of said county, this fifteenth day of October, A. D. 1857.

THERON BOSTWICK,
Clerk.

NEWAYGO COUNTY.

In the matter of an application of Chauncey P. Ives and others for the erection and organization of a new township.

It appearing to the board of Supervisors that application has been made, and that notice thereof has been signed, posted up and published, as in the manner required by law, and having duly considered the matter of said application, the board order and enact that the territory described in said application, described as follows, to wit: Townships fourteen and fifteen north of range seven west; also townships fourteen and fifteen north of range eight west; also townships fourteen and fifteen north of range nine west, and townships fourteen and fifteen north of range ten west, be and the same are hereby erected into a township to be called and known by the name of "Leonard." The first annual township meeting thereof shall be held at the post office called Leonard, on the first Monday of April, A. D. 1858, at nine o'clock in the forenoon, and at said meeting Jesse C. Shaw, Benoni Evans and Washington Seaman, three electors of said townships, shall be the persons whose duty it shall be to preside at such meeting, appoint a clerk and keep open the polls, and exercise the same powers as the inspectors of elections at any township meeting, as the law provides.

State of Michigan, County of Newaygo, ss.:

I, John H. Standish, clerk of the county aforesaid, and of the board of supervisors thereof, do hereby certify that I have carefully compared the foregoing copy of any order of said board, with the record thereof in my office, as clerk of said board, and the copy thereto attached of the map or survey of the new township of Leonard, in my office, and furnished to said board on the application for the erection and organization of said townships, and that said copies are true copies. And I further certify that the foregoing order of said board was passed by them at their meeting, held at the village of Newaygo, in said county, on the fifth day of January, 1858, as appears by their record.

In testimony whereof I have hereunto set my [L. S.] hand and affixed the seal of the circuit court of said county, this twelfth day of February, 1858.

· JOHN H. STANDISH, *Clerk.*

By HIRAM BAKER, *Deputy Clerk.*

In the matter of the application of G. W. Green and others for the erection and organization of a new township.

It appearing to the board of supervisors that application has been made, and that notice thereof has been signed, posted up and published, as in the manner required by law, and having duly considered the matter of said application, the board order and enact that the territory described in said application, described as follows, to wit: Being townships sixteen and seventeen north of ranges nine and ten west, be and the same is hereby erected into

27

a township, to be called and known by the name of the township of Green; the first annual township meeting thereof shall be held at the house of John Parrish, on the first Monday of April, A. D. 1858, at nine o'clock, A. M., and at said meeting, William A. Green, George W. Green and George J. Barker, three electors of said township, shall be the persons whose duty it shall be to preside at such meeting, appoint a clerk, open the polls, and exercise the same powers as the inspectors of election at any township meeting, as the law provides.

State of Michigan, County of Newaygo, ss:

I, John H. Standish, clerk of the county aforesaid and of the board of supervisors thereof, do hereby certify that I have carefully compared the foregoing copy of an order of said board with the record thereof, in my office as clerk of said board, and the copy thereto attached of the map or survey of the new township of Green, in my office, and furnished to said board on the application for the erection and organization of said township, and that said copies are true copies; and I further certify that the foregoing order of said board was passed by them at their meeting held at the village of Newaygo, in said county, on the fifth day of January, 1858, as appears by their record.

In testimony whereof, I have hereunto set my [L, S.] hand, affixed the seal of the Circuit Court of said county, this eleventh day of February, 1858.

J. H. STANDISH, *Clerk.*

By HIRAM BAKER, *Deputy Clerk.*

OCEANA COUNTY.

In the matter of the application of Benjamin Moe, Wm. R. Wilson, C. B. Moe, Oliver Swaine, Darwin P. Swaine, Nelson Wright, Sanders D. Ward, Amos Wright, C. W. Bullen, A. Swinson, Lachlan McCullum and H. D. Clark, for the erection and organization of a new township.

It appearing to the board of supervisors, that application has been made and that notice thereof has been signed, posted up and published, as in the manner required by law, and having duly considered the matter of said application, the board order and enact that the territory described in said application, described as follows, to wit: Towns thirteen (13) and fourteen (14) north of range fifteen (15) west, be and the same is hereby erected into a township, to be called and known by the name of the township of Greenwood; the first annual township meeting thereof shall be held at the house of Wm. R. Wilson, on Monday, the fifth day of April, 1858, at nine o'clock in the forenoon, and at said meeting Oliver Swaine, C. B. Moe and Nelson Wright, three electors of said township, shall be the persons whose duty it shall be to preside at such meeting, appoint a clerk, open and keep the polls and exercise the same powers as the inspectors of election at any township meeting, as the law provides.

State of Michigan, County of Oceana, ss:

I, Luther L. Alexander, clerk of the county aforesaid and of the board of supervisors thereof, do hereby certify that I have carefully compared the foregoing copy of an order of said board with the record thereof, in my office as clerk of said board, and the copy thereto attached of the map or survey of the new township of Greenwood, in my office and furnished to said board on the application for the erection and organization of said township, and that said copies are true copies; and I further certify that the foregoing order of said board was passed by them at their meeting held at

Benona, in said county, on the twenty-eighth day of December, 1857, as appears by their record.

> In testimony whereof, I have hereunto set my
> [L. S.]   hand, affixed the seal of the Circuit Court of
> said county, this first day of February, 1858.
>
> LUTHER L. ALEXANDER,
> *County Clerk.*

———

In the matter of the application of Nelson Glover, Sylvanus G. Rollins, James Brooker, Ire Jinks, Joseph Beath, Daniel Wentworth, John Spoor, Isaac D. Green, Victory Satterlee, Jacob Schaumpf, Robert McAlister and Alexander Black, for the erection and organization of a new township.

It appearing to the board of supervisors that application has been made, and that notice thereof has been signed, posted up and published, as in the manner required by law, and having duly considered the matter of said application, the board order and enact that the territory described in said application, described as follows, to wit: Town fifteen (15) north of ranges fifteen (15), sixteen (16), seventeen (17), eighteen (18) and (fractional part of) nineteen (19) west, be and the same is hereby erected into a township, to be called and known by the name of the township of Elbridge; the first annual township meeting thereof shall be held at the house of S. G. Rollins, on Monday, the fifth day of April, 1858, at nine o'clock in the forenoon, and at said meeting, H. H. Fuller, Geo. W. Light and Ire Jinks, three electors of said township, shall be the persons whose duty it shall be to preside at such meeting, appoint a clerk, open and keep the polls, and exercise the same powers as the inspectors of election at any township meeting, as the law provides.

State of Michigan, County of Oceana, ss:

I, Luther L. Alexander, clerk of the county aforesaid and of the board of supervisors thereof, do hereby certify that

I have carefully compared the foregoing copy of an order of said board with the record thereof, in my office as clerk of said board, and the copy thereto attached of the map or survey of the new township of Elbridge, in my office and furnished to said board on the application for the erection and organization of said township, and that said copies are true copies; and I further certify that the foregoing order of said board was passed by them at their meeting held at Benona, in said county, on the twenty-eighth day of December, 1857, as appears by their record.

In testimony whereof, I have hereunto set my [L. S.] hand, affixed the seal of the Circuit Court of said county, this first day of February, 1858.

LUTHER L. ALEXANDER,
County Clerk.

ONTONAGON COUNTY.

COUNTY CLERK'S OFFICE, }
May 80, 1857. }

State of Michigan, County of Ontonagon, ss :
BEFORE THE BOARD OF SUPERVISORS.

In the matter of the application of the township of Pewabec, heretofore made and acted upon, for an alteration of the boundaries of Ontonagon and Pewabec townships, the same having been informal and defective.

It now appearing to the board that application has been made, and that notice thereof has been signed, posted up and published in the manner required by law, and having duly considered the matter of said application, the board order and enact that the territory described in said application, as follows, to wit : "By taking from the township of Ontonagon and adding to the township of Pewabec, town forty-nine (49) north range forty (40) west, and town fifty (50) north range forty (40) west, and section thirty-one (31) and thirty-two (32) of town fifty-one (51) north range thirtyaine (89) west, be and the same is hereby set off from said township of Ontonagon and attached to the township of Pewabec, and that the boundaries of said townships, "Ontonagon" and "Pewabec" shall conform to the above alterations, and are hereby established in conformity thereto.

EDWIN EMMONS,

Chairman.

D. PITTMAN,

Clerk.

State of Michigan, County of Ontonagon, ss:

I, Daniel Pittman, clerk of the county aforesaid and of the board of supervisors thereof, do hereby certify that I have carefully compared the foregoing copy of an order of said board with the record thereof, in my office as clerk of said board, and the copy thereto attached of the map or survey of the townships of Ontonagon and Pewabec, in my office and furnished to said board on the application for the alteration of the boundaries of said townships, and that said copies are true copies; and I further certify that the foregoing order of said board was passed by them at their meeting held at the village of Ontonagon, in said county, on the thirtieth day of May, A. D. 1857, as appears of record.

In testimony whereof, I have hereunto set my [L. S.] hand and affixed the seal of the District Court of said county, at Ontonagon, this sixth day of July, A. D. 1857.

D. PITTMAN,

County Clerk.

SAGINAW COUNTY.

In the matter of the application of Robert Ure and others, for the detaching and setting off of certain territory from the township of Thomastown and annexing the same to the township of Saginaw.

It appearing to the board of supervisors that application has been made, and that notice thereof has been signed, posted up and published as in the manner required by law, and having duly considered the matter of said application, the board order and enact that the territory described in said application, bounded as follows, to wit: all that part of town number twelve (12) north of range number three (3) east, lying on the east side of the Tittabawassee river, now embraced in the organized township of Thomastown, be and the same is hereby detached from said Thomastown and annexed to said township of Saginaw.

The above order was adopted by the following vote: Yeas—Messrs. Andrus, Berry, Card, Fisher, Hodgman, Lewis, Loeffler, Ross, Schmidt, Schnell, Smith, Smock, Swartout and Turner, (14.) Nays—Messrs. Burns, Haines and Hess, (3).

A. S. GAYLORD,
Chairman.
HEMAN B. FERRIS,
Deputy Clerk.

State of Michigan, County of Saginaw, ss:

I, Heman B. Ferris, deputy clerk of the county aforesaid and of the board of supervisors thereof, do hereby certify that I have compared the foregoing copy of an order of said board with the record thereof, in my office as clerk of said board, and that said copy is a true copy; and I hereby further certify that the foregoing order of said board was passed by them at their meeting held at Saginaw City, in said county, on the fourteenth day of October, 1857, as appears by their record.

In testimony whereof, I have hereunto set my
[L. S.]   hand and affixed the seal of the Circuit Court
of said county, this thirtieth day of December,
A. D. 1857.

HEMAN B. FERRIS,

Deputy Clerk.

—

In the matter of the application of Joel Draper and others,
for the erection and organization of a new township.

It appearing to the board of supervisors that application
has been made, and that notice thereof has been signed,
posted up and published, as in the manner required by law,
and having duly considered the matter of said application,
the board order and enact that the territory described in
said application, bounded as follows, to wit: Township
number eleven north of range one east, and township number eleven north of range two east, be and the same is
hereby erected into a township, to be called and known by
the name of the township of Fremont; the first annual
township meeting thereof shall be held at the house of
Thomas Guilford, on the first Monday of April, A. D. 1858,
and at said meeting, Nathan Herrick, Thomas Guilford and
Joel Draper, three electors of said township, shall be the
persons whose duty it shall be to preside at such meeting,
appoint a clerk, open and keep the polls, and exercise the
same powers as the inspectors of elections at any township
meeting, as the law provides.

The above enactment was made by more than two-thirds
of all the members elect, viz: Yeas—Messrs. Andrus, Berry,
Burns, Card, Fisher, Haines, Lewis, Loeffler, Ross, Schnell,
Smock, Turner and Chairman, (13.)   Nays—none.

A. S. GAYLORD,

Chairman.

HEMAN B. FERRIS,

Deputy Clerk.

State of Michigan, County of Saginaw, ss:

I, Heman B. Ferris, deputy clerk of the county aforesaid and of the board of supervisors thereof, do hereby certify that I have carefully compared the foregoing copy of an order of said board with the record thereof, in my office as clerk of said board, and that said copy is a true copy; and I further certify that the foregoing order of said board was passed by them at their meeting held at Saginaw City, in said county, on the thirteenth day of October, A. D. 1857, as appears by their record.

In testimony whereof, I have hereunto set my [L. S.] hand and affixed the seal of the Circuit Court of said county, this thirtieth day of December, A. D. 1857.

HEMAN B. FERRIS,
Deputy Clerk.

——

In the matter of the application of Ira McKinney and others, for a new town.

It appearing to the board of supervisors that application has been made, and that notice thereof has been signed, posted up and published, as in the manner required by law, and having duly considered the matter of said application, the board order and enact that the territory described in said application, as follows, to wit: All that portion of fractional sections number twenty-eight (28) and twenty-nine (29) in township number fourteen (14) north of range five (5) east, that is covered by a recorded plat of the village of Portsmouth, also all that portion of section number thirty-two (32) that lies on the east side of Saginaw river, and entire sections thirty-three (33), thirty-four (34), thirty-five (35) and thirty-six (36) in town number fourteen (14) north of range number five (5) east, and all that portion of town number thirteen (13) north of range number five (5) east that lies on the east side of Saginaw river, save

28

sections twenty-one (21), twenty-two (22), twenty-seven (27), twenty-eight (28), thirty-two (32), thirty-three (33) and thirty-four (34), and town number thirteen (13) north of range number six (6) east, be and the same is hereby erected into a township to be called and known by the name of the township of Portsmouth; the first annual township meeting thereof shall be held at the school house in the village of Portsmouth, on the first Monday of April, 1858, and at said meeting, Ephraim Smith, Jesse M. Miller and William Daglish, three electors of said township, shall be the persons whose duty it shall be to preside at such meeting, appoint a clerk, open and keep the polls, and exercise the same powers as the inspectors of election at any township meeting, as the law provides.

The above was adopted by this vote: Yeas—Messrs. Andrus, Berry, Card, Fisher, Hodgman, Lewis, Ross, Schnell, Smith, Swarthout, (10.) Nays—Messrs. Burns, Haines, Loeffler, Smock and Turner, (5.)

A. S. GAYLORD,
Chairman.
HEMAN B. FERRIS,
Deputy Clerk.

—

State of Michigan, County of Saginaw, ss:

I, Heman B. Ferris, deputy clerk of the county aforesaid and of the board of supervisors thereof, do hereby certify that I have carefully compared the foregoing copy of an order of said board with the record thereof, in my office as clerk of said board, and that said copy is a true copy; and I further certify that the foregoing order of said board was passed by them at their meeting held at Saginaw City, in said county, on the fourteenth day of October, 1857, as appears by their record.

In testimony whereof, I have hereunto set my
[L. S.] hand and affixed the seal of the Circuit Court
of said county, this thirtieth day of December,
A. D. 1857.

HEMAN B. FERRIS,
Deputy Clerk.

SANILAC COUNTY.

An act of the board of supervisors of the county of Sanilac,
passed unanimously at the annual meeting of said board,
in October, 1857, organizing, by a series of resolutions,
the townships of Bingham, Maple Valley, Elk and Marion.

On motion of Alanson Goodrich,

Resolved, That, in compliance with the requisition of
more than twelve freeholders of the townships of Sand
Beach and Dwight, in the county of Huron, (attached to
the county of Sanilac for judicial and legislative purposes,)
due notice of such application having been given, that
towships fifteen north of ranges twelve, thirteen, fourteen
and fifteen east, be taken from the present organized townships of Sand Beach and Dwight, and organized into a new
township to be called Bingham; and that the first township
meeting be held on the first Monday in April, 1858, at the
house of William Wilson, and that William Wilson, Lewis
Bonnell and James R. Frank be appointed to act as inspectors of election at the first annual township meeting, and
to give due notice thereof.

On motion of James McLean, and for like reasons,

Resolved, That township nine north of range thirteen
east, be taken from the township of Speaker, and organized
into a new township by the name of Maple Valley; and
that the first township meeting be held on the first Monday in April, 1858, at the house of John H. Beckett, and
that John H. Beckett, Stephen Y. Rockwell and Hiram

Steinhoff, be and they are hereby appointed as inspectors of election at the first annual meeting of said township.

On motion of Ezra Van Camp, and for like reasons,

Resolved, That townships ten north of ranges thirteen and fourteen east, be taken from the township of Buel, and organized into a new township, to be known as the township of Elk, and that the first township meeting for said township be held on the first Monday in April, 1858, at the house now occupied by Ransom R. Pierce, in said township, and that Ransom R. Pierce, Nathaniel Vannest and John Ryan, be and they are hereby appointed as inspectors of election, at the first annual meeting of said township.

On motion of Alanson Goodrich, and for like reasons,

Resolved, That townships thirteen north of ranges twelve, thirteen, fourteen and fifteen east, be taken from the present township of Austin, and organized into a new township by the name of Marion; and that the first township meeting be held on the first Monday in April, 1858, at the house occupied by Andrew J. Wright, and that Andrew J. Wright, Samuel Abbot and John Snyder, be and the same are hereby appointed as inspectors of election, at the first annual township meeting.

And it is further ordered that all four of the above organizations shall take effect from and after the first annual township meeting in each of said new townships respectively.

Lexington, October 14, 1857.

DANIEL WIXSON,
Chairman.

RANDAL WIXSON,
Clerk.

State of Michigan, County of Sanilac, ss:

I hereby certify that the foregoing is a true copy of the act of the supervisors, and the following diagrams true copies of the original, now on file in this office.

In testimony whereof, I have hereunto set my
[L. S.] hand and official seal, at Lexington, this fifth
day of January, 1857.

RANDAL WIXSON,
Deputy County Clerk.

TUSCOLA COUNTY.

In the matter of the application of E. Battelle, John D.
Hays, James C. Luce, S. M. French, M. B. French, John
Morse, Benjamin Griswold, Joseph Cooley, E. B. Hays,
H. Hobert, John A. Hays, E. French, Jas. Gaunt, Geo.
Wilkinson, Joseph Spencer and E. Spencer, for the erec-
tion and organization of a new township.

It appearing to the board of supervisors that application has been made, and that notice thereof has been
signed, posted up and published, as in the manner required
by law, and having duly considered the matter of said application, the board order and enact that the territory described in said application as follows, to wit : township thirteen and fractional township fourteen north, of range seven
east, be and the same is hereby erected into a township, to be
called and known by the name of the township of "Gilford."
The first annual township meeting thereof shall be held at
the school house on sec. 36 in said township 13 N. R. 7 E.,
on Monday the fifth day of April next, at 10 o'clock in the
forenoon ; and at said meeting, E. B. Hays, Hamilton Ho-
bart and E. Battelle, three electors of said township shall
be the persons whose duty it shall be to preside at such
meeting, appoint a clerk, open and close the polls, and exercise the same powers as the inspectors of election at any
township meeting, as the law provides.

State of Michigan, County of Tuscola, ss:

I, John Johnson, clerk of the county aforesaid, and of
the board of supervisors thereof, do hereby certify that I
have carefully compared the foregoing copy of an order of

said board with the record thereof in my office as clerk of said board, and the copy thereto attached of the map or survey of the new township of Gilford in my office, and furnished to said board on the application for the erection and organization of said township, and that said copies are true copies. And I further certify that the foregoing order of said board, was passed by them at their meeting held at Vassar, in said county, on the 13th day of January, 1858, as appears by their record.

        In testimony whereof, I have hereunto set my
[L. S.]   hand and affixed the seal of the Circuit Court
          of said county, this 28th day of January, 1858.
                    JOHN JOHNSON,
                             County Clerk.

In the matter of the application of Hiram Bailey, Alden Bird, H. F. Cooper, A. Walmsley, Wm. Edgar, Hugh Leed, J. W. Salsbury, Wm. Jacobs, Wm. H. Winton, John Bird, A. P. Cooper, Lorenzo Teachout, and Burton Herney, for the erection and organization of a new township.

It appearing to the board of supervisors that application has been made, and that notice thereof has been signed and posted up, as in the manner required by law, and having duly considered the matter of said application, the said board order and enact, that the territory described in said application, bounded as follows, to wit : Townships thirteen and fourteen north of range number eleven east, be and the same is hereby erected into a township to be called and known by the name of the township of Elkland; the first annual township meeting thereof shall be held at the house of H. F. Cooper, on section twenty-eight, in township fourteen north of range eleven east, on the first Monday of April next, at ten o'clock in the forenoon, and at said meeting H. F. Cooper, Alexander Cooper and John Bird, three electors of said township, shall be the persons

whose duty it shall be to preside at such meeting, appoint
a clerk, open and keep the polls, and exercise the same
powers as the inspectors of election at any township meeting, as the law provides.

State of Michigan, County of Tuscola, ss.:

I, John Johnson, clerk of the county aforesaid, [and of
the board of supervisors thereof, do hereby certify that I
have carefully compared the foregoing copy of an order
of said board with the record thereof in my office, as clerk
of said board, and the copy thereto attached of the map
or survey of the new township of Elkland, in my office,
and furnished said board on the application for the erection and organization of said township, and that said copies
are true copies. And I further certify that the foregoing
order of said board was passed by them at their meeting
held at Vassar, in said county, on the 14th day of October,
1857, as appears by their record.

In testimony whereof, I have hereunto set my
[L. S.]   hand and affixed the seal of the circuit court
of said county, this 1st day of December, A. D..
1857.   JOHN JOHNSON,
                                        Clerk.

ANNUAL REPORT

STATE TREASURER FOR 1856.

Lansing, Nov. 30, 1857.

To His Excellency, KINSLEY S. BINGHAM, *Governor of the State of Michigan:*

In obedience to the requirements of law, I have the honor to submit to you my Annual Report, showing the condition of the finances of the State at the close of the present fiscal year.

Accompanying this Report, will be found the Ledger Balances, and the table of accounts of the several trust funds.

The Report will also contain a tabular statement of the receipts and disbursements for the years 1855, 1856 and 1857, as well as an estimate of the probable receipts and disbursements for the ensuing fiscal year. I have deemed it proper to make these tables in order that you may fully understand the present condition of the finances of the State, and the probable demands upon the Treasury for the ensuing year.

Comparison of the Receipts and Disbursements for the fiscal years 1855, 1856 *and* 1857.

The amount in the Treasury at the close of
    the fiscal year ending Nov. 30, 1854, was $553,004 08
Receipts during the fiscal year 1855,........   588,896 93
                                 —————————
    Total,........................... 1,141,401 01

29

Disbursements for the same period,........	624,777 88

Leaving on hand at the close of the fiscal year 1855, and at the commencement of 1856,	516,623 13
Amount received during the fiscal year of 1856, was...........................	511,271 70

Total,...............................	1,027,894 83
Disbursements for same period,.......·.....	639,879 06

Leaving on hand at the close of the fiscal year of 1856, and at the commencement of 1857, ...;...............	388,015 77
Receipts for the fiscal year 1857,...........	450,653 85

Total,....................................	838,669 62
Disbursements for same period,...........	679,979 19

Leaving on hand at close of fiscal year 1857, and commencement of next,...........	$158,690 43

This table, it will be observed, commences with the balance in the treasury at the close of the fiscal year of 1854. The amount on hand at the time, as shown by the Report of my predecessor, was $553,004 08. It is proper for me to observe in this relation, that the administration with which he was connected did not close its official functions until the 31st of December, one month after his Report was made; the disbursements from the Treasury during this period, amounted in the aggregate to the sum $83,962 71, leaving actually in the Treasury at the close of his official term, the sum of $469,041 37.

I have been thus explicit in this matter, that erroneous impressions on this point may be corrected.

You will observe by the inspection of these tables, that the surplus funds have been reduced during these years as follows:

1855,	$ 36,380 95
1856,	128,607 86
1857,	229,325 84
Total,	$394,313 65

This has been caused by the disbursements above mentioned—the payment of a large amount of State indebtedness—the increase of the payment of interest on State bonds, growing out of the adjustment of the "Five Million Loan"—by the payment of appropriations made by the Legislatures of 1855 and 1857, for the Deaf, Dumb and Blind, and Insane Asylum, House of Correction, Agricultural College, erection of new buildings at State Prison, University, Normal School, the increased expenses of the State Prison, and the steady diminution of receipts for the same period, which will be found in the following table:

Comparison of the amounts received into the Treasury from all sources during 1854, 1855, 1856 and 1857.

For 1854,	$610,699 97	
" 1855,	588,396 93	
Diminution for 1855,		$22,303 04
For 1855,	588,396 93	
" 1856,	511,271 70	
Diminution for 1856,		77,125 23
For 1856,	511,271 70	
" 1857,	450,653 85	
Diminution for 1857,		60,617 85
Showing a diminution of receipts in three years by comparison,		$160,046 12

The funds were largely increased in the Treasury during the fiscal year of 1854, by the proceeds of the sales of State Lands. Since that period the sales of lands have rapidly fallen off, as will be seen by the following comparative table:

Comparative Table of the Sale of Primary School, University, Normal School and Asylum Lands, for 1854, 1855, 1856 and 1857.

Amount sold in 1854,........... $409,675 73
"   "   1855,.......... 159,648 89

Decrease in 1855,..................... $250,026 84
Amount sold in 1855,.......... 159,648 89
"   "   1856,.......... 110,671 98

Decrease in 1856,.................... 48,976 91
Amount sold in 1856,.......... 110,671 98
"   "   1857,.......... 50,254 55

Decrease in 1857,.................... 60,417 43

Making the total aggregate decrease of sales
as compared, ... $359,421 18

The sales of these lands for 1854 exceed the combined amounts of 1855, 1856 and 1857, in the sum of $89,100 31. But little dependence can therefore be placed upon receipts into the Treasury from this source.

The amount received for interest on the surplus funds for the years 1855, 1856 and 1857, is as follows :

1855, ... $29,928 43
1856, ... 21,699 34
1857, ... 9,856 78

Total,................................. $61,484 55

The falling off of the amounts received for 1856 and 1857, is occasioned by the rapid decrease of the funds.

STATE DEBT.

The present indebtedness of the State is as follows :

University Bonds, principal due July 1, 1858,				$99,000 00
Pontiac R. R. Bonds,	"	"	"	97,000 00
Penitentiary	"	"	Jan. 1, 1859,	20,000 00
"	"	"	" 1, 1860,	40,000 00
Full paid 5,000,000 loan bonds, due Jan. 1, '63,				177,000 00
Adjusted 5,000,000	"		" 1, '63,	1,718,685 00
The part paid $5,000,000 loan or adjusted bonds, when funded, will amount to,....				113,399 72
Outstanding Internal Improvement War'nts,				3,832 76
Internal Improvement Warrant Bonds, interest stopped, and payable on demand,..				550 00
Total,.............................				$2,269,467 48

The following class of bonds have been paid and taken up during the years 1855, 1856 and 1857:

Bonds paid in 1855.

General Fund Bonds,...........$21,000 00		
Internal Improvement Bonds,.... 13,100 00		
Adjusted Bonds,............... 23,103 86		
		$57,203 86

Bonds paid in 1856.

General Fund Bonds,...........$79,000 00		
Adjusted Bonds,............... 3,636 93		
		82,636 93

Bonds paid in 1857.

Adjusted Bonds,............... $2,269 46		
Internal Imp. Warrant Bonds,.... 4,600 00		
Outstanding Internal Improvement Warrants,........... 325 59		
		7,195 05

Total,................,.................	$147,035 34

The interest paid upon the funded debt of the State for the fiscal year just closed, amounted to the sum of $128,-401 11. The interest paid to the several trust funds for the same period, amount to the sum of $61,086 27.

In my last Annual Report made to the Legislature, I submitted to that body an estimate of the disbursements and receipts for 1857 and 1858; the footings of these tables were as follows:

Disbursements for 1857 and 1858,......... $1,026,732 15
Receipts   "   " 947,543 77
Showing a deficit of means to meet disburse-
      ments of...........................   79,188 38

Being well satisfied that the various State Institutions, through their officers, would ask for the usual appropriation to enable them to complete and put the same in successful operation, I deemed it proper that these estimates in detail should be laid before the Legislature, in order that the proper Committees, in making their Reports relative to these appropriations, should fully understand the condition of the Treasury, and the prospective demands upon it for the years mentioned, and in case appropriations were made, that the necessary means should be provided to meet the same. Appropriations were made for the Asylums, House of Correction, Agricultural College, State Prison, University, Normal School, State Agricultural Society, and various other public objects, payable from the public Treasury on call during 1857 and 1858, amounting to over $325,000. To meet these appropriations, and the deficit in the Revenue before mentioned, the Legislature authorized the raising of a State tax for 1857 and 1858, equal to five-tenths of a mill on the taxable property of the State, as equalized by the State Board of Equalization in 1856. This tax would amount for three years to $137,000. The Legislature also provided by Act No. 106, authorizing the sale of the Swamp Lands, that seventy-five per cent. of the principal arising from the sale of these Lands, should be loaned to the State, "*and appropriated to the payment of the outstanding indebtedness of the State, secured by its bonds or stocks, in the order in which they shall fall due.*"

It was supposed that these Lands would have been put into the market and offered for sale, as soon as the act should take effect, and that the surplus funds of the Treasury would be greatly increased by the sale.

The Commissioner of the Land Office, after a careful examination of the law, decided not to offer the Lands for sale in consequence of the imperfections of the act, and published his determination on the subject by an official circular, on the 5th of May last. In consequence of the withdrawal of these lands from market, the revenue expected to have been received from such sale has been entirely cut off. It will therefore readily be perceived that means from some source should be provided to meet the accruing demands upon the Treasury for the ensuing fiscal year.

The following tables will show the real and prospective demands upon the Treasury, as well as the estimated receipts for the ensuing fiscal year of 1858:

Estimate of Disbursements for 1858.

Pontiac R.R. bonds, due July 1, '58,	$	97,000 00
University bonds, " "		99,000 00
Penitentiary bonds, due Jan. 1, '59,		20,000 00
Int. Imp. warrant bonds, on dem'd,		550 00
" warrants on demand,....		3,832 76
Interest on the funded State debt,		
due July 1, 1858, and Jan. 1, '59,		129,364 02

Total am't of State debt, principal and interest, falling due and payable in 1858,..........	$349,746 78
Primary School Interest,...................	118,151 79
University "	35,000 00
Normal School "	12,000 00
Expenses of Supreme and Circuit Courts,....	30,000 00
Awards of the Board of State Auditors,.....	60,000 00
Compilation of the Laws,.................	30,000 00
Expenses of State Prison,.................	25,000 00

Salaries of Public Officers,	15,000	00
State Library,	500	00
Coroner's fees,	800	00
Exchange and Commissions in paying principal and interest on bonds,	2,500	00
Wolf Bounty,	800	00
Unpaid Appropriations,	90,529	82
Total,	$770,028	39

Estimated Receipts for same period.

Cash on hand Nov. 80, 1857,	$158,690	43
Railroad Specific Tax,	140,000	00
Bank "	7,500	00
Plank Roads,	1,795	68
Mining and Manufacturing Co.'s,	6,000	00
Licenses,	500	00
Primary School Interest,	70,000	00
University "	18,500	00
Normal School "	3,500	00
State Tax for 1857,	85,000	00
Total,	$491,486	11

Leaving the sum of $278,542 28 to be provided for, to meet the actual and probable demands upon the treasury.

I desire to call your attention, especially at this time, to the fact that the General Fund account is largely overdrawn, and consequently is indebted to the several Trust Funds to the amount of $496,692 28. Under the present condition of the finances, and as the semi-annual interest on the State debt falls due on the 1st of January, 1858, amounting to the sum of $64,682 01, the payment of which, and the regular disbursements in the mean time, will reduce the surplus funds by the 1st of January, 1858, to about $75,000; and as the expenses of the State Government must be sustained and met, I do not see how further payments of appropriations can be made. I shall, therefore, decline their further payment until provision is made to meet the same.

I herewith submit the annual Reports of the Michigan Insurance Bank, Farmers' & Mechanics' Bank, and Peninsular Bank.

All of which is respectfully submitted.

S. M. HOLMES,
State Treasurer.

Treasurer of the State of Michigan, in account with the State of Michigan.

DEBIT.

1857.

Nov. 30. To balance in Treasury, Nov. 29, 1856, $388,015 77

Rec'pts on acc't of	General Fund,	280,904	58
"	" Int. Impt. "	33,346	94
"	" Pri. School "	26,203	82
"	" " Interest,	66,667	65
"	" University F.,	9,032	47
"	" " Int.,	18,380	96
"	" St. Build. Fund,	1,596	99
"	" Asylum "	3,357	61
"	" N. S. Endow. "	1,525	67
"	" " Interest,	3,000	55
"	" Swamp L. Fund,	1,876	37
"	" " Int.,	4,628	99
"	" M. C. R. R. Dep.,	131	25

Total,.............................. $838,669 62

Treasurer of the State of Michigan in account with the State of Michigan.

CREDIT.

1857.

Nov. 30. By am't paid on acc't of Gen'l Fund, $341,915 07
    "   "   " Int. Imp,   "   127,563 55
    "   "   " Pri. Sch.   "   316 31
    "   "   "   " Interest, 108,151 79
    "   "   " University "   34,796 23
    "   "   " M. C. R. R. D'p'sts,   34 14
    "   "   " State B'ld'g Fund,   4 94
    "   "   " Asylum   "   56,945 67
    "   "   " Norm. Sch.   "   80
    "   "   "   " Int.,   10,063 18
    "   "   " Swamp Land "   187 51
By balance Nov. 30, 1857,.......... 158,690 43

Total,............................. $838,669 62

Ledger Balances.

DEBIT.

1857.

Nov. 30. To cash,.........................$158,690 43

"   " General Fund,.................. 496,592 38

"   " Internal Improvement Fund,..... 285,813 45

"   " St. Mary's Canal,.............. 1,774 72

Total,.............................$942,870 98

Ledger Balances.

CREDIT.

1857.
Nov. 30. By Primary School Fund,...........$630,742 94
    " University Fund,............... 146,161 33
    " Primary School Interest,........ 36,430 78
    " University Interest, ... 401 45
    " Contingent Fund,............... 392 35
    " Mich. Central R. R. Deposits,.... 2,153 52
    " Treasury Notes,............... 731 00
    " State Building Fund,........... 9,618 21
    " Asylum Fund,................. 19,094 24
    " Normal School Fund,........... 17,033 47
    " Normal School Interest,........ 3,571 48
    " Mich. Southern R. R. Deposits,.. 206 72
    " Swamp Land Fund,............ 53,336 15
    " St. Joseph Valley R. R. Deposits,. 115 00
    " Swamp Land Interest,........... 22,873 76
    " Oakland & Ottawa R. R. Deposits,. 8 58

Total,..............................$942,870 98

General Fund.

DEBIT.

1857.

Nov. 30. To balance Nov. 29, 1856,......... $182,432 91
Warrants paid during fiscal year,   341,915 07
Am't transf'd to University Int.,   16,821 00
"   "   Primary S.   "   43,296 41
"   "   Normal S.   "   968 86
"   "   Swamp Land "   3,687 04
"   "   Nor. S. Appr'n,   7,700 00
"   "   Asylum   "   62,500 00
"   "   Int. Imp't Fund,   136,606 80

Total,.............................. $795,928 09

Internal Improvement Fund.

DEBIT.

1857.

Nov. 30. To balance, Nov. 29, 1856,........ $309,772 51
Warrants paid during fiscal year,   127,563 55

Total,............................... $437,346 06

Primary School Fund.

DEBIT.

1857.

Nov. 30. To warrants paid during fiscal year, $ 316 31
Balance, ...   680,742 94

Total,.............................. $631,059 25

General Fund.

CREDIT.

1857.

Nov. 30. By receipts during fiscal year,......$299,335 71
Balance, ... 496,592 38

Total, ...$795,928 09

Internal Improvement Fund.

CREDIT.

1857.

Nov. 30. By receipts during fiscal year,......$ 14,915 81
Am't transferred from Gen'l Fund, 136,606 80
Balance, ... 285,813 45

Total,.............................$437,336 06

Primary School Fund.

CREDIT.

1857.

Nov. 30. By balance, Nov. 29, 1856,........ $604,855 43
Receipts during fiscal year,..... 26,203 82

Total, ...$631,059 25

Primary School Interest.

DEBIT.

1857.

Nov. 30. To warrants paid during fiscal year, .$108,151 79

Balance,...................... 36,430 78

Total,............................. **$144,582 57**

University Fund.

DEBIT.

1857.

Nov. 30. To balance,........................$146,161 33

Total,................................$146,161 33

University Interest.

DEBIT.

1857.

Nov. 30. To balance Nov. 29, 1856,.......... $ 4 28

Warrants paid during fiscal year,. 34,796 23

Balance, ... 401 45

Total,................................. **$35,201 96**

State Building Fund.

DEBIT.

1857.

Nov. 30. To Warrants paid during fiscal year, $ 4 94

Balance, ... 9,618 21

Total,............................. **$9,623 15**

Primary School Interest.

CREDIT.

1857.

Nov. 30. By balance, Nov. 29, 1856,......... $34,618 51
           Receipts during fiscal year,..... 66,667 65
           Am't transferred from Gen'l Fund, 43,296 41

   Total,............................ $144,582 57

University Fund.

CREDIT.

1857.

Nov. 30. By balance, Nov. 29, 1856,........ $137,128 86
           Receipts during fiscal year,..... 9,032 47

   Total, ... $146,161 33

University Interest.

CREDIT.

1857.

Nov. 30. By receipts during fiscal year,.... $18,380 96
           Am't transfer'd from Gen'l Fund, 16,821 00

   Total, ... $35,201 96

State Building Fund.

CREDIT.

1857.

Nov. 30. By balance, Nov. 29, 1856,.......... $8,028 16
           Receipts during fiscal year,...... 1,596 99

   Total,............................ $9,628 15

31

Asylum Fund.

DEBIT.

1867.

Nov. 30. To Warrants paid during fiscal year, $56,945 67
            Balance, ... 19,094 24

Total, ... $76,039 91

Normal School-Fund.

DEBIT.

1857.

Nov. 30. To Warrants paid during fiscal year, $ 0 80
            Balance, ... 17,033 47

Total, ... $17,034 27

Normal School Interest.

DEBIT.

1857.

Nov. 30. To Warrants paid during fiscal year, $10,063 18
            Balance, ... 3,571 48

Total, ... $13,634 66

Swamp Land Fund.

DEBIT.

1857.

Nov. 30. To balance, ... $53,336 15

Total, ... $53,336 15

Asylum Fund.

CREDIT.

1857.

Nov. 30. By balance Nov. 29, 1856,.........	$10,182	30
Receipts during fiscal year,......	3,357	61
Am't transferred from Gen'l Fund,	62,500	00
Total,.............................	$76,039	91

Normal School Fund.

CREDIT.

1857.

Nov. 30. By balance Nov. 29, 1856,.........	$15,508	60
Receipts during fiscal year,.....	1,525	67
Total,.............................	$17,034	27

Normal School Interest.

CREDIT.

1857.

Nov. 30. By balance Nov. 29, 1856,..........	$1,965	25
Receipts during fiscal year,......	3,000	55
Am't transferred from Gen'l Fund,	8,668	86
Total,.............................	$13,634	66

Swamp Land Fund.

CREDIT.

1857.

Nov. 30. By balance Nov. 29, 1856,.........	$51,459	78
Receipts during fiscal year,.....	1,876	37
Total,.............................	$53,336	15

Swamp Land Interest.

DEBIT.

1857.

Nov. 30. To warrants paid during fiscal year, $ 187 51
　　　　 balance, ... 22,873 76

　　　Total, ... $23,061 27

Contingent Fund.

DEBIT.

1857.

Nov. 30. To balance, ... $392 85

　　　Total, ... $392 85

Treasury Notes.

DEBIT.

1857.

Nov. 30. To balance, ... $731 00

　　　Total, ... $731 00

Michigan Central R. R. Deposits.

DEBIT.

1857.

Nov. 30. To warrants paid during fiscal year, $ 34 14
　　　　 Balance, ... 2,153 52

　　　Total, ... $2,187 66

Swamp Land Interest.

CREDIT.

1857.
Nov. 30. By balance Nov. 29, 1856, ... $14,745 24
Receipts during fiscal year, ... 4,628 99
Am't transferred from Gen'l Fund, 3,687 04

Total, ... $23,061 27

Contingent Fund.

CREDIT.

1857.
Nov. 30. By balance, Nov. 29, 1856 .... $392 35

Total, ... $392 35

Treasury Notes.

CREDIT.

1857.
Nov. 30. By balance, Nov. 29, 1856, ... $731 00

Total, ... $731 00

Mich. Central R. R. Deposits.

CREDIT.

1857.
Nov. 30. By balance, Nov. 29, 1856, ... $2,056 41
Receipts during fiscal year, ... 131 25

Total, ... $2,187 66

Mich. Southern R. R. Deposits.

DEBIT.

1857.

Nov. 30. To balance,..................... $206 72

Total,............................. $206 72

St. Joseph Valley R. R. Deposits.

DEBIT.

1857.

Nov. 30. To balance,..................... $115 00

Total,............................. $115 00

Oakland & Ottawa R. R. Deposits.

DEBIT.

1857.

Nov. 30. To balance,..................... $8 58

Total,............................. $8 58

St. Mary's Canal Fund.

DEBIT.

1857.

Nov. 30. To balance,..................... $1,774 72

Total,............................. $1,774 72

Mich. Southern R. R. Deposits.

CREDIT.

1857.

Nov. 30. By balance, Nov. 29, 1856,............ $206 72

Total,................................. $206 72

St. Joseph Valley R. R. Deposits.

CREDIT.

1857.

Nov. 30. By balance, Nov. 29, 1856,............ $115 00

Total,................................. $115 00

Oakland and Ottawa R. R. Deposits.

CREDIT.

1857.

Nov. 30. By balance, Nov. 29, 1856,............. $8 58

Total,................................. $8 58

St. Mary's Canal Fund.

CREDIT.

1857.

Nov. 30. By balance,...................... $1,774 72

Total,................................. $1,774 72

Statement of the Condition of the Peninsular Bank, December 26th, 1857.

LIABILITIES.

Due Depositors and Corporations,..........	$98,691	54
" other Banks and Bankers,.............	39,371	02
Circulation outstanding,...................	123,856	00
Capital Stock,...........................	347,500	00
Bills payable,...........................	46,061	65
Total, ...	$655,480	21

RESOURCES.

Due from other Banks and Bankers,.........	$12,473	44
Cash, viz: Gold, Silver, Cheques and Items,..	5,900	66
Bills discounted and other debts due this B'k,	353,329	88
Bonds and Mortgages,....................	17,172	94
Michigan State Bonds (6 per ct. stocks),.....	163,683	71
Profit and Loss,.........................	15,712	57
Expense account,........................	1,328	00
Bank Note Plates, &c.,...................	2,402	85
Bank Fixtures,..........................	3,426	63
Banking House and Lot,..................	16,560	10
Personal Property,......................	2,187	71
Real Estate, including Pine Lands in Sanilac County, ...	61,351	71
Total, ...	$655,480	21

STATE OF MICHIGAN, } ss.
  Wayne County, }

Henry T. Stringham, the Assistant Cashier of the Peninsular Bank, being duly sworn, deposes and says that the above exhibit gives a true statement of the affairs of said Bank, as the same appears by the books thereof, on the

32

26th day of December, (1857,) eighteen hundred and fifty-seven.

H. T. STRINGHAM.

Sworn and subscribed before me, on this 26th day of December, 1857.

S. M. HOLMES,
State Treasurer.

Statement of the Condition of the Farmers' and Mechanics' Bank of Michigan, January 8th, 1858.

LIABILITIES.

Special Stock Account,		$204,294 95
Office Notes,	$46,200	
Less amount on hand,	1,212	
		44,988 00
Due Banks and Bankers,		17,025 75
" State Treasurer,		223 00
" City Treasurer,		16,138 14
" Depositors,		7,633 38
Bonds and Bills Payable,		41,475 00
Certificate Account,		7,442 92
Sundry Accounts,		1,892 53
Excess Resources,		16,238 82
Total,		$357,352 49

RESOURCES.

Cash and Cash Items,	$4,143 76
Personal Estate,	1,250 00
Real Estate,	27,612 68
Stocks,	1,650 00
Bonds and Mortgages,	72,877 84
Land Contracts,	6,518 36
Due from Banks and Bankers,	1,449 41
Michigan State Stocks,	80,000 00

Discounted Bills,	130,390	47
Sundry Resources,	3.,459	97
Total,	$357,352	49

STATE OF MICHIGAN, } ss.
County of Wayne, }

Clement M. Davison, Cashier [of the Farmers' and Mechanics' Bank of Michigan, being duly sworn, deposeth and saith that the foregoing statement is true, to the best of his knowledge and belief.

C. M. DAVISON,
Cashier.

Subscribed and sworn before me, January 9th, 1858.

S. M. HOLMES,
State Treasurer.

Statement of the Condition of the Michigan Insurance Company, of Detroit, December 23d, 1857.

LIABILITIES.

Capital Stock,		$200,010 00
Profits,		38,889 10
Bank Notes in Circulation,	$178,290	
Less on hand,	18,965	
		159,325 00
Certificate Account,		29,220 49
Due to Banks and Bankers,		22,579 14
Depositors,		183,819 22
Total,		$633,942 95

RESOURCES.

Cash on hand—Coin,	$22,530 79
Notes of other Banks,	31,223 00
Due from Banks and Bankers,	52,384 99
State Stocks,	77,133 60

Bills Discounted,........................	407,808	42
Bonds and Mortgages,...................	38,525	98
Real Estate,............................	4,331	17
Total,.........	$633,942	95

STATE OF MICHIGAN, } ss.
Wayne County. }

Henry K. Sanger, Cashier, being sworn, says the above is a true exhibit of the condition of the Michigan Insurance Company on the 23d day of December, A. D. 1857, according to the best of his knowledge and belief.

H. K. SANGER,
Cashier.

Subscribed and sworn before me, a Notary Public, County of Wayne, this 23d day of December, 1857.

C. N. GANSON,
Notary Public, Wayne County, Michigan.

INDEX.

A.

CPSIA information can be obtained
at www.ICGtesting.com
Printed in the USA
LVHW040836070223
738797LV00003B/217